The fates were guiding him . . .

Aames increased his stride, narrowing the distance between himself and the girl. He began surveying the neighborhood for likely places to take her. There were several alleys and one area that was dense with ungroomed hedges. He foresaw no problems in apprehending the girl. She was whistling and dancing her way down the sidewalk as she listened to the music in her headphones. She wouldn't hear him coming up on her until it was too late.

Aames was less than forty feet from the girl when he reached into his shirt pocket and removed one of the darts. The flight wasn't attached, but that was the way he wanted it. He had no intention of throwing the weapon. He closed his fingers tightly around the shaft so that only the sharpened tip was exposed.

Now she was only thirty feet away from him. He could read the lettering on the back of her denim jacket. "Prince Is Bitchin'."

Twenty feet away. She blew a bubble and snapped her fingers to the music only she could hear.

Fifteen feet . . .

DEADLY AIMS

DEADLY AIMS
Ron L. Gerard

PaperJacks LTD.

TORONTO   NEW YORK

AN ORIGINAL

PaperJacks

DEADLY AIMS

PaperJacks LTD.

330 STEELCASE RD. E., MARKHAM, ONT. L3R 2M1
210 FIFTH AVE., NEW YORK, N.Y. 10010

PaperJacks edition published October 1986

This is a work of fiction in its entirety. Any resemblance to actual people, places or events is purely coincidental.

This original PaperJacks edition is printed from brand-new plates made from newly set, clear, easy-to-read type. No part of this book may be reproduced or transmitted in any form or by any means, electronic or mechanical, including photography, recording or any information storage or retrieval system, without permission in writing from the publisher.

ISBN 0-7701-0448-7
Copyright © 1986 by Ron L. Gerard
All rights reserved
Printed in Canada

DEADLY AIMS

Chapter One

Two museums dominated Hancock Park in the heart of the Los Angeles Wilshire District. One, the Los Angeles County Art Museum, held a growing collection of fine art from all ages. The other boasted rebuilt skeletons and ancient bone chips excavated from the La Brea Fossil Pits, whose pockets of tar still dotted the park grounds, giving off an ever-present, primordial smell of raw pitch. Surrounded by huddling pines behind the art museum was a small enclosed observatory, built around one of the black, gleaming pools. The building was old and in need of major renovation, but since the Museum of Natural History across the park had opened its doors a few years before, attendance at this smaller attraction had steadily dwindled to the point where it was unlikely that funds would be allotted for a fresh coat of paint, much less a full-scale upgrading of the facilities. Already visiting hours at the observatory had been cut back to three days a week, and there was talk of closing its doors permanently at the end of the year. In the meantime, it was necessary for someone to stand guard over the indoor pit when it was open for viewing.

J.T. Aames thrived on odd jobs, and his job at the observatory was one of the oddest. Wearing a gray uniform and polished shoes, and with a walkie-talkie clipped to his belt, he had little to do but keep an eye on the pit and answer occasional questions from visitors. He had held the job for six months now, and the only difficulty he had to contend with was his tendency to nod off when things got too slow.

Tonight, however, Aames was far from bored. For the first time since he had moved back to Los Angeles, in late spring, the promise of rain was in the air. A lover of storms, he was filled with a joyous anxiety, wondering what magic the night would bring. The forecasts had kept people away for most of the day and, as the sun set, Aames was alone in the observatory, pacing at the top of a wide concrete staircase that spiraled down to the pit's edge and a display of bones that had been dredged up from the site years before. When a muffled din of thunder sounded from the coast, Aames grinned and rubbed his palms, as much with anticipation as to fight the November chill. The space heater he was supposed to have on cold nights was sitting on a janitor's bench somewhere in the basement of the art museum, waiting for a new filament to come off back-order from the manufacturer.

Soon raindrops began to drum on the roof. Aames lit a cigarette and cupped his fingers around the warmth of the match. When the flame burned down, he cast the match into the pit, where it floated a moment, then succumbed to the black pull of bubbling tar and vanished. High winds pushed the storm inland, and lightning flashed through slots of smoky glass in the rounded walls. A thunderous blast shook the building.

"Yes!" Aames blew smoke through his grin. The downpour formed puddles on the observatory roof, and drips squeezed through cracks in the ceiling, echoing hollowly as they landed. The chamber felt like a cave to Aames, despite the persistent glow of the fluorescent lights. He clapped in time with the next blow of thunder, enjoying the sound. Sidestepping one of the leaks, he walked to a donation box set near the main entrance. The box was made of clear plastic and mounted on a wooden pedestal. Inside were crumpled dollar bills and an assortment of coins. Aames leaned forward and pressed his lips against a slit in the plastic. The interior fogged with smoke from his lungs, and when he pulled his lips away a ghostly tendril curled up through the slit.

"A sign," he beseeched the wisp. "Gimme a fucking sign."

He could see himself in the clouded plastic as he licked his fingertips to tame a strand of hair that had broken the cling of Vitalis. Gray was invading his scalp and beard. He looked a decade older than his thirty years. And he liked it that way.

It was twelve minutes to closing time. Aames took the key ring from his belt and sprang a small lock at the base of the donation box. He tilted the box on its hinges and let smoke spill away from the money. He stuffed half the cash into his pockets and put the rest in a locker built into the pedestal. In the locker was also a miniature TV. Aames took it out before locking up the money and played with the dials as he walked away. The set ran on batteries and flashed an image that came into focus when he pulled up the antenna. He set the TV on a vending machine filled with color slides of the tar pits and the creatures that used to roam Los Angeles before they were sucked into the ooze.

It was election night, and the man on the screen was spouting early returns. Britland looked as though he was on his way out as President, courtesy of a toothy senator named Houril, who had won his clout during hearings on the Fenster scandal. Aames finished one cigarette and started another as he watched. Maybe the sign would come from there.

He was trying to plumb the hidden meanings of a panty commercial when a drenched man in a three-piece suit staggered into the observatory. His dark hair was slicked to his skull from the rain, and his round, plump cheeks were flushed above a crooked smile.

"I'm closing," Aames told the man.

"I just want to get out of the rain for a minute." The man shook himself, showering drops. "Is that okay?"

Aames flicked the last of his cigarette to the floor. It rolled to the rainwater and went out with a hiss. "Suit yourself. I lock up at seven."

"Fine. Thanks." The man looked around and sniffed the air, making a face at the smell. "Whew! Pretty fragrant here, eh?"

"You get used to it."

"Reminds me of when I used to reseal driveways back in high school."

Aames wasn't in the mood to chat. He turned back to the TV. A photo of George Britland was on the screen, along with numbers giving him only 46 percent of the tallied vote.

"Say, you got an extra smoke?"

Aames looked up. The man had come over beside him. Aames pulled out two cigarettes. The man took one and wedged it between his lips. "Thanks. I've got a light." Aames stared at the man as he coaxed flame from his lighter. There was something strange about him, something more than a clash between the fine cut of his clothes and his casual demeanor. Ominous, Aames thought. Gimme a sign.

"My name's Gasner. Mike Gasner."

Aames could smell liquor on the man's breath. Just a drunk. Aames kept his name to himself. Gasner reached for a bulge in his breast pocket and removed an aluminum flask done up with filigree. He held it out to Aames. "Want some?"

"After you."

Gasner unscrewed the cap and took a long swallow, then

handed the flask back, smirking. Aames took it but didn't drink. "Something funny?" he asked Gasner.

"How do you know I haven't taken the antidote?" Gasner's smile cocked the other way, slyly.

"What are you talking about?" Aames turned down the TV and stared at the man.

"You're paranoid," Gasner said. Aames's heart thumped at the accusation. "You think I'm going to poison you and make off with the bones."

Aames laughed dutifully, relieved. He sampled the flask. It held brandy, sweet and warm. He let it roll slowly down his throat. Gasner took the flask back and finished it, then glanced over Aames's shoulder at the TV. "Who's winning?"

"Houril."

"Who'd you vote for?"

"I don't vote."

"Why not?" Gasner lurched suddenly, veering to one side and banging against the vending machine. Aames reached for his TV before it could topple over and turned it off. As Gasner steadied himself he continued, "Hell, that's what democracy's all about!"

"I have enough people trying to run my life without electing them to do it."

"Good point." Gaser licked his finger and scored the air. One for Aames. Gasner closed his eyes a moment, laying rails for a new train of thought. "I'm from Bakersfield. Down here for a convention. Rotarians. And a little business. Staying at the Brea."

"That's a ways from here."

"Yeah, I been wandering around. Got primed for some pussy at that showbar on Sixth Street and started sniffing around after dinner. Looks like I got rained out, though."

"Don't give up yet. There's ladies that make the rounds near here."

"Oh, yeah?" Hope lit the man's bloodshot eyes. "Here? Near the museums, for cryin' out loud?"

"Why not? Highbrows like a little on the side, same as everyone else."

"Now that's what I could use," the man laughed. "An artful fuck."

Aames smiled tightly. "You go for blondes? Like Britland's daughter? You know, Jane?"

"Way I like 'em best is willing." Gasner laughed to himself. He tried to blow smoke rings, pursing his lips like a fish. It didn't work. He made a face and strolled to the nearby railing. Staring down at the pit, he said, "Quite a heap of bones you got there. Big bastards, too. My favorite dinosaur's triceratops."

"Those aren't dinosaur bones." Aames pointed to a placard on the railing. "Everything here's strictly Pleistocene. It's all explained there."

Gasner ignored the placard. He still wanted to talk about triceratops. "Great head with all those horns, don't you think?"

Aames realized the man might be giving him a sign. He'd had to decipher more cryptic omens in the past. He left the TV and joined Gasner at the railing. He'd play along for now. "I'm a pterodactyl fan myself."

"Those always bothered me." Gasner dropped his cigarette and crushed it under his brogues. Aames hung on the man's words, trying to read between the lines. "When I was a kid, I had this whole set of dinosaurs made out of plastic, and they all looked great, except for the goddamn pterodactyl. Had its head turned sideways so it looked like a hammerhead shark with wings. Bothered the hell outa me, so I finally lit a match under the neck and twisted it when the plastic got soft. Almost worked, but I twisted too hard and the head fell off. A real pisser . . ."

Aames stiffened and eyed Gasner. What did he know? The Rotarian kept his gaze on the black pool below them. "I suppose you know that even though they could fly, pterodactyls were actually of the reptilian persuasion."

"What?"

"Of course!" Gasner's latest dose of brandy kicked in, making him more loose and vibrant. He stared into space, seeing reptiles with wings. "And in their earliest incarnations, they even had teeth and tails, so they looked more like..."

He fell silent at the sound of spiked heels banging the concrete behind him. Both men turned to see a woman come in from the rain, holding a wet *Los Angeles Times* over her head. Aames had seen her around before and was cheered by her arrival. It was a good sign. She wore a short, clinging skirt and a tank top, both the color of rust, darker in spots from the rain. Her henna wig was slightly askew, and Aames saw that her real hair was blonde. Thunder backed the revelation as Aames's grin grew across his face.

"Look at the pair o' dactyls on *her*," Gasner whispered to Aames. He took a step forward. Holding his arms out to the woman, he boomed, "Behold, the goddess of wind and rain!"

Aames wondered if the woman knew Gasner, but she seemed equally perplexed by the Rotarian's outburst. "What a night!" She pitched her paper to the floor and shook her head until Aames thought her wig was going to fly off into the pit. It didn't. "I'll be lucky if I don't catch pneumonia."

"You might try wearing clothes," Gasner suggested.

"They get in my way." She hugged herself as she moved toward the man. "Jesus, what's that smell?"

"Something ex-stinked." When Gasner didn't get a laugh, he gestured over the railing. "Tar pit."

She glanced down. "How about that. I always wondered what they kept in here."

"Yeah, this pit's a real rascal." Gasner rocked happily on his soles. "My friend here says if they didn't keep it locked up the damn thing would run off. Can you imagine the havoc an escaped tar pit could wreak on a city this size? Good God, it staggers the imagination!"

The woman shivered. "I don't know what you're on, pal, but don't offer me any, okay?"

Aames took off his coat and handed it to her. "Lousy night for business. Here."

"Thanks." After she had the coat on, the woman found Aames's cigarettes and helped herself. Gasner lit one for her, but she had her eyes on Aames. "So how about it? You wanna date?"

Before Aames could reply, Gasner stepped between them. "He's dry and warm as can be," he protested with a mock Shakespearean lilt. "I, however, am chilled to the bone and wanting for a woman's caress . . . and, have no fear, for I carry the coin of the realm!"

The woman raised an eyebrow and said to Aames, "Is this guy for real?"

"I don't know him."

"He said you were his friend."

"He also said this tar pit would run off if I let it."

The woman turned back to Gasner. "What do you have in mind?"

"Well, my friend Mr. Aames here was just about to close for the night . . ."

Aames was shocked to hear his name. He watched Gasner reach into his vest pocket for a pair of folded twenties. The Rotarian handed one of the bills to Aames. "I was thinking you might like to dash outside for a bite to eat."

"And lock you two in, I suppose."

The woman grabbed the other twenty, saying, "Of course. We need our privacy, after all."

"Ah, excellent!" Gasner clapped his approval.

"I ought to make you take me somewhere with a little more class," she chided.

"Any port in a storm, love." Gasner gave Aames another wink. "Right, Mr. Aames?"

Aames noticed his name tag on the coat the woman was wearing. The print was large enough for Gasner to have read it. It was a small revelation, but Aames rallied behind it. Sometimes the signs worked in mysterious ways. "Fair enough." He slipped the gift twenty into his pocket. "If I'm going, though, I'd like my coat back."

"Fine." The woman returned it and slid to Gasner's side. "I won't be needing it."

"Spoken true," Gasner beamed. "I'm hot enough for two!"

"What's that you were saying about me being a goddess?" She pinched Gasner's cheek and rubbed against him.

"You came in my time of need. Surely you're heaven sent."

"I haven't come at all . . . yet." She stroked the man's leg. His body rolled with the contact, and he craned his head so their lips could meet. They docked like space pods going through maneuvers. Aames stopped by the vending machine for his TV. At the doorway he paused to look back. They'd broken their kiss and were watching him.

"How long do you want?" Aames asked them.

"Nine inches." The woman lowered her hand to the man's crotch. He was halfway there.

"I'm not greedy," Gasner said. "Half an hour should do it."

The woman bartered. "Fifteen minutes, unless you've got more where that twenty came from."

"I do indeed."

"I'll come back in a while and knock," Aames told them. "You can let me know then. Have fun."

"Oh, we will," Gasner predicted. "We will."

Aames stepped outside and locked the door. He waited a moment, sure he'd hear them through the door, reveling in their grand prank. But there were no sounds, apart from the thunder and rain that fell around him. Aames couldn't figure it out. It wasn't supposed to be like this. It was all wrong. Frustration knotted him from within, and he took deep breaths as he grabbed for his wallet. An inner fold yielded a yellowing photo of a young blonde woman with lively eyes that fading newsprint couldn't dim. He gazed at the picture and pressed his ear to the door. He could hear them now, caught in their lust near the railing. He set down the TV and clutched his groin. He thought of himself in Gasner's place with the woman in the photo as the focus of his affections. He was growing hard when he suddenly pulled his hand away and staggered from the door. No. Not like this. It wouldn't do. It wouldn't do at all.

He put the photo away before going out into what was left of the storm. A thin drizzle was filtering through the tall pines, and he slipped the TV inside his coat to keep it dry. A pair of carved sloths loomed motionless before him, wet and shiny. Despite the rain, caked shit from pigeons and black gouts of tar still mottled their stony hides. They stared in the direction of a clearing, where a bear-like megathore sat on a huge rock. Elsewhere in the park were life-sized replicas of mammoths, dire wolves and saber-toothed tigers, all striking poses near the outdoor pits. Aames strode along an asphalt walk that ran between the two museums and came out near the largest of the pits. A mammoth was shoulder deep in the black pool, its great head reared and its trunk curled upward between rounded tusks, roaring mute outrage at its fate to a mate and offspring on the nearby bank. A few yards away, through brush and a barred fence, the last spurt of rush-hour traffic hissed along the wet pavement of Wilshire Boulevard, flanked by tall buildings that threw their reflections into the rain-pocked surface of the ebony pit.

Aames crossed the street to buy more brandy at a convenience store. At the checkout stand, an old man with a dirty beret was talking to the clerk as he poured Grape Nuts into a yogurt cup and mixed it with a plastic spoon. "And I say good riddance to Britland," the old man grumbled between bites, watching Aames out of the corner of his eye.

"Oh, come off it!" the clerk snarled through his mustache. "Britland's the best damn President we've had since Roosevelt, and you know it!"

"Good riddance to Roosevelt, too!"

Aames set his brandy on the counter and paid with some of the money he'd taken from the donation box. As the clerk rang up the sale, he asked, "What about you? You vote for Britland?"

"I don't vote," Aames told him. The clerk was a fat man with dull eyes, and Aames didn't want to waste time on him checking for omens. He paid for the brandy and left, backtracking through the park to a rambling complex of apartments and condos overlooking the pits. The apartments were large neocolonial affairs with columned fronts and extended red canopies that ran from plush lobbies to curbs lined with luxury cars. Haloed streetlights threw the shadows of swaying palms across well-groomed lawns. Aames knew one of the groundskeepers and had a key to a work shed tucked behind the first parking structure.

Inside the shed, humidity had already roused the musty smell of grass clippings and fertilizer. There were no windows, and when Aames switched on an overhead light, sixty watts battled the darkness. Mowers, edgers and spreaders were set in a neat row under a workbench stocked with well-kept tools. The fertilizers and pesticides were piled on shelves across from the bench. A dart board was mounted on the end wall. Aames set his TV and brandy on the bench, then slipped off his coat and went through its pockets for his cigarettes and a small leather case. After lighting up, he tugged the Velcro catch on the case and pulled out three unassembled darts. One by one, he put them together, tightening shafts to heads and fitting the hard plastic flights into their grooves. He took his time, finding comfort in the ritual. He'd tried out more than a dozen sets of darts over the years before finding these, which felt perfectly balanced and weighted in his hands. They were thin and long, twenty grams of tungsten and nickel alloy, with inch-long tips that pricked his thumbs when he checked their sharpness.

After sipping his brandy, Aames stepped to a line of

scuffed duct tape stuck to the floor, less than eight feet from the board. With both toes on the tape and his feet aligned with his shoulders, he bobbed up and down several times, breathing in and out. When he was ready, he bent a few inches at the knees and flicked his forearm and wrist three times in quick succession. With a sound like gentle hands knocking on soft wood, the darts flew into the board. The first and second darts pierced the outer bullseye, but the third glanced against the shaft of the second and landed outside the coveted circle. Aames stared at the results, showing no sign of emotion other than a stiffening at the corner of his lips. All three of the darts had slammed the target so hard that the tips were fully embedded in the compressed cork, and he had to jerk hard to pull them out.

Aames's next toss was the same as the first, except that this time the third dart passed neatly between the other two and into the black dot of the double bullseye. His reaction was no different from before, although there was a faint upward curl to his lips now. After retrieving the darts, he paused for another drink and flicked on the portable TV. A correspondent was reporting live from Britland headquarters in Washington, and Aames leaned close for a better view, eyeing the screen intently. He was looking for signs.

Chapter Two

Jane Britland-Hatch felt trapped. No matter how much she felt herself changing, improving, those around her still saw the old Jane. She was sure of it. As long as she was weak, they remained strong. It was their conspiracy. If they had their way, she'd play out her tragedy to its logical end instead of having the gall to think she could walk away from it. Even in the sanctuary of the restroom she could hear them through the walls, and she was sure they were all talking about her above the chink of cocktail glasses as they nibbled their *hors d'oeuvres*. They had her pegged and were comparing notes on the latest developments with The President's Broken Daughter, Newly on the Mend. The poor girl; all she's been through. What kind words of encouragement could they lay on her next? What sweet, condescending gush of sympathy could they dole out with kid gloves to hide their secret glee? She knew the smug, superior looks they cast when she turned her back, the hushed whispers and tongue-clucking they traded when she moved beyond earshot. To her face they wished her well and hoped for her success, but in their secret hearts she knew they yearned for her to fall. The tumbler of amber temptation hadn't been left on the sink by accident; one of them had set it there with cool deliberation, filled with her favorite Scotch and chilled with round bobbing cubes of ice, beckoning her to hold the sweating glass in her hands. I'm your cool, wet friend, dear Jane, the one who truly listens and understands. Why do you shut me out when I can make things good for you again . . . ?

She looked away from the drink and continued brushing her golden hair. Each stroke brought a crackle of static that tingled her scalp, reminding her of the hospital. Electroshock therapy made simple. Why pay costly medical bills when you can cure your psychic ills in the comfort of your own home? Introducing the new Brain Brush, with staticlinic bristles. Brush to the right for depression. Fifty strokes and all's right with the world. Afraid? Just brush up and down . . .

The ungreased hinge of the restroom door grated as Dora Britland rushed in, sniffing hard and dabbing her eyes with tissue. "It's happened," she told her daughter. "God damn it, I can't believe it!"

Jane slipped the brush into her purse. "I'm sorry."

"Shit!" Dora's mascara started to run. She held her arms out to her daughter. "Oh, it's terrible!"

Jane stepped into her mother's embrace, but there was a part of her that despised the gesture and she felt stiff. They clung to one another like mismatched parts in a puzzle. Dora was caught between rage and anguish, giving off ragged sobs that shook her small body beneath the shell of designer silk.

"Mother . . ."

"It was those network bastards, making their goddamn projections before the polls were even closed. Your father didn't stand a chance!" Dora's bouffant filled Jane's face, and the smell of hair spray made her nauseous. She turned her head and stared at the drink as her mother droned on.

"I'd like to get those newsmen in a dark room and . . ." She couldn't come up with a vile enough revenge and left the sentence dangling as she pulled away from her daughter, letting out a long sigh instead. "What's the use? It's over now."

Jane said nothing. Dora took a deep breath and went to the mirror. Her gaze fell on the drink. As she picked it up, the cubes struck the sides of the glass like chimes. She smelled the liquor and eyed her daughter over the rim.

"It's not mine," Jane told her. "Someone left it."

"Jane . . ." Dora tipped the glass, and Scotch spilled into the sink. "Jane . . ."

"I told you, someone left it!" Jane exploded. "Give me a little credit, would you? Or is that asking too much?"

Dora recoiled, and a glimmer of fright sparked in her eyes. She set the glass down; her lips formed a tight smile. "Jane, honey, of course I believe you."

"Come off it, mother. I know that self-righteous sniff in your voice."

"Please, Jane, not now." Dora retreated into her purse for her makeup kit. She turned back to the mirror and spoke to her daughter's reflection. "Your father needs us. He's facing the press in five minutes, and we have to be there with him."

Jane watched her mother apply the makeup. She could see the resemblance between them and took comfort in the thought that her own looks might weather the years as well. Jane had just turned thirty and, in the wake of her other problems, the milestone had not been a pleasant one. It had been an added reminder of lost years she could never have back.

"How's Dad taking it?" she asked her mother, no longer angry.

"In stride." Dora turned, her lips a shade brighter. "You know your father. He always takes things in stride. I do the fretting for both of us. He runs the country and I get the ulcers. They can't say we aren't a good team."

Jane forced a smile. "Sorry I snapped at you."

Dora screwed her lipstick back into its case. "I deserved it, honey. And I owe you the apology. I jumped to the wrong conclusion when I should have asked questions first."

Jane shook her head. "I blew up before you said a word."

"Tell you what." Dora moved away from the sink to join her daughter. "Why don't we save our apologies for another time? Right now we have a show to put on."

"Cheese time?"

Dora nodded and mouthed the word "cheese." Jane did the same, and they both laughed. Dora stepped forward for another embrace, and this time Jane offered less resistance, although she held her breath against the fumes from her mother's hair.

"Okay, let's go get 'em."

Jane followed her mother into the chaos of Britland headquarters. Secret service agents immediately fell in beside the two women and escorted them past campaign workers and reporters vying for their attention.

"Mrs. Britland, two of the three networks have projected that your husband has been defeated by —"

"No comment," Dora interrupted, her smile in place for the cameras bobbing above heads in the background. The reporter swung his microphone toward Jane.

"Jane, is is true that — ?"

"Will you excuse us, please?" Jane raised her voice for all the reporters to hear. "Please?"

Flashbulbs continued to pop amid the hubbub as, avoiding the spate of questions, the two women followed the agents toward a backstage area. The several hundred people gathered in the vast chamber were clumped mostly in small groups under red, white and blue crepe bunting slung from the chandeliers. Patriotic balloons had begun to lose their helium and were floating down from the ceiling into kicking range. A Dixieland band jammed near the stage, trying to keep spirits up in the face of the bad news that had been building by the hour. The reporters eluded by Jane and Dora finally wandered off in search of other notables they could collar in hopes of getting some air time. One senator and longtime Britland supporter was already being pumped up as a potential candidate against Houril four years from now. Several unattended children frolicked near the serving tables, devouring cookies and mints as they stomped on fallen balloons.

Jane and Dora were led past more security officers to the backstage area, where a sprightly young woman in tweed greeted them. "Daddy's ready to go on." Her eyes were red from crying.

"We're ready, too, Regina," Dora said. "You could use some eyedrops, though."

"I have some," Jane volunteered, reaching into her purse.

Dora walked off to join her husband, who was standing in the wings, reading over a thin stack of index cards filled with remarks his speechwriter had been polishing since the polls had turned against him during the aftermath of the Fenster affair five months ago. Jane gave her kid sister the eyedrops and watched her put them in. In some ways Jane envied Regina, but the sisters were too close for it to have tainted their relationship. When Jane's life had been at its lowest point, Regina and her father had been there to support her; two sets of helping hands rescuing her from oblivion.

"Where's Andrew?" Jane asked, looking around for her husband.

Regina blinked as the drops splashed against her eyes. "He went for a drink. He'll be right back. How do I look now?"

"Fine, Regina. You look fine."

"I can say my contacts are acting up."

"You can say you're sad," Jane told her. "There's nothing wrong with that. Let Mother go through her stoic routine by herself."

Regina thought it over. "I can say I'm stoned."

"That would go over nicely, kiddo. With both of us looking like basket cases, the press would have a field day."

"Jane, stop talking like that." Regina handed the eyedrops back. "I mean it. You have to quit running yourself down all the time. It's not right."

"Hey, it was just a joke."

"It wasn't very funny."

They dropped the topic as Dora and George Britland rejoined them, surrounded by more agents. The President was a slim man of average height, with eyes as gray as his thinning hair. He embraced his daughters and cracked a warm smile that lent charisma to his otherwise plain features. "Well, are we nice and gracious here?"

Regina pouted. "I want to tell the people who voted for Houril to go to hell."

"So do I, Reggie, but that's not the way it's done." George kissed his daughter. "We're going to go out there and make those same people feel guilty as sin because we're so damn nice."

"Barf."

George turned to Jane. "You okay?"

Jane nodded. Inside, though, she felt petals of a blooming dread. She hadn't been in a large public gathering since leaving the hospital, and all the courage she had mustered to see this day through was deserting her.

Regina's husband, Scott Kendall, came to her side. He carried a young boy in his arms.

"Hey dere, widdle Darren, how's my precious boy?" Regina cooed as she rubbed noses with the infant.

"He's drier than he was ten minutes ago," Scott said. "He keeps it up and he's going to be the Pampers poster boy."

Jane watched her sister kiss Scott and take the child. More envy. More anger at her jealousy. And then The Thirst, nagging her. Close your eyes, Jane. Picture your liver rotting. Remember the headlines. Drink and you drink your way to doom.

Out in the main room, the Dixieland band fell silent while a spokesman for the party launched into a brief speech. Shortly after the mention of Britland's name, the band resumed playing. George looked at his wife as he took her hand. "Well, dear, they're playing our song."

The First Family left the backstage area, and a cheer went up as they faced the throng, which had begun to sing along with the Woody Guthrie standard the band was playing. It was the official song of the presidential campaign, its lyrics changed slightly to suit the cause.

> Britland is your man.
> Britland is my man.
> From California
> To the New York Island.
> From the redwood forests,
> To the Gulf Stream waters,
> Britland was made for you and me . . .

The standing ovation was loud and raucous, bursting with pride in the face of defeat. Banners with Britland's name were hoisted and waved in the air as the chorus was repeated. As the Britlands started up the steps leading to the stage, Andrew Hatch weaved through the crowd, downing the last of his drink before joining his wife. His thick build filled out his well-cut blazer, and his brown tie was only a faint shade lighter than his salon tan.

"Leased out the restroom, did you?" he whispered. Bourbon on his breath teased Jane's nostrils. She ignored the remark and looked away from her husband as they crossed the stage, taking up positions behind the podium. Lights glared at them as the entire family acknowledged the ongoing tribute from supporters. Even after the President gestured for quiet, the crowd launched into a final round of song. Jane stood between Regina and Andrew, squinting at the brightness to avoid staring into the faces of those before her.

"Must be a real thrill for you, huh, Jane?" She pretended she hadn't heard, but Andrew knew better. "With the old man getting the boot, it'll be easier for you to hide in your room."

"Can't you save it for another time, Andrew?" Jane cocked her head as she spoke and saw one of the secret service agents watching her. Jack Damascus. The one with the eyes. Pale green with strange dark flecks, unlike any eyes she had ever seen. She liked to think they were sensitive eyes, clues to an inner quality he kept hidden behind his emotionless exterior. He had been assigned to the President almost two months ago, when Jane was in the hospital, and she had yet even to talk to him, partly because she found him intimidating, partly from a sense of shame at the circumstances that made her a hot topic on the Washington gossip circuit. She wondered what he thought of her, how he saw her. Alcoholic? Spoiled neurotic? Nail in the coffin of her father's campaign? Or maybe he was different from the others. Maybe he would understand. Maybe he would listen. As she watched his eyes, she found herself hoping they were green lights, telling her to proceed.

"Touchy, touchy." It was Andrew, stirring her from her thoughts. Jane refused to let herself be baited further. She stared straight ahead, easing her smile. The brink, she thought to herself. I'm finally at the brink, and I'll be damned if I'll let him push me over. She wanted it as a statement of defiance, but the thought took shape dressed in fear and became a proclamation of her vulnerability. In the glaring lights she felt naked, exposed. It took all her concentration to hold back the scream of suppressed rage and self-hatred that lurked deep inside her.

At last the bedlam on the floor began to subside. George Britland maintained his grin, letting the applause die to a patter. Jane could sense his timing and guessed to the second when he would come in with the start of his concession speech.

"You people sound like you've been partying since the polls opened." A few whoops sounded from the throng, setting up his punchline. "From what the networks tell me, I wonder if you forgot to vote . . ."

Chapter Three

The first thing Aames noticed about her was that she'd straightened her hair. He couldn't believe it. He turned down the volume and leaned closer to the small set for a better look. The image on the screen abruptly changed to a close-up of the President, and Aames could only glimpse part of Jane's shoulder in the background.

"God damn it, let me see!"

He slapped the side of the set with his palm. George Britland continued to fill the screen. The only other member of the First Family in clear view was Andrew Hatch, staring blandly at the back of his father-in-law's head. Aames focused his irritation on Hatch. He was the one who made her do it, Aames figured. That fucker, that goddamn shit-eating Ivy League fucker with his capped teeth, high-priced clothes and bigshot ways. Who the hell did he think he was, screwing her looks up like that?

Aames reached for his wallet and pulled out the newsprint photo of Jane. He stared at the soft curls framing her half-turned face. That was how she was meant to look.

When the light caught her curls just right, it was as if a halo had settled about her head, lending her its radiance. How many times had he called her "angel"?

"You fuckass!" Aames beaded the screen with his spit. "Make her change it back!"

Unaware of his accuser, Hatch shifted on his feet and picked a shred of confetti from his lapel. The camera panned slightly to one side, and Jane came into view. Aames looked again at her long blonde hair. Seething, he closed his eyes and attacked his brandy, squirming at the liquor's mad rush down his throat. He couldn't swallow it fast enough, and the excess spilled down his beard. When the bottle was empty, he flung it away from him. It bounded intact off the dart board before bursting against the concrete floor. Glass shards pinged off the equipment and clattered around Aames's feet. One piece ripped a small gash in one of the fertilizer bags, spilling a trail of round pellets.

Aames stared wildly at what he'd done. How could he be so reckless? Someone could have heard. He reached for the light bulb and turned it till the room went dark. His fingertips burned from the bulb's heat. He shrank back in the gloom. By the dim glow of the TV he made his way to a round wastebasket in the corner and sank to his knees. The liquor came up on him, still warm and mixed with food. Sweat squeezed through his brow. He pressed his fingertips against the coolness of the floor for relief and grabbed a pair of hedge shears with his other hand. He stared at the door and waited. All he could hear above the drone of the TV was the renewed thump of rain on the corrugated steel of the shed roof. No one came to the door. Purged of the brandy, Aames's discomfort left him and, by degrees, so did his fear. With the storm back in full force, he still had time, still had another chance. He screwed the bulb back in and quickly cleaned his mess. He had dropped Jane's photo on the workbench, and as he put the clipping away he turned his attention back to the TV.

The President had finished his speech, and the cameras

were now on the crowd as it gave him a rousing, sad-edged cheer. Aames wished he was there so he could make things right once and for all. When the cameras cut back to the stage, Britland was sharing hugs with his wife and daughters. Now Aames had a clear view of Jane, and he watched her carefully for a telling gesture. She kissed her father's cheek and moved back next to her husband as Britland waved again at his supporters. Hatch was clapping his hands and looking away from Jane. Regina buried her face in her sister's shoulder, and Jane stroked her head. Regina still wore her hair in curls, and Aames thought he could see longing in Jane's eyes as she touched them.

"You can change yours back," Aames whispered at the screen. "You know you want to."

Then he saw it, the true sign he had been seeking.

Jane patted her sister a final time on the shoulder, then turned in response to something her husband said. For a brief second, Jane and Andrew traded stares for the nation and, sixteen hundred miles away, J.T. Aames sensed the war that raged between them. A blink in time was all he needed.

"They're through." He spoke the words with matter-of-fact conviction, then repeated them, his voice rising. "They're through."

The screen image cut back to a broadcast booth, where the anchorman began an analysis of the President's speech. Aames turned off the set and lit a cigarette to blunt the taste of vomit. Thunder rattled the shed, and the rain beat down harder. He knew the meaning at once. The storm was calling him. He looked at the watch and realized how long he had been gone from the observatory. He slipped his darts into their case without dismantling them, grabbed his coat and the TV and left. The rain stung his face, and shafts of lightning seared through the darkness as he hurried from the housing project. Clogged sewers were already forcing rainwater back into the streets, and

Aames had to leap from the curb to avoid plunging into a small river that coursed down the side street. He encountered no one and welcomed the solitude. It gave him a final chance to ready himself. There would be no more diversions. As he fitted his key into the observatory door, he saw himself about to step to center stage, ready to enact the climactic scene of tonight's wondrous drama.

"Well, hallelujah to ya!" Gasner howled with sarcasm when Aames stepped into the observatory. "We were beginning to think you'd run off on us."

"The rain slowed me down."

"Not to worry. We bided our time well."

Aames tuned out the man's laugh and stayed near the door as Gasner approached him. Over the man's shoulder, he could see the woman watching him from the vending machine. They were both dressed, showing no signs of their tryst save for a scythe-like smear of lipstick on the man's cheek.

"She's a morsel, my son." Gasner put a hand on Aames's shoulder. "High priced, but worth every penny, you mark my words."

Aames held the door open. "I'm glad you enjoyed yourself."

"Only problem is you could use a bed in there. Cement's murder on the knees." Gasner chuckled, peering past Aames at the storm. "Still a doozy, isn't it?"

Aames knew what the man was hinting at. "Sorry, but it's my turn now." He freed a few cigarettes from his coat and held them out. Gasner took them, lit one, turned up the collar of his coat and sighed. "Well, here goes . . ."

Aames watched Gasner head out into the rain, then closed the observatory door and locked it. When he turned around, the woman was only a few feet away.

"What about me?"

Aames took out the twenty Gasner had given him. "I thought you might want to stay out of the rain a while longer."

She eyed the bill, then looked into Aames's eyes. "What's your pleasure?"

"Do it without the wig."

"Come again?"

"I like real hair. Take off the wig."

She snickered. "You some kind of naturalist or something?"

"What do you mean?"

"No additives." She pulled off the wig, revealing short blonde hair, slightly curled from the dampness in the air. "*Ta da!* The real me. Satisfied?"

Aames stepped to one side and set his TV on the donation box. When the woman reached out for his money, he grinned and shook his head, pulling it away from her.

"You're just full of games, aren't you?"

"That's right." Aames turned his back on her and headed for the railing. The new storm front was moving overhead, and he felt its power surging through him, filling him with confidence. At the rail, he swung one leg over the top bar, then the other.

"What the hell are you doing?" the woman shouted.

Holding onto the railing with both hands, Aames turned around and spread his legs, keeping his feet firmly planted on the edge of the staircase as he leaned backwards out over the pit. He tightened his grip with his right hand, then pulled his left hand away, waving the twenty dollar bill in the air a moment before tucking it inside his pants, just behind the front zipper. The grin was still twisted on his face as he eyed the woman.

"You want it, Jane, you're going to have to come and get it."

A smile curled her painted lips as she sashayed across the floor toward him. "Naughty boy," she purred. "You like to play dangerous."

"So do you, Jane."

"My name's not Jane, sweetheart." She reached the railing and crouched so she could squeeze between the top bars and reach for Aames's pants. "I'm Georgia. Like the state. When I'm through with you, you're going to have Georgia on your mind."

As she leaned out and began to unfasten his belt, Aames looked down at her, seeing only the top of her head and the gentle curve of her back. Yes, Jane, he urged her on silently, his body swaying to her touch. He heard the soft grating of his zipper, then the crinkle of the money she pulled from his pants. When her hands lowered his shorts and took his flesh, her fingers were cold but soft, roaming playfully up and down. Then came the moistness of her lips, the deft flicking of her tongue, making his loins throb. His breathing grew shallow and his lips dry. He was barely able to whisper above the rising storm. "Jane . . ."

Once again he firmed his grip on the rail, this time with his left hand, freeing the right to grope for his coat pocket. In his excitement, his legs began to quiver, making it hard to move his hand with any certainty. At last he reached the pocket, and his fingers moved past the unfastened clasp of his carrying case until they closed around one of his darts . . .

Chapter Four

Only a small number of those on hand for the President's concession speech were invited for a later gathering at a hotel across the street. The chosen few mingled in a conference room less festively appointed than the campaign headquarters, primarily because a crew had just finished removing a large victory wreath and a number of other boastful flourishes originally set up by optimistic aides. Instead of a band, piped Muzak drifted quietly from ceiling speakers, to be drowned out by the small talk of those openly contemplating the prospects of life after Britland. Verbal irons were being cast into conversational fires, and the rubbing of elbows was accompanied by the fervent establishing of eye contact as eager climbers sought the likeliest route to self-betterment in the wake of their leader's defeat. The President himself was conspicuously absent, having excused himself early so that he and Dora could dine alone and make peace with their future.

Jane was only a little more at ease in this smaller crowd. Most of the faces were familiar, but that was hardly reassuring. She hadn't spoken to many people since her stay at the hospital, and she dreaded the thought of having to make casual conversation about her ordeal. Fortunately, most of the people in the room were wary of bringing up the subject, and in most cases she was able to ward off acquaintances with a fragile smile and a slight nod of the head that conveyed her desire to be left alone.

"Something for you, ma'am?" A tuxedoed waiter hovered in front of her with a loaded tray of drinks balanced on his fingertips. He added, "That's cider on your right."

"Thank you." Jane took a glass and clutched it as if for reassurance as the waiter moved on to a huddle of cabinet members enveloped in a thick cloud, which they nurtured with each smoke-filled breath. She watched the men, both intrigued and repelled by the ease with which they carried themselves. She wondered how much of their poise and self-confidence they owed to their tunnel vision of the world around them, a vision that conveniently excluded anything not directly connected to their personal goals. Why couldn't she impose some of that single-mindedness on her own life instead of feeling constantly obliged to consider all the possible consequences of any action? Why couldn't she just be selfish, at least once in a while? The conscience was meant to be a benevolent guide, not this cruelly inhibiting despot. Jane closed her eyes and tried to do the same with her mind. Shut up, shut up, and get off the couch. You already spend enough time with your analyst. Why rehearse for the next session?

When she opened her eyes again, she saw a bulbous, veined nose drifting across the rim of her glass and, behind it, the ruddy features of a man with mirthful eyes and limp hair receding like a coastline eroding under the defiant waves of his furrowed brow.

"Hmmmmm, a fine cider, eh, Jane?"

Jane eyed the man coldly. "Sorry to disappoint you, Ed."

"Not at all." Ed Lobyia, a longstanding fixture at the

Washington Daily, used his column like a voodoo priest sticking pins in dolls. He'd been the first to break the story of Jane's drinking problems, devoting a string of columns to rumors and innuendoes that had inevitably affected the President's re-election campaign just as the polls were showing him and Houril in a dead heat. Britland's steadfast support of his daughter may have won her heart, but there were those who claimed it had cost him the election.

"I assure you, Jane, we're all heartened by your recovery." Lobyia's eyes twinkled above his courteous smile. "Tell us, how are you holding up?"

"You sound like you're on camera, Ed." Jane sipped her cider. "How did you manage to get in here? Did someone forget to check under all the rocks outside?"

Again the smiling grin. "Seriously, Jane. How about an update? We're all behind you. Let us know how it's going."

"If you want a quote from me, Ed, why don't you make one up? You're good at it."

Lobyia finished his drink and snatched a replacement from a passing waiter. His tongue clucked like pressed keys on a word processor. "Now, now. Mustn't bite the hand that needs you."

Regina emerged from the throng and linked arms with her sister, guiding Jane away from Lobyia's Cheshire cat leer. "That bastard," Jane seethed.

"He's right on one count, you know. You can't beat the press by antagonizing it."

"He's not the press." Jane watched Lobyia latch onto a group of men in suits. He said a few words, and the men laughed into their drinks. Jane was sure he'd made some joke about her. She continued to glare at him while she and Regina stopped next to a table laden with snacks. Her sister attacked a bowl of dip with celery sticks.

"You know what I mean, Jane. Say anything to guys like him and they'll twist it into something else."

"I don't need a lecture, thank you." Jane settled for a breadstick. "Okay?"

Regina wiped her lips with her napkin. "Sorry. Look, I'm going to track down Scott and Darren. I've had enough. You want to split with us?"

"I want to, but I won't."

"You sure?"

Jane smiled. "I promised myself I'd stay at least an hour. I need the practice."

"What for? The one good thing about Dad's losing is that we get to chuck the limelight. We're old news. Free at last."

"I know, but I need to do this anyway."

Regina kissed his sister's cheek. "Good luck, then."

"Thanks."

Regina left. Jane finished her breadstick, took a deep breath to disperse the butterflies in her stomach, then worked herself back into the crowd. She found a haven among the long-winded who talked nothing but shop and spent her rationed hour without being drawn into a discussion that had to do with her. Only half-listening, she let her eyes roam the room. Andrew had stationed himself near the bar with a pair of reporters and some members of the campaign staff. One of the female aides was a lean redhead dressed in white and blue stripes so she looked like a flag with curves. The men seemed willing to pledge allegiance to her if she'd given them the chance. Most of her attention was on Andrew, however. Watching them, Jane recalled the tabloid rumors that her husband's increased involvement in the campaign during her hospital stay had been motivated by more than altruism. She wanted to believe that the gossip was no more than Ed Lobyia's wishful conjuring, but she recognized the telltale subtleties of her husband's mating dance with the redhead. The sly wink, the cocked eyebrow, the fleeting smirk; he lavished them on the woman with a maestro's grace. Several times his gaze wandered far enough to meet Jane's, but he wouldn't be deterred from his gestural tango with the redhead. Jane wasn't sure if he was bluffing innocence or indulging in malice against her. The Thirst came back, leaping off the tray of a passing waiter. She eyed the drinks. The champagne looked the same as the cider. A quick drink and she could mask her breath with *hors d'oeuvres*. No one would have to know.

She decided instead to leave. There were sliding glass doors near the snack table, and Jane let herself out onto the veranda. By the railing were a pair of Secret Service agents wearing custom suits and toting the walkie-talkies that kept them in touch with other agents posted on the hotel grounds. They were Strull and Greene, the agents most frequently assigned to her protection. She nodded to them as she moved to the opposite railing. The veranda overlooked a small park lined with bare-limbed cherry trees. The night was clear, but a dome of city light obscured the stars.

"I want to go for a walk," she told the men. "Alone, if you don't mind." She started for the stairs and heard footsteps behind her. When she reached ground level, they had already caught up with her.

"We have a job to do, ma'am. Sorry."

The other agent added, "We'll keep our distance as best as can, but —"

"Yes, yes, I know." Jane draped a shawl across her shoulders and walked past a flower bed filled with dying zinnias. A gravel walk circled the park within the boundary of cherry trees. Through the naked branches she saw the Washington Monument poking up into the night, lit from all sides. She doubted that any landmarks would be erected in her father's honor. He'd been a good President, but there had been no great event during his term that might have elevated him to the likes of a Lincoln or a Washington. Instead, he had been forced to settle for the blandness of mere competence, presiding with minimal fanfare and a low profile, adopting a course that would better the nation in small ways while staying out of any international forays that might have shifted the country's focus away from self-improvement. Had it not been for the indiscretions of one lone appointee, he probably would have been elected for another term. As it was, though, the Fenster business had come during a summer that was short on other news, and too many headlines had created a plank that the electorate decided both Fenster and George Britland should walk. Then, too, there had been the scandal of Jane's drinking and related antics, the wild sprees and reckless behavior that had led to her stay at the hospital.

"Figured I'd find you out here."

Andrew was approaching her along the path, drink in hand.

"I didn't ask you to look for me."

"What's the matter now?"

Jane looked over Andrew's shoulder and saw the two agents standing under a nearby tree. She lowered her voice. "I've had my problems, but none of them has to do with my eyesight."

"Meaning what?"

"What's her name?"

"Who?" His voice was sullen. "What are you talking about?"

Jane moved a step closer. Light from the veranda let her get a good look at her husband's features. He was in his war stance, jaw clenched, eyes filled with indignation, tongue poised to take the offensive, daring her to provoke him further. She refused to back down. "I don't have to tolerate it, Andrew. I won't."

Andrew's lips twisted in a sneer. "There's a lot you can't seem to tolerate these days, Jane. Be more specific."

"Well, aren't you the smug one! The man on top of it all, looking down his nose at —"

"Back off, Jane."

"I intend to." She'd often mulled over this long-dreaded moment, rehearsing a range of phrases with which to break the news. None of that eloquence came to mind now, though. "I want a divorce," she said bluntly.

Andrew's eyes narrowed. "Oh, that's rich."

"I might have known you'd find it amusing."

"Hardly. There's a big difference between ridiculous and amusing."

"Wake up, Andrew. It's over. In a few months you won't be the President's son-in-law any more. You'll have to find another route to the easy life. You don't have any use for me now, and I sure don't need your abuse any longer, either."

Andrew jostled the cubes in his glass, the rattler poised to strike. "That's low, Jane."

"The things you've done behind my back these past two years are lower than anything I could possibly dream up." The words were coming back to her now, rushing out in fury. "You've slept around and exploited your place as a member of my family, and all —"

"That's enough!" Andrew's hand shot out and clamped Jane's wrist. He pulled her further from the agents, then shifted his grip to her shoulders. "Listen up, you fucking martyr. You want to know why I want other women? Is that what this is all about? I'll tell you. Maybe I wanted some pleasure out of life for a change. Maybe I was fed up with your goddamn self-pity. You like to think you're the only goddamn person on this earth with problems . . . fine! More power to you. Maybe you never get tired of feeling sorry for yourself, but I sure as fucking hell get sick of having you stuff your misery down my throat until I'm choking on it!"

"Andrew, shut up!"

"I'll shut up when I'm damn good and ready."

"And take your hands off me!"

Andrew loosened his fingers and took a step back. "You and your fucking nonstop mourning. You turn every petty little foul-up into a goddamn soap opera, and then you wonder why I hate to be around you. Did it ever occur to you it's no fun having sex with someone who's too obsessed with her precious little hang-ups to enjoy herself?" His already strident voice rose another octave, mocking Jane.

" 'Dear Diary, I couldn't come tonight because I couldn't help thinking maybe he wanted to be with someone more attractive than me. Oh, poor me. What am I ever to do? Gee, I think I'll have a drink.' "

Jane lashed out with the flat of her hand, striking Andrew across the face. "Get away from me!"

Andrew laughed, rubbing his cheek. "You don't have to ask twice, sweetheart. I'm gone. Go ahead, polish your halo and put horns on my head if it makes you feel better. Jesus, you're pathetic."

Jane stood still as Andrew stormed back toward the hotel, passing close to the Secret Service agents. "Beware, the Wicked Bitch of the East," he warned them. Strull and Greene said nothing, but as Andrew was bounding up the steps, Jane could hear them laughing quietly.

"Something funny, gentlemen?" she asked them, her voice hoarse from the tight reins she was keeping on her emotions.

"No, ma'am."

"I won't have to put up with the likes of you much longer, either," Jane told them.

Agent Greene grinned back at her. "No, ma'am, just until the new boss swears in."

"It won't be that long if I can help it." Jane left the men and headed for the staircase. She felt numb, empty. Someone else was putting her through the motions of climbing the steps. In her mind, she was still back beneath the cherry trees, staring at some strange mirror her husband had held up to her. The reflection made her want to scream.

Chapter Five

J.T. Aames lifted the hose from the wall and directed a thin, pressurized stream at the muddy tracks visitors had left inside the observatory during the day. Near the upper railing there was also a pool of blood, and Aames stared impassively as the red puddle was washed over the side. The hose reached all the way to the railing. He made sure there would be no lingering stains on the concrete. Down in the pit, Georgia slipped into the tar's embrace, her body twisted oddly by her fall. Her head was tilted back so that her lifeless eyes stared up at her slayer. Blood still drained from the single puncture wound in her left temple, just below the hairline. Sperm glistened on the lipstick smeared around her mouth, which hung open at an unnatural angle.

Aames finished hosing down the steps, then held his dart under the spray to rid it of blood. By the time he'd turned off the water and looped the hose back on its hanger, Georgia had been dragged completely beneath the tar. He lit a cigarette as he stared at the black pool, making sure she didn't reappear. He flicked off the lights and let himself out, locking the doors behind him. As he shut off the water main servicing the building, he listened to the distant rumbling of the departing storm, now bound for the desert.

As Aames was walking away from the building, a three-wheeled security vehicle rounded the nearest stand of pines and a searchlight flashed in his face. Aames stopped and squinted at the light. A short, overweight man leaned out and stared at Aames over the beam.

"Wanna lift, J.T.?"

"Get the light outta my face first, White!"

"Oh, sure. Sorry."

Aames squeezed into the vehicle, which was barely large enough for both men. Johnny White was in his late fifties and had been on the park's payroll longer than any other employee. Prior to working security, he'd been part of the crew handling the first excavation of the pits. He was counting the days to his retirement. Twenty, not counting weekends and holidays. As he drove to the main building, which housed the time clock, he slipped a cigar from his pocket and poked it into his mouth.

"Lakers playing the Celtics tomorrow night, J.T. You wanna lay a bet?"

"I'll lay five on Boston," Aames said. "By ten."

"You got it, sucker." White veered the cart to avoid worms that had crept onto the sidewalk, then pulled to a stop near the side entrance. "Here you go. Say, how'd that roof hold up in the rain?"

"It didn't." Aames climbed out.

"Figures." White gave Aames a nudge on the shoulder. "Better make sure and cash your paycheck, J.T. Lakers are gonna kick ass on Boston, mark my word."

"We'll see."

White left his cart running and followed Aames inside to refill his coffee thermos while Aames punched out for the night. They left the building, the older man resuming his patrol, and Aames walking the other way to the corner bus stop. An old woman sat on the damp bench, shivering in her wool coat and babushka. A plastic bag was set between her knees, and her hands were stuffed inside it to keep warm. When Aames approached her, she eyed him cautiously and drew herself into an armadillo-like ball. She pulled her hands out of the bag, revealing knitting needles and a half-done pink bootie. She held the needles like weapons in her gnarled fingers.

"Evening, ma'am." Aames's voice was calm, polite. Scoutmaster material. "Rain sure brings down the temperature, doesn't it?"

She bobbed her head, relaxing slightly as he came close enough for her to see his uniform. She put the needles to work on the bootie. Aames glanced down Wilshire. Traffic was thin, and passing vehicles left wakes on the wet street. A bank one block over flashed headlines on its business sign. "HOURIL DEFEATS BRITLAND." "LOW-RATE LOANS AVAILABLE HERE." The posted time was 7:39. The bus came a minute later, right on schedule.

The old woman had back problems and could barely rise from the bench. Aames offered her a hand and helped her up onto the bus. She flashed a senior citizen's card to the driver and settled into the bench seat across from him. Aames took a seat next to her. Taking his time, he looked the other riders over. Poor bored fools, he thought. Wallowing in their insignificance. Worthless simpletons. Christ, did he hate them. He'd like to line them up in a row and throw darts at them until they all dropped dead. The world wouldn't miss them. His eyes met those of a teenage girl wearing a trendy Madonna ensemble, heavy on the jewelry and makeup. Chomping gum, smug, thinking she was the cat's meow. She wrinkled her nose at Aames and looked the other way. Bitch. Of all the passengers, she was the one he'd like most to follow off the bus until he was sure they were alone. He'd wipe that slutty smirk off her face, stick her with something besides his dart.

The bus was heading east. As they passed the Brea

Hotel, Aames wondered if the Rotarian had made it back yet. What was that fool's name? Gasser, Gasshole, something like that. Bakersfield. Gasshole from Bakersfield. What a fucking moron.

The girl got off the bus in front of the Wiltern. There was a crowd filing into the jade-green theatre. The girl stopped to talk with someone. Aames stayed in his seat. He'd let her go this time. The bus continued past a few more landmarks, the Ambassador Hotel and MacArthur Park, then crossed over the Harbor Freeway into downtown Los Angeles. Skyscrapers huddled in clusters, wet and sparkling, spotted with random light where folks were working overtime. Neon lights reflected off the sidewalks, and parked cars hugged the rolling curbs.

Aames helped the old woman get off near the main library, then transferred to another bus that took him a few blocks north to the fringe of Little Tokyo. The smell of won ton and fried squid rode the steam tumbling out from an alley between two small restaurants near the bus stop. Aames bought a takeout order of sushi and carried it inside his coat as he walked the final few blocks to the city's old warehouse district. The area was going through a rebirth of sorts. Many of the old buildings had been converted into art galleries, studios and specialty shops. Some structures had been flattened to make room for new condominiums, but most of the art crowd and the *nouveau riche* types still preferred retreating to the suburbs after dark, with good reason. For each transformed structure and pastel-painted facade there were at least a few architectural eyesores with boarded windows and graffiti-scrawled walls, doorways and alleys reeking of piss and Thunderbird and littered with cardboard mattresses and food wrappers scavenged from trash cans and dumpsters by those who called these streets home. The storm had sent most of the transients scurrying for shelter, but Aames had to sidestep two panhandlers who emerged from a darkened recess, begging for loose change. When they tried following him, Aames whirled around to face them, a dart held out before him like a midget stiletto. The drifters cowered away, then slipped back into the shadows.

At the corner of Bowman and Hardwick stood a three-story brownstone, formerly a packing plant for one of the city's independent produce firms. Now the padlocked front doors bore a "FOR LEASE" sign. Aames circled around to the side of the building and used a key to let himself in through a steel-plated door. A yellow buglight illuminated the dingy inside staircase, and Aames picked up a few pieces of junk mail from the floor before climbing wrought-iron steps to the loft. The upper floor had been divided into three cavernous efficiency apartments. Two of the rooms had been readied for occupancy, and Aames lived in the one furthest down the narrow hallway. His place was large but sparse and bleak, the furniture shabby and mismatched. A mini-cooler and hot plate next to a free-standing sink comprised the kitchen area. The single window overlooked the back alley, and even that view was obstructed by a bulky fire escape that clung to the side of the building like an unwieldy fungus. There was little insulation, and the night chill had seeped through the brick walls. Aames set down his sushi on a weathered oak table and fired up a forced-air heater. There was a rattling through exposed ducts, then a weak flow of heat. Aames took a beer from the cooler and sat down, leaving his coat on as he ate. He chewed slowly, placing the evening in perspective. The brief surge of power and elation he'd felt with Georgia was long gone, replaced by a vague depression, a sense of discontent. After he finished eating, he went to the wall behind his flimsy single bed and pried loose one of the bricks, revealing a cavity inside which was a small bound book of blank pages. He had filled nearly a quarter of the book over the past few months. He flipped open to the latest entry, turned the page and unscrewed the cap of his pen.

I tried it tonight with a whore, he wrote, *but it was no good. It has to be Jane . . .*

Chapter Six

Jack Damascus stalked down the deserted street, pistol in hand. It was quiet, deathly quiet. No traffic, no pedestrians. And yet he knew that somewhere along the block lurked a man who had killed before and would kill again to buy a few more hours of freedom. The late morning sun threw long shadows across the asphalt. Damascus kept a wary eye on each darkened niche and doorway. His ears sorted through any faint noise stirred up by the breeze gusting down the street, tugging at his jacket. Knowing the difference between a rustling scrap of paper and the tread of crepe soles could mean the difference between life and death. Tension cranked tighter inside him with each step, but he forced himself to maintain his steadfast concentration, to breathe in slow, regular intervals. His gun was held out to one side, lingering just inside his field of vision. His finger rested gently against the trigger. The safety catch was off. On his right was a pharmacy. The storefront windows reflected the glint of sunshine, making it difficult for him to see through the glass. He narrowed his eyes, squinting through the glare. This was one time he could have used his supposedly ever-present sunglasses. There seemed to be people at the counter in the pharmacy. Nothing appeared out of the ordinary.

To his immediate left Damascus heard shuffling and saw a sudden movement in the shadows of an alley. Even before the sensations had firmly registered in his mind, the agent had whirled to a crouch and whipped his gun into firing position. He stopped short of squeezing the trigger, however, and shouted, "Freeze!"

The figure in the alley ignored his command and continued to move. Damascus still held his fire. Emerging from the shadows was a life-sized silhouette of a woman pushing a baby carriage. The figurine rolled along an unseen track, crossing the alley and disappearing inside the entrance of the adjacent building.

Damascus exhaled and slowly rose from his crouch. He was just beginning to lower his gun when a new sound caught his attention. He spun back around and spotted another figure in the doorway of the pharmacy. It was the gunman, poised to fire at Damascus. Damascus twitched his trigger finger six times, emptying his gun into the targeted silhouette, which had swung into view on a set of hinges. All six shots struck the target in the chest area, and five of them left holes in the circle representing the would-be assassin's heart. Damascus took a closer look at his handiwork. Not bad.

He was at Hogan's Alley, a state-of-the-art weapons course erected at the Secret Service training center in Beltsville, on the outskirts of Washington. It was here that Damascus had been groomed for his present job of protecting the First Family, and he returned to these former stomping grounds on a regular basis to make certain his reflexes were still up to par.

"Nice piece of shooting, Jack."

Damascus turned to see a tall, burly man approaching

him down the middle of the mock street. Nick Boihr, his immediate supervisor, was in charge of the First Family detail. In his late forties, with sandy hair cut close to his scalp and jowly features, he had long ago been nicknamed Bulldog Boihr. Like Damascus, he was dressed in a three-piece suit the color of coffee.

"Thanks, Nick." Damascus slid his gun into his shoulder holster and shook the other man's hand. "What's up?"

As the men headed back to the administration building, Boihr pressed the knuckles of his right hand against his left palm, cracking them one at a time. "Got some ruffled feathers that need tending to, Jack. I'm going to have to do a little juggling of personnel for the next couple of months."

"Oh." Damascus slowed his pace so Boihr could keep up with him. "So there's something to the rumors after all."

"Yeah, afraid so. You're going to have to start pulling a few shifts a week guarding Jane instead of the President. Apparently she locked horns with Strull and Greene again last night, and word got back to Britland."

They headed up the walk to the admin. building. Damascus held the door open for his boss. "I've seen it coming."

"You don't mind, then?"

"I can handle it."

"You're sure? You know what she's been through. You'll be walking on eggs."

"I'm light of foot," Damascus cracked. "I know the situation."

Boihr started working the knuckles of his other hand. "Good. I picked you because you've got more psychology background than anyone else available. It oughta come in handy."

"Right."

Boihr gave the agent a slap on the back and took his

leave. Damascus gathered up his things from the check-in counter, then left the building and headed for the parking lot, grinning to himself at the news. "Well, I'll be..."

Chapter Seven

"Are you sure this is something you really want to do?"

"Positive." Jane's voice was firm. "I know myself, Tim. I can't put it off again, or I'll probably talk myself out of it. I don't want to do that."

"It's just that this seems like an incredibly drastic action to be taking so soon after going through rehab."

Tim Black was a junior partner at the law firm of Katache, Reef and Black, which had recently been profiled in the *Washington Post* as one of the up-and-coming legal firms on Capitol Hill. Jane had gone to college with Tim more than ten years ago, and they had maintained their friendship over the years. He had handled her legal affairs on several occasions, and although divorce wasn't his specialty, he was the first lawyer Jane had thought of after her confrontation with Andrew the night before. He had a low-key demeanor and a sharp mind, both attributes that Jane was glad of as she proceeded with plans to terminate her marriage.

"I know what you're saying, Tim, and I appreciate the concern." Jane rose from her chair and began to pace the penthouse office, which afforded a clear view of the Capitol only a few blocks away. "But I'm not about to wait for a convenient time. It has to be done, and I'm just going to have to be ready to cope, that's all."

"Do you think he'll put up a fight?"

"I don't know . . . yes, probably. If only to save face."

Tim moved out from behind his desk and filled a ceramic mug with hot water from a bubbler by the window. As he dipped a tea bag into the cup, he said, "How about something for you?"

"Yes, please." Jane turned from the window and watched Tim prepare the tea. "As long as I don't go back to drinking, I'll get through this."

"Well, that's one of the things that has me worried. Here." Tim handed her one of the cups, then carried his own back to the desk. "There's no such thing as a clean break when it comes to divorce. I'm not saying it has to get ugly, but you have to realize you're going to be dragged through the wringer before this is through. I've seen some pretty tough customers ground up by the proceedings."

Jane sipped her hot tea cautiously. "My father has always maintained that adversity gives a person a chance to find out what they're really made of. I think I'm stronger than I've let myself be lately. I want to find out just how much stronger."

"This is sure a heck of a way to go about it."

"I can't go on coddling myself," Jane insisted, trying to convince herself as much as Tim. "And I know I can't go on living with Andrew."

"You could try a separation."

Jane shook her head. "We had our separation when I was in the hospital. It just made things clearer. Tim, I want a divorce, and I want it as soon as possible. I've got friends at A.A. I can turn to if the strain really starts getting to me.

I'm as ready for this as I'm ever going to be. Will you help me?"

Tim sighed, and forced a smile. "Yes, of course I will. I have to be in court for the rest of the day, but I'll start drawing up the papers first chance I get. Can I reach you at home if I need information?"

Jane nodded as she finished her tea and set the cup down. "Thanks, Tim. I appreciate it. And I know you've got another appointment, so I'll show myself out."

"I have to run a quick errand anyway." Tim went to the door and held it open for Jane. "Come on, I'll walk you out."

Jack Damascus was in the hallway, gazing at the paintings hung on the paneled walls. He followed Tim and Jane from a distance as they headed for the elevators at the far end of the building.

"Do you have plans for after the divorce?" Tim asked. "It might help to have something else to focus on if things get rough, you know."

"Well, I haven't been much of a success as a housewife or a socialite, that's for sure." Jane smiled wryly to mask the shame she felt. "I guess I'd like some sort of career."

"Doing what?"

"I'm not sure. My analyst says my biggest problem is that I never got around to deciding what I wanted to be when I grew up. A classic Peter Pan type, female version."

At the elevators, Tim pressed the down button, and a bell rang somewhere inside the wall. "Seems to me I recall you did a lot of writing back in college. Whatever happened with that?"

"Dead end." Jane flinched at the memory. "I came out of college with this fancy notion I was going to start turning out Pulitzer Prize material full of meaty insights. I sent some things out, but the only person who ended up beating a path to my door was the mailman. I have enough rejection slips from that one fling to wallpaper the White

House. They were all form letters, too. I decided to take the hint."

"From what I hear, a lot of submissions get sent back without being read. The curse of not having connections. Maybe it'd be different now."

"Maybe yes, maybe no. At any rate, back then I gave it up. Cold turkey." She laughed. "I went out in style though, I have to say. I was still living back in L.A. at my folks' ranch, and one night I started up a huge bonfire near the stables and tossed in this old footlocker I'd filled with my typewriter and everything I'd written. Once it caught fire I walked away, and I haven't looked back since. The only things I write these days are Christmas cards and grocery lists."

"Could be you just needed to get away from it for a while, hmmmm?"

"Are you my lawyer or my shrink?" Jane teased. The doors of the elevator slid open behind her. Damascus went in first and held them for her.

"I'm a friend, Jane."

"I'll remember that when I get your bill."

When she was alone in the elevator with Damascus, she leaned against the carpeted wall and sighed.

"You all right?" he asked her.

"Yeah, me all right." There was sarcasm in her voice.

Damascus could see she wasn't interested in further conversation. The elevator made one other stop on the way down, then let them out in the main lobby, which was roughly the size of an auto showroom, with plush couches as large as sports cars. Ed Lobyia was sitting on one of the couches. Spotting Jane, he vaulted to his feet and came toward her. A gaunt, scar-faced photographer loomed behind him holding his trusty Nikon and making a few quick adjustments to the flash bar.

"So, Jane, I take it you've put the wheels in motion, eh?" Lobyia pulled a microcassette recorder from the pocket of his suit coat.

Jane forced her way past him. "None of your damn business, Ed."

"On the contrary," Lobyia countered, as his associate began snapping pictures of Jane. "I want to be sure I have my facts straight."

Damascus took a step forward to intervene, but Jane had already charged the photographer, wrenching the camera from his hands.

"Hey, what the hell . . . ?"

Jane lurched out of the building and pitched the camera across the sidewalk as if it were a flat stone she was trying to skim across a lake. The street was clogged with noon-hour traffic, and the Nikon was crushed under the wheels of a taxi pulling into the pickup zone. Seeing his camera demolished, the photographer shrieked and strode toward Jane, fists clenched. "You're gonna pay for that one, sweetcakes!"

Damascus and another agent intercepted the man before he could reach Jane. Jack slapped a full nelson on the man, pinning his arms behind his back and warning, "I think we'd all better cool down here, friend."

"That was my best camera, damn it! I've got a job to do!"

Jane pried open her purse and pulled out a handful of twenty-dollar bills. She wadded them in her fist, then flung them down at the cameraman's feet, shouting, "There! That should make us about even, jerk!"

"Not by a long shot!"

A limousine pulled up alongside the curb, and the second security agent opened the rear door for Jane. Damascus waited until she was inside the vehicle before letting go of the photographer. Back in front of the building, he could see Ed Lobyia photographing the commotion with a small Instamatic. The columnist grinned when he saw the agent watching him.

"In this line of work, it's good to have a little backup." Lobyia put the camera away as his comrade joined him.

He advised Damascus, "I don't need to tell you we already have grounds for a lawsuit. I'd appreciate it if you didn't feel obliged to practice your wrestling holds on me."

"You're on thin ice, Lobyia," Damascus warned.

"Not as thin as your client," the columnist countered. "She'll crack before anything under my feet ever does."

Lobyia strolled away, soothing his sidekick as Damascus got inside the limousine with Jane. The driver pulled out into traffic and headed west.

"That wasn't very smart, if you don't mind my saying so," Damascus told her.

"I *do* mind," Jane shot back. "Look, I'd like to spend a few minutes without someone riding me, okay?"

Damascus shrugged his shoulders. It was going to be a long two months.

Chapter Eight

J.T. Aames dreaded his first few hours back at work. It was almost impossible for him to keep away from the railing that overlooked the tar pit, and whenever there were no visitors, he would stare intently into the dark pool, fearful that Georgia would surface. She didn't, though, and as the day progressed, his worries gradually gave way to confidence and a renewed sense of power. He had taken a life and discarded it like refuse, and no one was any the wiser. Despite his initial paranoia, he knew the body would never rise from the tar on its own, and there was no scheduled excavation at the pit for at least another three years. By then he would be far away from here. The omens had served him well after all.

Perhaps he could not have Jane, but nothing need stop him from having others. If he tried hard enough, he was certain he could make future encounters more gratifying. He could prolong the moment, add some drama, maybe throw in an element of the chase. That was it! Instead of just fantasizing on the bus, he could breathe life into those idle schemes, actually stalk those special women until he had them alone. Yes, he could make a challenge of it, the thrill of the hunt.

Work could not end soon enough once his mind was set on his new endeavor. Several times he had to catch himself when the anticipation wore at his nerves and made him impatient with visitors. Once he shouted at two children for throwing pebbles into the pit, triggering an argument with their parents. Later, as he was about to close, a bearded man who had been sketching a bone display at the edge of the pit asked if he could stay long enough to finish his drawing.

"No way," Aames told him. "You have to leave."

"Please. Just a few extra minutes?" The man had thick-lensed glasses that obscured his eyes as he looked up at Aames.

"Give me a break, would you?" Aames retorted. "Come back tomorrow and finish it. The bones aren't going anywhere."

"You don't understand," the man pleaded. "I've never drawn this well. I don't want to stop until I've at least filled in —"

"I'm closing. Period. Come back tomorrow."

The artist removed his glasses. His near-sighted eyes held an expression of disgust. "Thank you, so much," he said, "for nothing."

Watching the old man gather up his things, Aames cursed his temper. He had to be more cautious. Flare-ups would only leave bad impressions with people and help them to remember him. If he was going to make good with his new grand design, he would have to strive for anonymity, or at least treat people well. Like the old woman he had helped onto the bus. If he were ever caught, she would never finger him as a likely criminal. That nice young man? Why, he helped me on and off the bus, bless his heart.

"Look, sir," he finally told the man, who was by now

heading for the exit. "I didn't mean to jump on you like that."

"You were rather rude, I must say."

Aames looked contrite. "I know and I'm sorry. It's just that I'm in a bit of a hurry to make it to the hospital before visiting hours are over. My wife, she's just out of surgery, and . . ."

"Don't worry about it," the artist said, his features softening. "You were right. I can come back tomorrow. Hell's bells, if I can't draw well two days in a row I ought to give it up."

Aames held the door open for the man. "Good night to you, sir. My apologies again."

"Good night." The man tucked his sketch pad under his arm. "I hope your wife pulls through all right."

"I'm sure she will, but thanks for the thought."

They traded smiles, and then Aames quickly put things in order and locked up the observatory. After punching out, he reached the corner just as the bus was waiting for the light on the other side of the intersection. As usual, he had skimmed off the exact change for his fare from the donation box and, after boarding the bus, he moved to one of the back seats to give himself a clear view of the other riders. The teenage girl from the previous night was on the bus again, hiding from the world behind horn-rimmed sunglasses and bobbing in her seat to music pouring through radio headphones. She was a definite possibility, but Aames was more intrigued by a woman wearing fake fur over a short-skirted waitress's uniform. Aames guessed she was in her late thirties. What drew him most to her was her hair. It was long and blonde, with the remains of a perm curling it at the ends. From certain angles she looked vaguely like Jane. She was sitting by herself, applying lipstick with the help of a compact makeup mirror. Aames felt himself grow hard as he watched the round-tipped stick being drawn across her lips. Yes, she would do nicely. The fates seemed to be listening to J.T. Aames. Several moments later the waitress put away her compact and pulled the buzzer as she rose from her seat. Aames admired her legs as she headed for the rear exit. He liked dark nylons on a woman.

Aames was about to leave his seat when, through the window next to him, he saw a franchise restaurant at the corner where the bus was about to stop. He knew at once from the woman's uniform that she worked there. It would be impossible for him to get to her before she walked the few yards to the front entrance, and he was not about to wait until the restaurant closed to have a chance at her. He remained seated and smiled sourly, watching her climb down to the sidewalk and head for the building. Perhaps another time, he mused as the bus rolled on.

That left the teenage girl. A few blocks later, she headed for the front of the bus. Aames stepped to the back exit and instinctively patted his breast pocket, where his darts bulged faintly. Two other riders got off the bus with him and the girl. To Aames's frustration, they also accompanied her as she crossed the street and headed east on Wilshire, passing a new three-story complex and the local branch of the city library. Patience, J.T., he told himself as he walked alongside the Wiltern, following his prey from the south side of the street. Patience. At the next corner, the girl headed north on Hobart, splitting off from the other two people. Heartened, Aames waited for the traffic to clear and jaywalked to reach the side street.

There was no traffic on Hobart. Aames increased his stride, narrowing the distance between himself and the girl. He began surveying the neighborhood for likely places to take her. There were several alleys and one area that was dense with ungroomed hedges. He foresaw no problems in apprehending the girl. She was whistling and dancing her way down the sidewalk as she listened to the music in her headphones. She wouldn't hear him coming up on her until it was too late.

Aames was less than forty feet from the girl when he reached into his shirt pocket and removed one of the darts.

The flight wasn't attached, but that was the way he wanted it. He had no intention of throwing the weapon. He closed his fingers tightly around the shaft so that only the sharpened tip was exposed.

Now she was only thirty feet away from him. He could read the lettering on the back of her denim jacket. "Prince Is Bitchin'."

Twenty feet away. She blew a bubble and snapped her fingers to the music only she could hear.

Fifteen feet . . .

The blare of an auto horn abruptly ripped through the night, backed by a chorus of pubescent screams. Headlight beams shone on Aames from behind so that his shadow caught up with the girl before he could. She stopped dancing and lifted the headset from her ears as she looked over her shoulder at a station wagon that rolled to a stop next to the cars parked along the curb. All of the vehicle's windows were rolled down, and two teenagers were leaning out, waving their arms and calling to the girl.

"Hey, Earth to Wendy!" "Girl, you won't believe what we just scored tickets to. You are going to faint!!!" "Get your ass in here and we'll cruise to Shakey's!"

As the girl sauntered over to the curb and squirmed between parked cars to join her friends, Aames kept up his pace and walked by, taking deep breaths to control his anger. God damn them! Mouthy little bastards and bitches, driving around in daddy's car, trying to be important.

"Hey, who's your boyfriend?" he heard one of the girls tease. "Isn't he a little old for you?"

"Oh, shut up, Karen, you twit!"

"I don't know, he looks kinda cute to me."

The car rolled by slowly with half its riders still dangling out the windows. A young man with spiked hair howled at him, "Hey, dude! Wanna ride? Like, there's room on the roof, you know . . ."

Aames shook his head, forcing himself to ignore the youths. They weren't so anxious to return the favor.

"We're goin' to the moon. Wanna come?"

When Aames refused to respond, the boy in the front passenger seat squeezed out the window and supported himself by holding onto the roof rack with one hand while he lowered his pants with the other. "Okay, then, we'll bring the moon to you, dude! Check it out!!!"

The driver leaned on his horn again as the station wagon pulled ahead so that the exhibitionist, pretending to relieve himself of gas, was in full view of Aames. The girls giggled in mock horror at the display, and Aames's intended victim shrieked, "You better zip up quick, Tony! I think that guy's a fag!"

Enraged, Aames left the sidewalk and started after his tormentors. As he expected, the driver accelerated, and the others retreated inside the station wagon as it sped to the corner and raced through a yellow light at Sixth Street.

"Assholes." Aames spat in their direction. Smug little know-it-alls. They wouldn't be so cocky if he got them alone and pressed the tip of his dart against their heads. Excuse me, but who was that you called a fag? What's that, you got nothing smart to say now? Why not? None of your little friends around to impress, is that it?

He waited at the corner and boarded the next eastbound bus, which brought him downtown to San Pedro Street. It took him the entire ride to bring himself back under control. He finally decided that things had turned out wrong because he had failed to watch for the right omens. He had tried to impose himself on the elements. In future, he would have to be less eager. If he waited, the right moment would present itself to him, just as it had the night before. Patience and caution. He would need both to make things right, to keep from making mistakes.

Now Aames wanted nothing more than time to himself for quiet contemplation. He had to think things through. As he approached his building, he noticed a number of unfamiliar cars parked along the normally deserted curb, and when he let himself in the side door, the loud blare of rock music echoed down from the upstairs lofts. The staircase buglight had been replaced by a bluish bulb that cast its eerie glow on a dayglo orange arrow pointing in the direction of the music. Aames vaguely recalled mention of a party being planned by the girl in the apartment next to his, but he had assumed it was scheduled for the weekend. As he slowly trudged up the stairs, the cloying smell of marijuana and sandalwood grew stronger. He felt as if he had strayed into a time warp that took him a year back with each step until he reached the upstairs corridor and re-entered the Age of Aquarius. Vintage Fillmore West posters were tacked on the walls. Longhairs in bell-bottoms passed joints and wore head bands with peace signs. A Doors song ended and was replaced by a wandering Jerry Garcia guitar solo.

"Hey, J.T.!"

A short woman in a miniskirt and knee-high go-go boots broke away from the others and walked toward Aames. In the dim light, it took him a moment to recognize his neighbor. Her normally shoulder-length hair was tucked up underneath a beret. Like the others crowding the hallway, she was in her thirties, a baby boomer valiantly staving off the march into middle age.

"Uh, hi, Debra." Aames fumbled for his keys. Why tonight of all nights?

"Don't tell me you forgot about the party!" Debra accused playfully. "Look around! Ain't it great? It's like the sixties all over, isn't it? Look, why don't you change your clothes and join the fun? You *did* track down a costume like you promised, didn't you?"

"Well, no." Aames could barely remember his conversation with her about the party. "Not exactly."

"Did you hear that?" she called out to the others around her. She stepped in front of Aames to keep him from reaching his room. "My neighbor forgot to get a costume for the party! Can you believe that?"

"Nooooooo!!!" came the multi-voiced response, filled with drunken cheer.

"We can't very well let such an offence go unnoticed, can we?"

"Noooooo!!!"

"Then what should we do with him?" Debra asked the mob.

"Initiate him!" someone cried out.

"Yes, initiate him!" another voice shouted.

"Please, Debra," Aames said as he tried to get past her. "I've had a rough day."

"Good!" Debra grinned diabolically. "An initiation is just what you need, then. Come along . . ."

Another of the guests helped Debra guide Aames into her apartment. Close to twenty people were milling about the room, which was lit by a combination of strobes and black lights. There was a mirrored ball on the ceiling, and the air was hazy with smoke. Most of the guests were looking toward the middle of the room, where a man wearing a clear waterproof poncho over his Nehru jacket was lying on his back in the middle of an inflated rubber raft. His eyes were closed and his hands were clasped on his chest as if he were dead and awaiting burial at sea.

"What's wrong with him?" Aames raised his voice to compete with the music.

"Shhhhhh," Debra whispered back. "He's being initiated. Watch, and learn."

The man on the raft was far from resting in peace. He began to squirm, and even in the erratic light Aames could see that he looked ill.

"What's the initiation?"

"You'll find out soon enough."

The man on the raft opened his eyes suddenly and cupped a hand over his mouth as he bolted from the raft, stiff-arming his way to the nearest window, where he leaned out and retched violently into the alley.

"Nice try, Jerry," Debra called out to the sick man. She climbed up onto a chair next to Aames and waved to get the crowd's attention. Somebody near the stereo cued up the tone arm, stopping the music.

Debra announced, "You people have gotten soft over the years, I'm afraid. I mean, only three of you have passed the initiation so far."

"Who's next?" someone yelled.

"The next initiate will be my neighbor of four whole weeks, J.T. Aames!" Debra held up Aames's hand as if he were a prizefighter. He opened his mouth to protest, but was drowned out by the cheers of the crowd. Debra waved down the applause and continued: "Once again, the rules of the initiation are simple."

"Yeah, right," Jerry groaned from the sink, where he was rinsing his mouth.

"After donning the ceremonial poncho, the initiate will take his place in the Raft of Wonder and partake of the chosen fuel before beginning his journey of initiation."

"What?" Aames gasped.

"All right!" The man who had helped escort Aames into the room retrieved the poncho from Jerry and brought it back to the raft. He handed it to Aames. "Here you go, man. One size fits all."

Surrounded by the throng and bombarded by psychedelic lights, Aames felt disoriented, but could not bring himself to leave. A part of him was beginning to spark with curiosity. He stabbed his arms into the poncho and zipped up the front.

"Now sit down," Debra told him, guiding him into the raft. "Bruce! Is the fuel ready?"

Bruce was a Charles Manson lookalike hunched over the kitchen counter next to Jerry. He nodded without taking his eyes off his work. Once Aames was seated, Debra crouched to his level and said, "You get to pick your own soundtrack for the journey. Any music we've got, as long as it's from the sixties and is at least five minutes long."

"Soundtrack?" Aames was confused.

"Well, you know . . . for atmosphere. You see, the thing is, you have to put down all the fuel and then lie down in the raft until your music's over. That's all there is to it. If you can tough it out without getting sick, you pass the initiation and become an official Astral Traveler." Debra raised a suggestive eyebrow. "It's a very elite group, I'll have you know."

"Maybe someone else should —"

"Nothing doing, J.T. You've donned your poncho. There's no turning back. Now, what do you want to hear?"

Aames thought it over. Suggestions came at him from all around.

" 'In-A-Gadda-Da-Vida'!"

" 'Wipeout'!"

" 'Light My Fire'!"

" 'Mrs. Brown, You've Got a Lovely Daughter'!"

There was one song that seemed appropriate to Aames. "How about 'In the Hall of the Mountain King'?"

"Never heard of it," Bruce said.

"That's classical, isn't it?" Debra said.

"Yeah, it's real downer music," Jerry put in. "Like *Bolero* on quaaludes."

"J.T., I said it has to be sixties music. Remember?"

Aames nodded. "There was a band out of Detroit that did a rock version."

"Yeah, I remember!" another spectator cried out. "S.R.C. Scott Richard Case, or something like that."

"Well, we don't have the record here," Debra said. "Sorry, J.T."

"It's an instrumental," Aames said.

"Hey, we can hum it for him!" Bruce suggested. "How does it go?"

Somebody hummed a few bars, and there were cries of recognition all around. It was a familiar tune, after all. Most people thought it had something to do with either "The Pied Piper of Hamelin" or *Peter and the Wolf*. Debra quieted down the crowd, then signaled for Bruce to bring on the fuel. When he came out from behind the kitchenette counter, he was holding one of the raft's paddles out before him. Balanced on the flat of the oar was a sixteen ounce can of beer, a line of white powder and a rolled joint. Bruce carried the cargo with a solemn look on his face. He looked like an acolyte at a religious service. The crowd parted so that he could reach the raft. In the background, the gentle humming of "In the Hall of the Mountain King" began to fill the room.

"First you do the line of coke, then gravity-feed the beer," Debra told Aames softly. "After that, you lie back and smoke the entire joint, then close your eyes and ride out the song. Good luck, Initiate Aames."

Aames stared hesitantly at the offerings. He was no stranger to any of them. The humming grew louder around him, and the strobe lights continued to make the room seem like something from one of his own dreams. After a moment's deliberation, he leaned forward and picked up the empty pen chamber next to the cocaine. Placing the wider end just inside his right nostril, he inhaled half the powder, then repeated the procedure with the other nostril. The can of beer, which had been opened from the bottom, rested upside down on the oar. He raised the can to his lips and tilted his head back as Bruce leaned forward to pull the ring tab on the can's top. The beer surged down Aames's throat. A few ounces splashed down his chin and onto the poncho.

Already he was beginning to feel a detached light-headedness. The tightness in his chest and back eased as he dabbed the foam from his beard and waited for Bruce to light the joint and hand it to him. He drew in the pungent smoke and held it deep inside his lungs as he lay back in the raft. It was potent, mingling with the other substances he had just consumed to enhance the strange reality enveloping him. The play of the lights was making him dizzy, so he closed his eyes and concentrated on the music. The group was having fun and exaggerated the repeating notes into a parody of Grieg's tune. But Aames heard the music being performed by an unflawed symphony orchestra, lending drama to the vision blooming in his mind. He was back at the observatory, spread-eagled inside the railing, far above the bubbling tar, waiting for the inevitable crack of light from the opening door. Jane slowly walked in, a silhouette framed by the intense glare outside the chamber. She closed the door behind her and came fully into view. She wore a dark green dress with a neckline that reached down to the first hint of her breasts. Her eyes were on him, and her lips were turned up at the corners in a smile that assured him she knew his every desire. When she reached the railing, she dropped to her knees and leaned out between the bars, caressing his leg, pressing herself against it so that he could feel her softness through the fabric of his pants. Her hands rose to his groin and sought out his zipper. He looked down and saw her smiling up at him as her fingers slipped inside his pants . . .

Aames rocked with convulsions on the raft, wrenched from his fantasy by the ejaculation that streamed hotly down his leg. He sat upright and sprang from the raft, staggering through the crowd. His legs were uncooperative, and he fell several times on his way to the hallway. When hands reached out to help him, he swatted them away violently. Reaching his room, he dragged his key against the lock until it slid in, allowing him to escape the pandemonium. After he had thrown the deadbolt and reeled away from the door, he heard an urgent knocking and Debra's voice, asking him if he was all right. He shouted that he wanted to be left alone and slumped down on his bed. His hands groped through a drawer of his nightstand until his fingers fell on the blonde strands of a woman's wig. He pressed the hairpiece to his face and curled into a fetal position beneath the covers, shivering.

Chapter Nine

"A what?" Dora rattled her coffee cup against its china saucer as she stared at her daughter. "Jane, dear, you can't be serious . . ."

"I'm afraid I am, mother."

They were out on the patio in Jane's backyard, finishing breakfast. The President sat quietly across the table from his daughter, listening to the conversation. The morning sky was clear for the first time in more than a week, warming the yard. Behind them loomed the neocolonial home where Jane and Andrew had lived throughout Britland's term. White and pillared, the house had a certain aristocratic charm and had been profiled in an *Architectural Digest* spread just after the Hatches had moved in, before things had begun to go wrong with the marriage.

Jane watched as her mother turned and looked out at the landscaping, staring at nothing in particular. Two Secret Service agents stood near a brick barbecue at the end of the patio, their eyes on the yard's periphery of tall brick walls covered with creeping fig. As Dora sighed eloquently, Jane glanced at her father.

"I'm sorry, Jane." He reached past the coffee pot and gently rested one hand on top of his daughter's wrist.

"Well, this is just wonderful!" Dora inched her chair away from the table and crumpled her napkin before tossing it fitfully next to her plate. She stood up and turned her back on the others, as if to address the small birds gathered on a power line running from the house to a telephone pole half hidden behind a strategically planted spruce. "We Britlands are just filled with cheery news these days, aren't we?"

"Dora..."

"Oh, is the media ever going to have a field day with this!" Dora snorted. " 'The Britlands: Losers on a Roll!' " She whirled around and took a step toward the portable phone resting on the table. "Maybe I should give Regina a call and see what kind of contribution she's planning..."

"Dora, that's enough."

"Oh, is that an executive order?" Dora clicked her heels and straightened her spine as she snapped off a curt salute at her husband. "Yes, *sir*!"

"Mother, what is wrong with you?" Jane demanded. "Why do you have to bend over backwards to make this harder on everyone than it already is?"

"*I'm* making this harder?" Dora pressed the tip of one finger against her breastbone. "What on earth are you talking about? I *never* make things hard! I'm the optimist of the family, remember? You drink yourself into the hospital and gossip columns, and I put on a smile and tell reporters my daughter's just going through a temporary problem. My husband gets voted out of office because he refuses to stop defending a two-bit swindler he appointed his chief of staff, and I put on a smile and tell reporters that just because George Britland and James Fenster have been longtime friends and investment partners, that shouldn't mean my husband is too subjective to see dear

Mr. Fenster's tendency for indiscretion. . . . And now you're getting a divorce and I'm supposed to be *what* . . . thrilled? Should I throw a party maybe?"

"I knew you'd take it like this." Jane poured more coffee, spilling it in her anger. "And, yes, it wouldn't surprise me if deep down you might actually *be* thrilled by it all. Another chance to point out what a failure I am. Another chance to put on that long-suffering-mother act for the papers. Here she is, ladies and gentlemen, the next Rose Kennedy, poor woman! Such grace in the face of tragedy! How does she ever do it?"

The two women faced off from either side of the table. The President sat between them uncomfortably, an ineffectual buffer caught in the crossfire. Dora had the last word. "How dare you!" she demanded, then left the patio and stormed inside. Jane was about to follow, but her father reached out and motioned for her to stop.

"I think you should give each other a little space right now," he suggested.

Jane dropped back into her chair. A maid emerged from the house and gathered up the dishes with quiet efficiency. "Why do mother and I always fight?" Jane wondered aloud. "Why can't we get along?"

The President smiled, adding cream to his coffee. "If you can figure out the answer to that one, my dear, you might want to give Mr. Houril a call and see if he still has an opening for Secretary of State."

"Very funny." Jane had half a slice of coffee cake on her plate, and she rationed off another sliver to nibble on. Britland watched her, waiting for the right moment to resume the conversation.

"Speaking for myself, Jane, I feel badly about what's happened between you and Andrew. In a way, I feel that I'm partly to blame . . ."

"What are you talking about? Don't be ridiculous."

The President shook his head. "I'm serious. I know how much of a private person you are, and being thrust into the spotlight these past few years hasn't been easy for you. It's not fair that you had to be put under the microscope."

"Oh, come on, Dad! I'm a big girl. I can't hide in a hole all my life."

"By the same token, having your private life in the headlines hasn't helped matters any." The phone on the table jangled to life. "Excuse me a minute, Jane . . ."

Britland carried the phone across the patio, leaving Jane alone with the rest of her cake. When she finished it, she moved her chair to the shade, turning so she faced the yard. During her father's term in office she had spent some of her most peaceful moments out there. She reflected on all the hours she had spent tending to the plants that bordered the property, coaxing seedlings through the first stages of development, fighting off weeds, making early morning inspections to keep the snail population in check. Even now, with the first chills of winter forcing plants into their dormant phases, there was considerable beauty to behold, a beauty even more treasured because she knew her own efforts had made it possible. Andrew had helped her occasionally, she recalled, despite his professed hatred for gardening. There was one time in particular, just before she wound up in the hospital, when they had spent an entire day in the backyard, listening to the Orioles play a doubleheader with Boston while they laid out a brick border to separate the flower beds from the lawn. It was an ordinary, unexciting day, but toward its close, when they started up the barbecue to grill chicken for a patio supper, Jane found herself thinking that she might be able to overcome her drinking without treatment, and that she and Andrew might be able to salvage their marriage after all. They laughed over dinner, talked excitedly about the future. She forced herself to slowly sip one glass of wine, making it last the entire meal and leaving the rest of the bottle for Andrew. He'd already had a few other drinks, and the wine started to get the better of him. When the sun set and Jane suggested they go inside and slip into something comfortable, she picked up on the sudden change in his mood. When she pressed him for an explanation, he exploded with the news that sent her toppling over the edge . . .

A newspaper suddenly slapped down hard on the tabletop, jarring her from her reverie. She looked up to see Andrew looming over her as if her thoughts had summoned him forth like some vengeful genie, rage in his eyes. He'd gone to stay at their cottage on Chesapeake Bay the night of their argument, and he looked as if he'd hardly slept the whole time he was away. His suit was rumpled and his face unshaven.

"I should have figured you'd pull something like this." His voice was ragged, high-pitched.

"What are you talking about?"

"What the hell do you think I'm talking about?" Andrew stabbed his finger at the paper. "This!"

Jane glanced down and saw a front-page picture of her confrontation with the *Washington Daily* photographer. She had just flung the wads of money at his feet and had her hands on her hips. "Oh, my God . . ." Jane quickly skimmed through Ed Lobyia's column next to the photo, which boasted exclusive news of the pending divorce and speculated that Andrew's womanizing and exploitation of his status as the President's son-in-law had led to Jane's "booze-drenched downfall and current string of public temper tantrums."

"Pretty good, huh?" Andrew said. "Nice can of worms you've opened up there, Jane, girl. I sure as hell hope you think it's worth it."

"I hope you don't think I —"

"I mean," Andrew cut in, "I would have thought that you, of all people, would have had the decency to go about a divorce quietly. But no, you have to make a big scene and see how deep you can drag my name through the mud."

"I didn't tell him anything!" Jane persisted. "You know me better than that!"

"Oh, do I?" Andrew shook his head and laughed. "I

don't know you at all. The woman I married drowned in a bottle. You're an imposter, a whining, snot-nosed little bitch who—"

"I'll thank you not to talk to my daughter like that, Andrew." George Britland came back to the table, holding the portable phone in his palm. He set it down and stared at his son-in-law. "And you have a lot of gall, putting anyone down for their drinking. At least *she* owned up to her problem."

"I didn't come here to pick a fight with *you*," Andrew muttered.

"You look like hell, Andrew," Britland said. He had yet to raise his voice. "Why don't you go in and get cleaned up?"

"Me? Why?" Andrew's voice was thick with sarcasm. "Hey, I'm just playing my part here. You know, the low-down dirty bad guy. Give me a few weeks and I'll have a mustache so long I'll be able to twirl it."

Britland's expression remained calm. "I suppose you're going to tell me all these accusations against you in the paper are unfounded."

"No," Andrew countered firmly. "I'm going to tell you there's two sides to every story, and if Daddy's Little Girl thinks she can get away with calling me the cause of all her problems, she's in for a rude awakening."

"Get out of here," Britland said.

"This is *my* house, Mr. President."

"Fine, then we'll leave." Britland turned to his daughter. "You're welcome to stay with us, Jane."

Jane shook her head. "That's okay."

"Yeah, because I plan on going anyway," Andrew said. "I just came by to get a change of clothes and to let Jane have an extra copy of the paper for her scrapbook. She can paste it up in her collection of personal tragedies."

"Don't you think you've said enough?"

"Yes, I think I have." A cocked, saber-like smile cut through the stubble on Andrew's face. "Goodbye. I'll be back later with the pickup to get some more of my things."

Andrew left a dreary silence in his wake. Britland sat down next to his daughter and put a hand on her shoulder.

"Why did I let it come to this?" Jane fought back tears. "He's right, you know. I'm always either blaming other people for my problems or having them take care of things for me."

"Nonsense."

"No, it's true!" Jane found a tissue in her purse and dabbed her eyes. "I mean, just yesterday I got new Secret Service agents assigned to me because I bitched to you about the old ones."

"Jane, you're just going through an incredibly rough time. You have to understand that you've been saddled with an obscene run of bad luck these past few years. I don't think there's anyone who could have weathered all you've been through without needing some help."

Jane took a few deep breaths and brought herself under control. After taking a look at her watch, she said, "You have to be going or you're going to be late for that meeting with Senator Kandel."

"Screw Senator Kandel," Britland said. "The last thing I want to do is lock horns with that bastard!"

"Maybe, but one thing you still want to do as President is push through that Hardlum-Smith bill, remember? You're going to have to twist Kandel's arm to get it, and keeping him waiting isn't going to help your cause. Go on, I'll be all right."

Britland nodded and stood up. "Some father I am. You need help and I'm the one who ends up getting the advice."

"I'll be okay, Dad. I promise."

"Well, if you say so."

Jane led her father to the door. The Secret Service agents fell in behind them. "Don't forget we've got a date for the opera tomorrow night."

"Oh, right." Britland kissed his daughter's cheek.

"Well, you take care of yourself in the meantime, okay? If you want anything, just call."

Jane nodded. "I want to apologize to Mom before you guys go."

Britland chuckled as they headed inside. "Too bad they canceled 'Family Feud,' isn't it? We would have been a shoo-in as contestants once I was out of office."

Chapter Ten

Onstage at the opera house of the John F. Kennedy National Center for the Performing Arts, stage hands were going through a trial run with the latest version of the giant snake that would be used in the opening scene of the upcoming performance of Mozart's *The Magic Flute*. The director had a thing about grandeur and had vetoed the previous incarnation of the serpent as being too short and unslithery to create the effect he was looking for. The new, improved snake, modeled after a Chinese dragon he remembered from a Mardi Gras parade in his youth, required six people working in tandem beneath the framework to give it the appropriate sidewinding movement. Only three workers had been required to operate the previous beast, and this was the first day on the job for the additional force.

"Very good." The director left his front-row seat and clapped his way to the stage. He echoed his compliments to those responsible for the creation of the new snake, then turned his attention to a few other last-minute preparations for the following night's performance. As the serpent's operators climbed out from underneath the creature, they were approached by the stage manager, a tall, grim-looking gray-clad woman.

"I need the three new men to come with me." A sweep of her long-fingered hand gestured to one of the side rooms in the wings, where two men in three-piece suits stood on either side of the doorway. One of the men had a clipboard and pen, the other a walkie-talkie. "These men are from the Secret Service," the woman explained. "They've already run security checks on everyone else working here, and they need to ask you a few questions for everybody's peace of mind. Please cooperate."

As the newly hired workers entered the room, one of them cracked, "I didn't vote for Britland. I hope that doesn't make me a security threat?"

"Not necessarily," the agent with the clipboard deadpanned. "We just like to take a few extra precautions, that's all. The President might be a lame duck, but he won't be a sitting one, too, if we can help it."

Indeed, the regimen of security checks being made in anticipation of the President's appearance at the opera was staggering. While staff maintenance crews wandered about the interior of the theatre, replacing light bulbs and scraping gum from the undersides of seats, an officer roamed nearby, holding the leash on a German shepherd that was sniffing the premises for any scent of a possible bomb. Elsewhere, other man-and-dog teams were prowling not only the foundation and roof of the Center, but also the lavish foyer and the performance halls that flanked the opera chamber. Still more agents were identifying strategic locations from which trained sharpshooters could survey the environs of the center. The banks of the Potomac were being carefully monitored, as were the nearby Theodore Roosevelt Bridge and all other approaches to the center.

Jack Damascus arrived at the opera house just as one of

the German shepherds was being paid off with biscuits for its efforts. Getting out of his car, he addressed the dog's handler. "The hospital's got a fresh supply of O and B positive," he said, referring to the President's and First Lady's respective blood types. "Stimson, their head of surgery, will be on call all evening. He's got one of his best cutters coming to the opera, too."

"Great," the other man said. "Pass along word to Boihr before you head out, okay?"

Damascus tracked down his supervisor inside the management office, where he was penciling in security arrangements on a grid map of the travel route from the White House to Jane's house and from there to the Center. The older man had his coat off and his sleeves rolled up. After Damascus relayed the news from the hospital, Boihr motioned for Jack to look at the map. "You know anything about this shop on the corner here, Damascus?"

Jack nodded. "One-story coffee shop. No roof access. Should be no problem covering it."

"That's what I wanted to hear. It's settled, then. We'll take 'em this way." He flipped his pencil around and traced the itinerary with the tip of his eraser. "Should take a hair over twenty minutes, I figure."

"Sounds right."

"By the way, Jack, how's that new shift working out?"

"With Jane?" Damascus shrugged. "Okay, I guess. She keeps a guy on his toes. I could have sworn she was going to start duking it out with that photographer the other day."

"But how *is* she?"

"How do you mean?"

"Word is this divorce thing might knock her for a relapse. We don't want to have to deal with another rampage like the one she pulled before she got put in rehab."

Damascus remembered the incident well. It was during midsummer, when word was just beginning to circulate about the extent of Jane's drinking problem. The Secret

Service had bolstered its protection around her as a routine precaution, but she had somehow managed to slip away on her own for more than an hour, during which time she had put away half a bottle of cognac while stumbling through one of the rougher neighborhoods in the city, baiting any-one she ran into to take advantage of her. Miraculously, or perhaps because she was recognized, no one had taken her up on her offer, and she had ended up down in one of the subway stations, where she had unsuccessfully tried to throw herself in front of an approaching train before subway employees subdued her and put through a call to the White House. Jane had been placed in the rehabilitation hospital that night.

"She's going through a rough time, but she's clean," Damascus said. "I don't think she's going to fall back."

"I hope you're right," Boihr said. "Any problems just getting along with her?"

"Well, she's not thrilled with the whole idea of having a government-issue guardian angel at her side all the time, but I don't think that's anything new. I wouldn't like it either."

"Amen to that."

Damascus was about to leave the office when another agent came in, carrying a computer readout. "We come up with seven iffies within fifty miles of here," he said to Boihr. An iffy was someone on record as having made some sort of threat against the President in recent years, either verbally or in print. "They're all under surveillance now. You think we should widen the radius?"

Boihr shook his head. "I think we've got things covered well enough. You and Damascus better get a move on if you're going to make your shifts on time."

"Right."

Damascus left with the other agent, Seamus McTeague, who had been assigned to the First Family detail for most of the past four years. McTeague was pale and blue-eyed with blonde hair that grew in tight curls around his narrow head. He and Jack were long-time acquaintances who spent many an off-duty evening on the racquetball court or golf course, playing to see who'd pick up the tab for dinner. As they got into Jack's car and pulled away from the opera house, Seamus wadded tobacco into his briar pipe and puffed the bowl into life.

"So, tell me, Jackie ol' boy. Has it happened yet?"

"Hmmmm?"

Seamus shook his match out and stuffed it in the ashtray. "You know what I'm talking about," he chuckled. "Cupid started making a nuisance of himself yet?"

Stopping for a traffic light, Jack turned to Seamus. "You've got it wrong, Seamus."

Seamus shook his head. "We're talking chemistry here, Jackie. I've seen the two of you around each other. You've both managed to put on a good show most of the time, but there's been sparks. Now that you can't possibly keep your distance from each other, how long do you think it'll be till the inevitable happens?"

The light changed and Damascus eased through the intersection. "It'll never happen, Seamus. You're crazy."

"I've got a C-note says I'm not."

"I don't want to have to take your money like that," Damascus laughed. "Beside, it's against regulations to bet. You know that."

"Malarkey," Seamus barked. "Come on, Jack. You can own up to it now. She's getting a divorce, right? By the time Britland's out of office, she'll be available. It's a natural. Why fight it?"

"You ought to go to work for one of those tabloids, Seamus. They can always use a gossip with an overactive imagination."

"Ahhh, stubborn man." Seamus clucked his tongue and watched landmarks race past the car on their way to the suburbs. Jack fell silent behind the wheel, trying to shut out his partner's needling.

He couldn't.

Chapter Eleven

An electrical malfunction forced an unscheduled closing of Hancock Park's Page Museum of Natural History. Visitors were diverted to the observatory for a consolation glimpse at caramel-colored bones and one of the black pits. The stream of gawkers was the largest J.T. Aames had encountered during his stint as security guard, and their constant presence played on his nerves. One of the things he had liked most about this job was the isolation and solitude, the chance to let his mind wander to secret realms. Now, with the ongoing distractions, there was no time for daydreaming, and he reluctantly divided his attention between the onlookers and his portable television. Several times he had to raid the donation box to make change for youngsters who wanted to purchase photo packets from the old vending machine near the door. He was returning to his TV from one such errand when he caught the end of a teaser announcement about news of Jane Britland-Hatch's pending divorce. Aames turned up the volume, but when the program cut away to a commercial he cued the sound back down. His pulse was already racing from the news. This was too good to be true! What an omen! He gaped, mesmerized, at the miniature screen. His mouth tightened, and he gnawed gently on the inside of his lower lip in anticipation. A second commercial came on, and at that point Johnny White entered the observatory and made his way through the visitors to Aames, one hand held out in front of him like a beggar.

"Been hiding from me all day, Aames." The man's palm floated in front of the small screen, blocking Aames's view. Aames looked up at White, who said, "Pay up, J.T."

"Huh?"

"Don't play dumb. Five bucks you owe me. You picked Boston by ten. The Lakers took 'em by thirteen. Sorry, kiddo, but you can't say I didn't warn you."

"Shit." Aames flumbled for his wallet, keeping one eye on the screen, where a dog in a clown suit was walking on its hind legs, pushing a dwarf lawn mower.

As White pocketed his winnings, he glanced over at the crowd. "Ain't seen this kinda business here in years. I sure picked the wrong weekend to sub for you. Say, what you got planned, anyway? Doin' something special?"

Aames shook his head impatiently. The walking dog, which had been peddling a no-nonsense lawn fertilizer, was gone, and the news was coming back on.

"Well, I gotta get back," White said. "Anything I should know about running things while you're gone?"

"You're the one who taught me the ropes, remember?"

White chuckled. "Hey, you think I don't know that? I was just pullin' your leg, kid. Lighten up. Take my advice and make sure you tie one on over the weekend. You been real on edge lately, y'know?"

Aames saw the first news item wasn't about Jane. He took his eyes off the tube and managed a grin at White. "Yeah, maybe I'll party down one night. Thanks for the idea."

"Don't mention it."

White left and Aames eased up the volume. When the segment on Jane's divorce began, the screen filled with the photo of her confronting the *Washington Daily* photographer, and the report quoted extensively from Ed Lobyia's column about the incident and speculated on the allegations that were likely to form the grounds for the divorce. When a head shot of Andrew Hatch flashed onscreen behind the news reporter, Aames felt his anger growing.

". . . likely fueled by a supposed string of extramarital affairs allegedly conducted by Hatch during the years of his marriage to the President's daughter," the reporter droned. "Hatch has given no official response either to the announcement of the divorce suit or the news of his wife's tangle with the media, but sources say he has already moved out of their Washington home to take up temporary residence at a family-owned vacation cottage on Chesapeake Bay . . ."

Aames absorbed the news with conflicting emotions. The official confirmation that things were over between Jane and Hatch gave him reason for joy and hope, but at the same time he couldn't help hating Hatch for what he'd done to Jane. It was a matter of honor. It wouldn't be enough for Aames merely to reclaim his beloved. Hatch had gone too far. He needed to be punished. Aames saw himself as the logical avenger.

Engrossed with his beckoning fate, Aames didn't notice a man approaching him until five slender fingers clasped themselves around his arm. Aames sprang away from the touch and whirled to find himself staring into the face of Michael Gasner. A rush of fear drowned Aames's musings over his destiny.

"Sorry. I didn't mean to startle you," Gasner said. "Do you remember me? I was here the other night. Georgia?" The man's voice was low, guarded.

"Yeah, I remember you." Aames forced himself to remain calm. "The Rotarian."

"Right. Mike Gasner. I, uh, got myself dragged here by my wife, of all people. Can you believe that?" The Rotarian gestured over his shoulder at a hefty, middle-aged woman who stood near the railing, gazing down at the pit. "She flew in this morning . . . said she wanted to surprise me. Christ, she's lucky she didn't come the other night or she would've gotten the surprise of her life, right?"

Aames nodded but said nothing.

Gasner lowered his voice even further. "That's what I wanted to talk to you about. You see, my wife'll be flying out tomorrow morning, but I'm sticking around another day after that, and I'd kinda like to get back in touch with Georgia, if you know what I mean . . ."

"What do I look like, a pimp?" Aames replied coolly. "I don't know the woman."

"You said she hung around here, though, right? You might see her again." Gasner slipped a ten-dollar bill into Aames's coat pocket. "Especially if you were keeping an eye out for her, eh?"

Aames sighed. "I can't make any promises."

"Just do what you can." The Rotarian pulled a business card from his pocket and scribbled something on it before handing it to Aames. "This is my room number at the Brea. Have her get in touch with me if you can."

"Like I said . . ."

"Yeah, yeah, no promises. Just try, that's all. That woman gives a guy his money's worth. You ever run into lips like hers? I bust my britches just thinkin' about it."

Two young boys had wandered over to where Aames and Gasner were talking. The Rotarian excused himself and went to rejoin his wife, allowing the boys to crowd in closer to Aames.

"We got a bet," the oldest youth said. "I say the tar pit here's only a few feet deep. My brother thinks it's deep enough to trap one of them hairy elephants."

"A mammoth," Aames corrected. "Some of the other

pits are big enough for them, but not this one. They figure it's only ten feet deep or so.''

"Then I win!" the older brother exclaimed, turning to his sibling. "You owe me twenty cents, Jonathan!"

Jonathan shook his head vigorously. "Uh-uh. Ten is more than a few. You said it was only a few feet deep. Nobody wins!"

They kept up the argument as they headed back to the railing, where Gasner and his wife were just getting ready to leave. He and Aames traded winks as the couple walked out of the observatory. Moments later, there was a loud gasp from young Jonathan as he pointed down through the railing.

"Billy! Look! Look!"

The other visitors quickly drifted toward the rail to investigate. Aames advanced warily and peered over the shoulders of the two boys. Their excitement was centered on nothing more than a series of bubbles that had worked their way to the surface of the pit and popped in slow motion, leaving round rings that quickly disappeared, leaving the surface undisturbed once more.

Chapter Twelve

The Marx Brothers were romping through their paces in *Duck Soup*. Scott and Regina sat on the floor, snickering at the screen. The bowl of popcorn between them was nearly empty. Their young son Darren wasn't interested in the movie, preferring to crawl about on all fours, leaving knee marks on the thick carpet. His attention eventually fell on a toy tractor lying on its side near the sofa, where Jane sat with a woolen afghan wrapped around her shoulders. The antics on the screen provided her with an occasional smile, but her mind invariably wandered to less comic terrains. As she watched her nephew play with the truck, making motor noises, she could not suppress a feeling of longing for the children she had never had. She wondered if things would have turned out differently if she'd become a mother.

Perhaps the challenge of parenthood would have forced her to stop dwelling on her personal problems. She marveled at the selfless ease with which her sister seemed to raise

Darren, remain close to Scott and still find time to advance her career at the marine biology lab, back in L.A., where she had gone to work after her college graduation. Jane wondered why it was that some people could be so adept at managing their day-to-day affairs when she could rarely even wake up in the morning without a shroud of gloom upon her, immobilizing her. Why did it have to be so damn difficult to be happy? Why couldn't she find contentment in the mere thought that she was alive, with a life full of promise waiting out there for her to discover?

In the room next to the den, Jack Damascus and Seamus McTeague sat at the dining table, involved in a game of chess. As Seamus pondered his next move, Damascus glanced into the den and saw Darren puttering his tractor across the floor toward him. There was a small truck under the table, and Jack set it into motion with his own sound effects. Darren stopped what he was doing and looked up at Damascus, puzzled. Damascus idled his truck next to the boy's tractor, then honked an imaginary horn and pretended to rev his engine. Darren laughed excitedly and prepared to race his tractor against the truck. Between the two of them they made enough noise to draw the attention of the others, and when the race was on, Darren's parents cheered him on. The boy thumped across the carpet on his knees, guiding his tractor on to victory when Damascus let the truck run out of gas and sputter to a stop.

"Yayyyyyy!" Darren cried out, raising his arms in triumph as he acknowledged the applause from the den. As Jane softly clapped, her eyes met Jack's and she smiled awkwardly before diverting her gaze.

"Thought you could distract me, huh?" Seamus chided as he skimmed his bishop across the board. "Guess again. Check."

Damascus returned to the table as Darren returned to the den, conducting his own grudge race between the two toys. After a pause of a few seconds, Jack reached over and leap-frogged his knight past Seamus's bishop, landing within striking distance of his opponent's king. "Checkmate."

Seamus puffed a cloud from his pipe and groaned as he scanned the board and realized his blunder. "Drat," he muttered. "You're a shrewd one, Jackie, I have to hand it to you."

"It's all in the wrists." Damascus helped his fellow agent put the chess pieces back into a box beneath the board. As he was slipping the box into a niche in the bookcase behind him, he noticed an old yearbook on the shelf and pulled it out. "Mind if I look at this?" he asked Jane.

"Go ahead," Jane said. "Just don't make any wisecracks about my freckles."

"Or my braces," Regina added.

For much of the past half hour, there had been periodic sounds coming from upstairs, and when Jack began to flip through the yearbook, Andrew Hatch came down the stairs with a large suitcase in either hand. He'd showered and shaved since morning, but the dark scowl was still stamped across his face.

"Want some help getting those to the car?" Damascus asked.

"I can manage."

Jane fingered the remote control to turn down the television, then rose from the sofa. "Don't get up on my account," Andrew snapped at her. "Anything else we have to say can wait. Better yet, let your lawyer talk to mine."

Jane left the den and caught up with Andrew as he was on his way out the door. "Look, I'm sorry it had to come to this, but —"

"Spare me, would you?"

Andrew left the house without looking back. Jane slowly closed the door and went back into the den, ignoring the concerned looks cast her way. Dropping back onto the sofa, she turned up the volume on the television. The Marx Brothers continued their mayhem, but no one was laughing any more.

"Listen, Jane." Regina stuffed Darren's pudgy arms into his jacket sleeves. "We've got dinner reservations at seven. Why don't you come along? We're having Chinese."

Jane shook her head. "Thanks, but I'm not that hungry. You guys go ahead."

Scott repeated the invitation, but Jane couldn't be swayed. She promised they'd get together for dessert after the opera the following night. Seamus accompanied Regina's family out of the house, leaving Jane and Damascus alone on the front porch. They stood quietly, watching the others get into their car and drive off. Jane crossed her arms in front of her and shivered at a stiff breeze that rolled across the landscaped lawn. A phalanx of thick, dark clouds was heading inland from the coast, filled with promise of the season's first snowfall.

"I hate the winters here," Jane said as they moved back inside. "Everything gets so cold and bleak. It makes me feel like I'm trapped in an Ingmar Bergman movie."

"Yeah, I know that feeling, too."

Jane turned up the thermostat. "Maybe I should take a vacation . . . somewhere nice and balmy. Miami or Bermuda."

"Why not fly back to L.A. with Scott and Regina?" Jack suggested. "They had some rain a couple of days ago, but supposedly things have cleared up."

"I'll have to think about that." Jane started cleaning up the den, gathering stray toys and drinking glasses. "I haven't been back home in . . . God, it must be more than three years now."

Damascus sat back down at the table and resumed looking through the yearbook. After a few pages, he grinned and remarked, "You're all over the place in here, Jane."

"I know. Isn't it terrible?" Jane came out of the kitchen

and joined Damascus at the table. "It's not so much that I was popular, though. You see, I was yearbook editor . . . and a bit of an egomaniac, I guess."

"Join the club," Jack said. "I worked on *my* yearbook, too, only I was head photographer. Made a lot of friends *that* year."

"I'll bet you did," Jane laughed, taking a seat next to him. As he went through the book, Jane supplied anecdotes to match some of the photos, happy for the chance to think about something other than the bleak present. There was an undeniable pleasure in looking back on a time when her life had been carefree and uncomplicated. For her, thoughts of high school brought back memories of the Beach Boys, skateboarding, slumber parties, clambakes on Zuma Beach and driving through the mountains around her home in the beat-up convertible her parents had helped her buy as an early graduation present. She'd had equally good times at school, and in most of the pictures she wore a wide, lively smile.

"Well, well, aren't you the glamorous one here . . ." Jack pointed to a prom picture that showed Jane in a floor-length evening gown with a revealing neckline. With her was a tall, thin youth with short hair and wide eyes, wearing a tuxedo a size too large for him.

"Boy, did I have to campaign to wear that dress," Jane recalled. "My mother kept telling me I was going to a dance, not a cathouse. Dad was on my side. Of course, if he only knew . . ."

"Who's the lucky guy?"

"Jimmy Aames. Everybody called him J.T., except for a few teachers that liked to get his goat by calling him James Aames."

"He looks pretty intense."

"You hit the nail on the head," Jane said. "That's what attracted me to him at first. We worked together on the yearbook. He was a real whiz at layout, took some of the pictures, too. We spent a lot of time working together, and the next thing we knew, we were caught up in this real fast-lane relationship. I'm talking real passion."

"What happened?"

"It got to be too much for me," Jane confessed. "I mean, we did some things I don't even want to own up to now. I broke it off a couple of weeks before graduation. J.T. dropped out of school and left town to live with his mother up in Oregon. Can you believe that? He left me this long, impassioned letter about how I'd broken his heart. I felt terrible that he was botching his chance for a diploma just because he felt this need to make a big statement."

"I guess we all had a heavy relationship like that in high school," Damascus said. "Mine wasn't quite that wild, but it came close. I broke up with a girlfriend, and she turned around and married the class bully out of spite. What a mistake. I saw her at a reunion a couple of years ago. Divorced with two kids . . ."

"Jimmy writes me these long, rambling letters every once in a while," Jane said. "And he always has a laundry list of all the new, bizarre things he's gotten himself into since the last time he wrote. I think I'm supposed to be impressed, but it always seems a little sad. Maybe it reminds me too much of things I've done that I'm not too proud of."

"You heard from him lately?"

"A little over a month ago, as a matter of fact, when I was still in rehab. He wrote to say he had the answer to all my problems and all I had to do was come live with him at this dude ranch in Nevada where he was working as a part-time cook and learning how to ride horses. There were about four pages of weird stuff about the time he took a handful of peyote buttons and went out to the desert to have visions. He said all he could think about was the kind of wonderful life we'd have if I got back together with him. And that's the most mundane of the letters he sent me."

"Sounds like a real character," Damascus reflected. "What did you write back?"

"Nothing," Jane admitted. "The truth is, I haven't answered any of his letters. I . . . I guess I didn't want to encourage him, you know? I figured I already had enough melodrama in my life."

Chapter Thirteen

The bus was ripe with possibilities for J.T. Aames, but he wasn't in the mood for games. His mind was still on Jane's divorce. He wanted to know more about it, to see if he could glean a signal from additional information. He got off the bus a few stops early and tracked down a large all-night newsstand with the widest selection of papers in the area. The stand stretched the full length of a storefront at the corner of Fifth and Standish and there were half a dozen people browsing through various offerings under the watchful eye of a crease-faced, gray-haired man in bib overalls and a thermal shirt. Near the man's feet was a resting Doberman that kept its own special vigil over the customers. Now and then the dog yawned, showing off tartared fangs.

"Do you have a copy of this morning's *Washington Daily*?" Aames asked the vendor.

"Nope," the old man said. "Sold out."

"Isn't that a copy right behind you?" Aames pointed to

a tabloid lying in a recess next to the vendor's three-legged stool.

"That one's already spoken for."

Across the top of the paper, Aames could see a headline touting Ed Lobyia's exclusive on Jane's divorce. He reached for his wallet and pulled out a twenty-dollar bill. "I'll give you five dollars for it."

The vendor shook his head. "I charge two bucks for the damn thing as it is. These things haveta get flown out here by air mail, you know. I'm damn lucky when I can get a same-day issue of this —"

"Ten dollars," Aames bartered, waving the bill like a wand in front of the man's face.

The vendor squinted at the currency. "What're those stains all over it? You trying to pawn some funny money?" Reacting to the tone in its master's voice, the Doberman began to growl its way softly to its feet. Aames took an involuntary step back and looked at the twenty, realizing it was the same one he'd given Georgia before he killed her. The stains were blood.

"I got it from the bank," he lied. "It must be good."

"Looks like that dye that sprays all over everything when there's a robbery." The vendor gave his dog a hand signal to silence it. The Doberman continued to stare at Aames as if it hadn't had its supper yet.

Aames went through his wallet and came up with an untainted tenspot, which the vendor finally accepted in exchange for the *Daily*. Much as he desired to sate his curiosity on the spot, Aames folded the paper under his arm and took it home. The building reeked from the party, and some posters still cluttered the hallway, but Debra wasn't home. He hadn't seen her since barging out of her apartment the night of his failed initiation.

Once inside his apartment, Aames snapped on his lights and quickly turned to Lobyia's column.

"Bastard," he muttered aloud as he read. "You goddamn prying bastard!" The initial volley was directed at

Lobyia, but by the time he was halfway through the column, Aames had refocused his anger on Andrew Hatch. What had she ever seen in him, anyway? He'd tried to warn her, as far back as the first time he'd read of her engagement. But either she had not received his letter or she had chosen to ignore his advice that no good would come of their marriage. He wouldn't rub it in when he saw her, though. He just had to make sure that Hatch was put out of the way for good. That would clear a path for him to get through to Jane.

When he'd finished reading, Aames flung the tabloid to the floor and began pacing. His nervousness persisted, and he assembled his darts and began throwing them at a board mounted on the wall next to the window. He forced himself to concentrate on his throwing, and the steady rhythm of his play helped give him a chance to think things through. He knew what needed to be done, and after a few games he had figured out a way to do it.

The night before Aames had left work at the Nevada dude ranch, he'd slipped into the management office to steal the petty cash, and he'd also helped himself to the ranch's answerphone. In all the time he'd been back in Los Angeles he'd received only six calls on the machine, but he still persisted in preparing messages and leaving the machine on whenever he left the loft. Tonight there were no responses, either. Aames switched the operating mode to record and pressed the activating button.

"This is J.T. Aames," he dictated, "and I can't get to the phone because I'm spending the weekend at Joshua Tree National Monument. I'll be back Sunday night, so if you want me to get in touch with you then, please leave your name and number when you hear the beep . . ." When the beep sounded, Aames switched the mode back to answer, then grabbed the yellow pages from under the bed and let his fingers do the walking through the listings for airlines. He dialed a number and waited. On the fourth ring he received a recorded message telling him to hold for the next available operator. Muzak cued up and poured through the telephone earpiece. Aames pulled the receiver a few inches away from his head and leaned across his bed, grabbing a tacky ceramic likeness of the Venus de Milo. Holding the statue like a club, he slammed it against the floor. Venus lost her head, revealing a hollow cavity in her torso that was filled with bills of various denominations. Aames upended the beheaded sculpture and shook the money out on the bed, then began counting it.

"Coast-to-Coast Airways," a cheerful woman's voice sounded on the line. "Thank you for calling. How can we help you?"

"Yes, this is Kent Rembo," Aames said. "I'd like to book a seat on the next available flight to Washington."

Chapter Fourteen

There was a little color left in the cloud-choked sky as Jane stared out the bay window of her bedroom. She wore a forest-green Dior evening dress that her parents had given her for her last birthday, and across her bare shoulders she had draped a shawl to ward off the chill creeping in through the window. Over the years, this corner of the room had become her favorite part of the entire house. There was a quiet intimacy to the area, and she could climb up into its padded recess during late afternoons to read by the light filtering through trees in the back yard. Between chapters she could set the book down and reflect on what she had read while staring out at the yard and feeling the sun's warmth on her face. Like her hours spent in the garden, those were times of simple contentment, times during which she felt at peace with herself and her life. And yet she hadn't spent more than a few minutes here in recent months; her anxieties had interfered so much with her concentration that reading had become a chore, not a pleasure.

A rapping of knuckles on the bedroom door roused her from her latest broodings. Dora peered into the room. "You almost ready, hon? The limo should be here any minute."

Jane watched the last glint of sun dip below the horizon, then leaned away from the window and turned to her mother. "I'm all set." She went to the dresser and retrieved a jade necklace from a teak jewelry box. "Can you help me put this on?"

"Of course."

The two of them faced the mirror as Dora stepped behind her daughter and fixed the clasp holding the string of green stones in place. She noticed Jane staring at a wedding portrait on the dresser, a picture of her and Andrew the day they had exchanged their vows. She was also aware of the gaping spaces in the walk-in closet off to her right, left by Andrew when he removed his things the day before. "It must feel strange here now."

"I still can't believe it," Jane murmured, eyes lingering on the photograph. "We were so happy then. I had so much hope for the future..."

"With time, you'll find that hope and happiness again, Jane. I'm sure of it."

Jane turned from the mirror and smiled sadly. "Spoken like a true mother."

"I mean it, Jane. And listen to me. You and I may get on each other's nerves from time to time, but deep down you know I'll never stop loving you."

"I *do* know that." Jane breathed deeply and picked up her clutch purse from the edge of the bed. "Well, we'd best be going, hmmmm?"

As the women left the room, Dora said, "Andrew switched tickets so he won't have to sit with us."

"He mentioned that to me yesterday. Who'd he switch with?"

"Somebody named Hunter Stead. He's with one of the oil companies. Have you ever met him?"

Jane shook her head. "No, but Andrew's mentioned

him a few times. I think they belong to the same health club."

Stead was waiting downstairs with George Britland and a handful of Secret Service agents, including Jack Damascus. Jane felt an instinctive aversion to Stead the moment she laid eyes on him. He looked like someone Dr. Frankenstein might have created if he'd been a Madison Avenue executive. He had that rugged yet polished look, wore a tailored Brooks Brothers suit, and sported a perfect tan and the kind of white-capped smile that finances dental tax shelters. After the President had introduced him to Jane, Stead said, "It's a pleasure to meet you, I must say. You look just stunning in that gown. It's a Dior, isn't it?"

"Yes. Thank you."

"You could be their spokesperson. Really."

"Thanks again." Jane blushed slightly. Catching Damascus's gaze, she rolled her eyes.

"In case you hadn't guessed," George Britland drawled, "Mr. Stead is a lobbyist. Flattery is his stock in trade . . . though that's not to say you don't look absolutely radiant tonight, Jane."

"Maybe we'd better go before my head swells too much to get through the door," Jane said.

Damascus peered through the living-room curtains. "The motorcade's here."

As the group stepped outside, Jane looked up at the stars that were dimly visible through the cloud cover. "It's such a nice night. I wish we could just walk to the opera for a change. It isn't all that far, after all."

"Maybe in the spring," Britland suggested, "when I've been officially demoted to a mere citizen."

"You'll never be a mere citizen, husband dear," Dora teased. "And forget the demotion nonsense. After January they promote you to Distinguished Elder Statesman."

The President grinned at Hunter Stead. "You're not the only smooth talker around here."

Scott and Regina were already waiting inside one of the three limousines idling in front of the house. A small contingent of motorcycle officers and agents in other security vehicles accompanied the motorcade. As they headed down the walk, Stead fell into step beside Jane. "I hope my being here isn't too awkward for you?"

"Oh, no," Jane lied. "We opera junkies get so keyed up for a performance that everything else seems to —"

"Take a back seat?" Stead finished her sentence for her, at the same time opening the rear door of the limousine and gesturing for her to get in.

"Yes, that's it." As Jane approached the limo, she glanced over at Jack Damascus. He sensed her unspoken plea and intercepted Stead before he could follow Jane into the back seat.

"I'm sorry, sir," he told the lobbyist, "but the President and First Lady are sitting back here with Jane. If you'll follow me to the next car . . . ?"

Stead was momentarily taken aback, but he quickly regained his poise. "Oh, sure. Fine. Well, I'll see you all there, I guess."

Jane smiled her gratitude at Damascus before the agent led Stead to the last limo. When George and Dora joined their daughter in the back seat, the President snickered, "I somehow get the feeling that Andrew is taking out some sort of perverted revenge on us."

"George! That's hardly funny," Dora chided.

"Oh, come on, Dora. Did you see that man's teeth? He's a trained piranha. Why, we hadn't had more than a sip or two of our drinks back at the house before he was already trying to grease the skids for whatever crap he's hoping to run past me by the time tonight's over."

"How so?"

"He mentioned there's an opening on their board of directors," George said. "He thinks it's possible they could wait to fill it until next February if I were interested. Of course, while I'm still President it'd be real swell if I'd go along with them on the depletion-allowance bill that comes up next week, right?"

Jane sighed as she looked out of her window at the motorcycle cops riding alongside their moving limousine. "I guess when Andrew decided to switch tickets he wanted to make sure he'd get somebody who'd remind us of him. How thoughtful."

Chapter Fifteen

Wet and glistening from its trip through a storm front that had drifted over the Appalachians, the Coast-to-Coast DC-10 touched down on the runway at Dulles International and taxied to a stop near its designated terminal. Ground personnel carefully maneuvered the enclosed exit ramp to the side of the plane and made the necessary connections to allow those aboard to disembark after their nonstop flight from Los Angeles. J.T. Aames patiently followed the stream of passengers down the ramp and into the terminal, where cries of welcome greeted those with friends and loved ones waiting for them. He ignored the various reunions and made his way to the gift shop, where he bought the latest edition of the *Washington Daily*. Once he had gone to the baggage claim area, he skimmed through the tabloid in search of the next cue for action. As anticipated, he found the information he was seeking in Ed Lobyia's column, which mentioned the First Family's plans to attend the opera that evening at the Kennedy Center. The columnist predicted an interesting evening, since both Jane and Andrew were ardent opera buffs and were both likely to be at the performance despite their recent separation.

When the luggage began tumbling down into view, Aames inched his way to the edge of the conveyor belt and awaited the arrival of his suitcase. Across the way, he spotted an attractive blonde woman in a sable coat standing beside a chauffeur, pointing out a tooled leather hatbox headed their way on the conveyor. As the chauffeur leaned forward to grab the box, the woman glanced up and saw Aames watching her. He refused to look away. She had long lashes, wide seductive eyes and an inviting smile. Aames felt a stirring in his loins as he pondered the thought of approaching her. Here was a challenge of another sort, no mere stalking of unsuspecting prey. This would require wit, charm and a good deal of shrewdness.

The arrival of his suitcase forced a decision, and Aames chose to leave the woman alone. There were more pressing matters to attend to. He had no time for surrogates. There was a car-rental agency operating out of the terminal, and Aames put down money for an inconspicuous Omega. During his stay at the dude ranch in Nevada, Aames had paid for a counterfeit driver's license in the name of James York, and the crease-faced man behind the counter accepted the indentification unquestioningly. Getting directions to a nearby tuxedo rental shop, Aames left the terminal and put his suitcase in the trunk of the car. Before slamming down the trunk lid, he opened the suitcase and removed his dart case. From previous trips, he knew he could transport darts in his luggage without arousing suspicion, whereas questions might be asked if he tried to carry them aboard the plane.

The tuxedo shop was closing for the night when Aames pulled into the small plaza where it was located. He had to bribe the manager with twenty dollars to get him to track down an outfit in the right size. Aames left a cash deposit, signed for the suit under his assumed name, and changed into the tuxedo before leaving.

The man at the shop had given him directions to the Kennedy Center, and as he drove through the crowded streets, Aames kept an eye on the skyline for the Washington Monument or some other landmark. Under cover of night, this section of the city didn't seem much different from parts of Los Angeles. The Southwest Freeway finally brought him within sight of the sprawling Tidal Basin, and soon he was surrounded on all sides by architectural tributes to bygone presidents. By the time he'd passed under the Arlington Memorial Bridge, putting the rain-swollen Potomac on his left, traffic was barely moving. Just as the Kennedy Center came into view several blocks away, Aames was forced to a complete stop by a police barricade. Lights flashed atop the squad cars that formed the barrier, giving Aames brief cause for concern, but within a few moments he was able to make out the front end of the motorcade passing through the intersection ahead of him. He was only seven cars back from the barricade, so he turned off his engine and joined the other motorists who had gotten out of their vehicles for a glimpse of the presidential party. All the limousines had tinted windows, so Aames couldn't see Jane, but he felt certain she was there, and he smiled broadly at the omen. How promising. After so many years and so many miles, here they were, within a few dozen yards of one another. Soon they would be much closer than that.

A middle-aged couple stood next to Aames as the motorcade rolled by. The husband, a stocky man in a trenchcoat, strained on tiptoes as he held a flash camera close to his face. "Come on, Mr. President," he urged. "Roll down yer window and wave, damn it!"

"Fat chance, Harry." The woman waddled back to their car on spiked heels that threatened to buckle under the unwieldy mass they were forced to support. "He ain't gonna be President for much longer, so he don't have to kiss up to common folk no more."

When the last of the security-flanked limousines drove by without any of its passengers revealing themselves, the husband lowered his camera and circled around to his side of the car. "Yer right there, Sylvia. That Britland was never much fer flashin' his mug around, even before we made him the big cheese. Always usin' that assassination mumbo jumbo to hide out from the folks that got him where he is."

Aames got back in his car and started up the engine. When the barricade was lifted, he drove another two blocks to a parking lot within walking distance of the Kennedy Center. As he was leaving the lot, he happened to glance up and saw men atop several buildings. Some had binoculars and walkie-talkies, while others held high-powered rifles with telescopic sights.

There was a long line trailing out from the entrance to the Center, and Aames was directed to take a place at the end of it. The patrons filed slowly into the building, and when Aames stepped out to get a better view of what was causing the delay, he saw that ticketholders were being asked to step through a metal detector like the ones used at airports. Every time a patron set off the detector's alarm, security officers moved in with wandlike devices to pinpoint the source of the buzzing, which was usually keys or pieces of jewelry. Aames reflexively patted the breast pocket of his tuxedo, feeling the contour of his dart case. As the line proceeded, Aames began to sniffle, then cough with increasing frequency. Finally, he apologized to the people next to him and excused himself, asking to have his place in line saved while he returned to his car, supposedly for cough drops he'd forgotten to bring along.

As he left the line and headed back to the parking lot, his cough left him. He slipped his darts from the tuxedo and secreted them inside the Omega before returning to the line, eventually passing through the metal detector without incident, having purchased a ticket to tonight's opera from a scalper moments before.

Chapter Sixteen

Despite Jane's subtle attempts to alter seating arrangements, when the First Family came to their private section of the balcony, she ended up next to Hunter Stead, who showed no signs of discomfort and failed to sense her unease. Mired in his long-held philosophy that charm conquers all, he kept up a constant banter, invariably finding a way to make a connection between any given topic and what seemed to be his assigned mission for the evening — getting George Britland to seriously consider a future position on the board of directors of Global Oil. The President was sitting on the other side of Jane, and he gracefully fielded Stead's barrage of chat as he glanced over the program notes. His patience quickly reached its limits, however.

"You'll have to pardon my gruffness, Mr. Stead," Britland said finally. "But if there's one thing I hate worse than a lobbyist, it's one who lobbies when I'm trying to settle into a good evening of Mozart. Now, do you mind . . . ?"

Stead raised his palms like someone placed under arrest. "Touché, Mr. President," he said with a disarming grin. "My apologies. Force of habit, you understand."

Britland nodded. "Of course." When Stead looked away, gazing at the crowd that was slowly filling the theater, the President winked at his daughter, who let out a long breath and pretended to wipe sweat from her brow.

Sitting behind the First Family, Jack Damascus and Seamus McTeague scanned the buzzing enclosure, locating the other agents posted near strategic exits and aisles. After a few moments, Damascus glanced down at Jane, who was seated directly in front of him. She'd taken off her shawl, and Jack admired the smooth contours of her shoulders and the delicate tapering of her slender neck. He sensed a tension there, and fought off a whimsical urge to reach forward and massage the soft flesh, to gently knead the taut muscles until she was completely relaxed and ready to lean her head back so that he could kiss her scented hair.

"Nice necklace, isn't it?" It was Seamus murmuring in his ear.

"Yeah."

"How many are there?"

"What?"

Seamus cocked an eyebrow and smiled slyly at his fellow agent. "The jade, Jackie. I thought maybe you were counting the stones."

The dimming of the house lights helped mask the redness creeping up Damascus's neck. He was going to have to lay off the daydreaming before it got him into serious trouble. Looking away from Seamus, he turned his attention to the orchestra pit, where a bearded conductor was readying his baton to begin the score. The whispers and coughs throughout the theater quickly subsided as the overture was played, the curtains opened to the first burst of activity onstage, and several thousand opera glasses were raised and focused on the feathered figure that scrambled in terror from the undulating rush of the new, improved serpent.

Far back in the upper balcony, one set of rented binoculars was trained not on the stage but on the presidential box seats. J.T. Aames had a clear view of Jane and the rest of the First Family from his seat. His hands trembled against the binoculars as he focused the lenses. He hadn't glimpsed Jane in person for more than ten years, and to see her now filled him with an almost giddy rapture that was enhanced by the strains of Mozart swelling from the orchestra pit. Jane's hairstyle still annoyed him, but in every other way her beauty lived up to his memories and expectations. She was intently watching the performance on stage, but he could see her inner turmoil reflected in the way her lips were pressed together, and the way she held her arms crossed protectively in front of her. Soon they would be together, and all would be well. But first, there were certain matters for him to attend to.

Seeing that Andrew Hatch wasn't beside Jane, he panned his binoculars to take in the others sitting near her. No sign of Hatch. Who was the man with her? he wondered. She couldn't be seeing someone else already. It wasn't possible. No, there had to be another explanation. But where the hell was Hatch? Aames had been counting on Hatch's being there. His absence changed everything. As the opera proceeded, shifting gracefully through moments of humor, solemnity and hopeful grandeur, Aames struggled to plan his next move. Every few minutes he would look back at Jane and Hunter Stead, trying to fathom their relationship. The man would periodically glance Jane's way, but she would never return his gaze, and Aames could see that she was going out of her way to avoid any contact with him. Good. Maybe he was just a relative. Aames took consolation from the thought, letting it take the edge off his frustration. He kept his attention on Jane, reveling in her every gesture and speculating more about their reunion. Should he take her into his arms that moment they were together, or should he hold back and let the first move be hers? It would be a shock to her, seeing him after all these years. He decided it would be better to let her get over the initial surprise. Then she would be the one who rushed to him. Yes, it would be much better that way. Now, he only had to figure out the best time and place to meet her.

Aames was still peering through his binoculars when someone suddenly leaned into his side, startling him. He turned just as the man next to him was blinking his eyes open. He'd fallen asleep and slumped into Aames. "Sorry," the man said.

Aames kept the binoculars on his lap for the rest of the act, wary that he might have drawn attention his way from his earlier gawking. After all, he could clearly see half a dozen Secret Service agents from where he was seated. When the audience applauded the cast before the intermission, Aames clapped too, all the while keeping his eyes on the presidential box. Seeing Jane and the others leave their seats, he too headed for the aisle and followed the other spectators to the Grand Foyer. He spotted more agents on the way and knew he was going to have to remain inconspicuous if things were to work out the way he wanted.

The Grand Foyer was brilliantly lit by eighteen massive Orrefors crystal chandeliers weighing a ton apiece, and the conversational hum of patrons swelled throughout the carpeted enclosure as lines formed at several bars offering a range of drinks. Aames bought a glass of champagne and lingered at the periphery of a crowd gathered around the First Family. He didn't want to show himself to Jane now, but he wanted to get closer to her none the less. There was a potted tree in one corner of the room that offered a semblance of cover, and Aames took up position behind it, lighting a cigarette as an excuse to stay put by the ashtray next to the tree.

Between Aames and the First Family, Jack Damascus and Seamus McTeague stood watching the crowd, making certain no one made any sudden, suspicious movements in the direction of the President or the rest of his party. No one made such a move until Andrew Hatch elbowed his way through the throng of well-wishers to his wife's side. He had a half-emptied plastic cup in his hand, and it clearly wasn't his first drink of the evening.

"Quite a show, huh?" he said loudly. "Domingo's in good voice tonight."

"So are you, Andrew," the President commented.

"So I am." Hatch swilled the rest of his champagne, then tossed the plastic cup in the direction of a nearby wastebasket, missing it by a good three feet. "Oops. Somebody better nab that rebound."

Jane shook her head in disgust and started to walk away, muttering, "I don't believe this."

"Don't believe *what*, Janie dear?" Andrew taunted as he moved to follow his wife.

"Andrew, you're drunk. Leave me alone."

"Oh, I'm making a *scene*, is that it?" Hatch laughed. "You don't want anybody practicing your specialty, right?"

Hunter Stead caught up with Hatch and put a hand on his shoulder to keep him away from Jane. "Hey, partner," he said casually. "Looks like you've tied one on. Maybe we ought to go get some fresh air. What do you think?"

Andrew waved away the suggestion. "Forget it. You wanna know what I think? I think we oughta switch places again. The bimbo you stuck me with isn't going to put out, and I don't want to have to spend another two hours smelling that drain cleaner she wears for perfume. I wanna sit with my wife."

"Well, there's no way I'm going to sit with you," Jane retorted. "Especially in your condition."

"In my condition?" Hatch laughed again. "Hey, what about all the times I stood by you when you were in *your* condition? Let's talk about that, why don't we?"

The altercation was drawing a larger crowd by the second, and other agents hurried over to try to bring things under control. Jane and Andrew traded a few more words, then Andrew made a threatening gesture at his wife, and

Damascus joined Hunter Stead in trying to restrain the man. Hatch broke free from their hold and started taking wild swings at his would-be captors. Damascus ducked one swing and returned another of his own, connecting with Andrew's jaw and sending the man staggering backwards until he lost balance and fell to the floor.

"I didn't want to have to do that," Damascus told no one in particular as he rubbed his knuckles.

"I did," Seamus grinned, as he watched Stead help Andrew to his feet and lead him away. Stead was having trouble steering Hatch on his own, and Seamus came to help. Aames stayed close to the potted tree and lit another cigarette as Hatch was brought within earshot.

"I think I ought to get him out of here," Stead told Seamus.

"Good idea. You know where he's staying?"

Stead nodded. "He's at the Diplomat. I'll drive him there. Give my regards to the President and his family. Not that they'll miss me..."

Aames waited until Stead and Hatch had left the building, then took his binoculars over to the vendor he'd rented them from.

"I want to turn these in," he said.

"Is there something wrong with them?"

"No, they're fine," Aames said. "It's me. I'm not feeling too great. I think I'm going to call it a night."

Chapter Seventeen

The Diplomat, a mirror-surfaced hotel on Virginia Avenue, boasted penthouse views of both the Washington Monument and the Lincoln Memorial. Despite its name, it wasn't a particularly prestigious establishment, although one of the travel guides had given its restaurant's cuisine and wines a three-star rating. Valets in crimson blazers stood near the front and side entrances, waiting to park cars for arriving guests. Hunter Stead drove past the attendants, however, and pulled into a parking space behind the hotel. Less than two minutes later, J.T. Aames arrived at the lot and backed the Omega into a spot from which he could see Stead helping Andrew Hatch to the back entrance. If anything, Hatch seemed drunker than when he had left the opera. And meaner.

"What a cunt! Can you believe that bitch, Hunter?"

"Shhhh, keep it down, Andy, would you?"

"Ah, fuck it!" Hatch veered from side to side, muttering a few words that were lost in the slur of his speech.

"I hate to be the one to say it, partner, but you're going to regret this, come tomorrow."

"Ah, fuck tomorrow, too!" Andrew fumbled for something in his coat. A pint of peppermint schnapps crashed to the sidewalk, scattering glass shards in a green pool of liquor. Hatch kicked at the glass as Stead struggled to hold him up. Fifty yards away, Aames was quietly slipping out of his car and heading toward them.

"Knock it off, Hatch!" Stead snapped. "Straighten up and fly right, God damn it! Show a little brains for a change, why don't you?"

Hatch stopped and wavered in place as he narrowed his bloodshot eyes at Stead. "You callin' me on? That it? You wanna fuck with me?"

"I'm not the type, asshole." Stead steered Andrew toward the doorway.

"Yeah, you're a pussy man, like me, right?" Hatch chortled. "Shit, man, the night is young. Let's go grab us some snatch somewhere. Whaddaya say?"

"I say forget it. The only thing you're going to grab are forty winks."

There were other people in the parking lot, so Aames made his way slowly to the hotel, waiting until Stead and Hatch were in the lobby before entering the building. He saw them get into one of the elevators, then went over and kept an eye on the numbers above the framed doorway. As the elevator ascended, the numbers lit up to indicate which floors it was stopping at. To Aames's relief, the elevator made only one stop, on the eleventh floor, before heading back down to the lobby. The doors to a second elevator rang open behind Aames, and he stepped in.

"Almost there." Stead helped Hatch down the corridor to his suite. "I hope you still have your key on you."

"Yup." Hatch reached into his pocket and pulled out a small glass vial filled with white powder. "Here ya go!"

"Put that away, you idiot!" Stead grabbed the cocaine.

"That's just what you need — to get your butt thrown in the slammer on top of everything else. Christ, would you sober up, Hatch?"

"You calling me on again?"

Stead opened the door and dragged Hatch inside. "You should be thanking me instead of giving me all this shit."

"Don't shout, man." Hatch staggered into the bedroom and toppled onto the bed. The alcohol was finally blunting his rage and luring him into a stupor.

"Look, you stay put," Stead advised him. "I'm going down the hall to get some ice."

"Good idea," Hatch murmured without opening his eyes. "Keep an eye open for some pussy while you're at it."

"Yeah, right, Romeo."

Stead stopped off in the bathroom to sample Hatch's cocaine. By the time he came back out, Andrew had passed out and was beginning to snore. Stead left the room and sorted through his pockets for change. At the end of the hallway was a small side room containing a bank of vending machines and a large ice-maker that churned out a steady supply of cubes from its rumbling bowels. As he reached for a plastic bucket, someone abruptly dodged out from behind the machine.

"What the hell?" Stead shouted at a four-year-old boy, who charged past him squealing with frantic joy as he ran off along the hallway. Another boy not much older appeared seconds later, taking up the chase with a steady whoop. "Hey, you little brats!" Stead shouted at them. "This isn't a damn playground!"

The boys fled to the stairway as Stead filled the ice bucket and returned to the hallway. He watched for them on his way back to the room, fighting back his temper, which had been sorely tested the whole evening. He had left Hatch's door ajar so he wouldn't have to set down the ice to unlock it. When he pushed his way in, he was startled by the sight of someone inside, heading for the bedroom .

"Who the fuck are you, pal?" Stead demanded.

Aames whirled around. In one swift motion, he jabbed his right hand forward, plunging the tip of his dart into the lobbyist's chest. Stead's eyes widened as he dropped the ice bucket and felt himself being forced back against the door, which closed behind him with a loud slam. The two men stood face to face as Aames twisted the dart and pressed against Stead with his full weight.

"P-p-p-p-please . . ." Stead whimpered hoarsely as blood bubbled in his throat, choking his plea. Aames took a step back, and Stead dropped lifelessly to the floor, staining the carpet with his blood.

"That you, Hunter?" Hatch called out drunkenly from the bedroom. "Back with some pussy so quick?"

Aames slowly walked to the bedroom and stood in the doorway, staring at the drunken man on the bed. Andrew had his back turned to Aames and was trying to sit up. When he finally managed to thwart gravity and raise himself, Hatch looked toward the doorway and realized for the first time that it wasn't Stead watching him.

"Hey, whaa — ?"

A dart slammed into Hatch's face, obliterating his left eyeball before the point lodged in his brain. A muted scream died in his throat as he twitched from the impact of two more darts striking him in quick succession. One punctured his neck, severing the carotid artery. The other embedded itself in his chest. Falling back, Hatch slipped off the edge of the bed and tumbled to the floor, forcing the darts further into his body.

Aames stood calmly over the dead man and nudged him with the tip of his shoe, then turned the body over so he could retrieve his darts. He carefully wiped the reddened shafts on Hatch's suit until the points were clean, then took them to the sink and rinsed them off further before putting them back in the case.

From the hallway just outside the kitchen area, he had a clear view of both bodies, which lay in contorted sprawls.

Aames didn't feel as if his vengeance was yet complete. He went into the suite's living room and pulled aside the curtains, gauging the length and strength of the cords.

The Diplomat Restaurant had an outside terrace for patio dining, and even though temperatures were steadily dropping at this time of year, there were a few diners willing to brave the chill for the pleasure of the outside view. Large butane heaters helped combat the cold, as did an outdoor fireplace that crackled loudly, while its flames devoured chunks of split pine. A young couple held hands across their table near the outer railing furthest from the fireplace. They were happily reflecting on the tourist haunts they had visited that day when the man suddenly frowned and pulled his hand away from the woman's. When she asked what the problem was, he pointed to the red splotches that had suddenly appeared on the sleeve of his camel's-hair jacket. The crimson downpour increased, splattering off the tablecloth and changing the color of their drinks, and the couple looked up. The woman screamed. Ten floors up, two men were hanging by their necks from one of the room terraces. Stripped of clothes and steadily leaking blood, the bodies twisted eerily in the night breeze.

Leaving the room, Aames slowed to a brisk walk and headed for the stairwell. The corridor was vacant, but as he reached the door, the two young boys came scrambling around the corner, playing tag. The lead youth collided with Aames and fell to the floor, crying out in pain. The other child was able to stop himself before running into Aames.

"Excuse me, mister," the boy on the floor apologized.

Aames stared at the boy. His right hand went for the breast pocket of his coat, but he changed his mind and held his hand out instead to help the boy to his feet.

"You should be more careful," he advised in a soft, kind voice. "Somebody could end up hurt."

"Yes, sir," the youth said. "We won't do it again. Promise."

"Good." Aames opened the door to the stairwell. "See that you don't."

The moment the door closed and Aames started down the steps, the two boys resumed their game with boisterous abandon, only to be stopped by the pair of security officers who bolted out of the elevators and strode purposefully down the hall to Andrew Hatch's room.

Chapter Eighteen

As she got out of the limousine and started up the walk toward her house, Jane hummed her favorite excerpt from *The Magic Flute*. Jack Damascus walked beside her, his eyes scanning the lawn until he spotted the agent assigned to watch over the property. The two men waved to one another, then Jack told Jane, "I have to confess, it's been a while since I've seen you in such good spirits."

"It's Mozart," Jane sighed happily. "The man was an absolute genius. The things he could do with music . . . . Didn't you just love it?"

"Well, actually, opera's never been my strong suit," Jack confessed. "It was nice to look at, though. Good sets and costumes. My favorite was the snake."

"Philistine!" Jane climbed the front steps and sorted through her keys. "You just need some more exposure, that's all. Listen, why don't you come in and let me play you something from *Don Giovanni*? If that doesn't move you, you're beyond all hope."

"Thanks, but Lew here's taking over for me now, so —"

"So that means you're off-duty and can relax," Jane countered quickly. "Maybe that's what you need to get in the proper frame of mind."

"Well, if you insist . . ."

"I do."

Jack excused himself long enough to speak with the other agent, then joined Jane inside. She put the opera record on her stereo, then retreated to the kitchen and placed a kettle over the range. "Tea, Jack?"

Damascus nodded, standing in the doorway so he could hear the music, which reflected a far more sorrowful side of Mozart than the opera he'd just heard. As he watched Jane bustling around the kitchen with a half-smile on her face, his curiosity finally got the better of him. "Can I ask you a question?"

"Sure. Fire away."

"When your husband was acting up back at the theater, I could have sworn you were on the edge of losing control, if you know what I mean. And now . . ."

"And now . . . I *have* gone over the edge," Jane said, taking tea bags from an antique tin box and dropping them into the teapot. "That little melodrama of Andrew's gave me a chance to see how insufferable people can be when they wear their weakness on their sleeves. He did me a favor, actually. He was right, you know, about the way I always used to be the one making scenes." The kettle began to whistle. She took it off the flame, poured boiling water into the pot, and when the brew was ready, filled two cups and brought them over to the table. Motioning for Jack to sit down, she went on. "Do you remember the other day, when I was telling my lawyer why I quit writing?"

"Vaguely," Jack recalled. "I wasn't listening closely enough to catch all of it."

"Well, I told him I gave up writing because I couldn't

take the rejections. That was only a fraction of the truth, though."

Jack stirred sugar into his tea. "Oh?"

Jane sat down across from him. She hesitated for a moment, then said, "During my senior year in college, I was a real hotshot on campus as far as the literary crowd went. A couple of my professors sent around some of my stories and even helped me sell one to *Esquire*. It was a real ego boost, and naturally I wanted to go myself one better. For my last advanced fiction writing class, I decided I was going to write a novella.

"My roommate at the time was going through some pretty intense things. Drugs, a string of lousy relationships, some family problems back home. Cindy was her name. She ended up being the model for the main character in this novella, and I made her out to be this real doomed heroine. Of course, I put a part of myself into the story, too, but once I'd finished the piece and turned it in, word got around that I'd written an exposé of Cindy. I tried to play down the comparisons, but people had already made up their minds. The story made the school literary magazine, then was picked up by *Atlantic Monthly*, so the damn thing would never die down. The gossip just destroyed Cindy. I came home one day and she'd moved. I didn't know where. A week later I found out she'd killed herself."

Jane's eyes glazed over and she stopped talking for a moment, glancing away from Damascus while she tried to reign in her emotions. When she resumed, there was a strained crackle in her voice. "She left a letter. I don't remember the exact words, but the basic message was that I'd betrayed her, ripped the scabs off her wounds and showed them off to everyone. Something like that . . ."

The music in the background mirrored the bleakness of Jane's story, and the retelling had been enough to undermine her brief show of good cheer. Watching her stare into her teacup, Jack wondered why she'd brought up the story in the first place. He told her, "That's quite a burden to have dumped on someone. But I still don't see the connection between that and tonight."

"Don't you?" Jane said. "For all these years I've been carrying around this load of guilt, letting it run my life for me. I've always had this attitude that I don't have a right to be happy after what I did to Cindy, and everything I've done has reinforced that. Seeing Andrew behave the way he did tonight gave me a chance to see what I must have looked like most of these past few years, and that was enough to make me realize how much I want to change."

"I see."

They sat without talking for a few moments, while an aria drew to a close. Then Jack raised his cup and proposed a toast. "Well, here's to changes for the better."

"Yes." Jane tapped her cup against Jack's. "What do you say we listen to the rest of the album in the other room? Are you enjoying it?"

Damascus smiled. "I take it this isn't a comic opera."

"You might say that. If you think I've just told you a sob story, you ought to read over the libretto of *Don Giovanni*. We're talking sad, here . . ."

In the other room they sat on the sofa and sipped their tea silently. Before the record finished playing, they heard a knock at the front door. Jack went to answer it. Lew, the other agent, stepped inside, his face drawn. He looked warily at Jane, who had turned down the volume on the stereo.

"Ma'am, I'm afraid I have some terrible news. It's about your husband."

Chapter Nineteen

Cherry trees lined the west bank of the Tidal Basin, and through their branches Aames could see the reflection of the Jefferson Memorial. He crouched behind the thickest of the trees and quickly stepped out of his bloodied tuxedo, checking carefully to be sure no one had spotted him coming here from the car, which he had parked just off the shoulder fifty yards down the road. Directly across the basin, a small flotilla of paddle boats bobbed at their moorings under a string of lights, and off to his left the fabled glow of the Japanese Lantern outlined the silhouettes of a young couple walking along the shore. Once into his street clothes, Aames wrapped the rental outfit around a large rock and cast it out into the dark water. The weighted parcel sank quickly, and he hurried off without waiting for the ripples to subside.

When he opened the door to the Omega, an overhead light blinked on and for the first time Aames noticed blood on the upholstery. Some of it wiped off when he rubbed it with a handkerchief, but a number of stains still remained. Cursing his luck, Aames took his suitcase out of the trunk and put the keys back in the ignition. If the fates were cooperative, someone would steal the car and be caught, drawing suspicion away from him. To further this plan, Aames walked to a pay phone near the Jefferson Memorial and put a call through to the police, giving his name as James York and reporting the theft of his rented Omega.

Barely a minute after the call, Aames flagged down a taxi driven by a Jamaican with inch-long dreadlocks spilling out from under his beret.

"Where to, mon?"

"Washington National," Aames ordered, holding his suitcase on his lap. As the cab lunged forward, his nostrils were assailed by the pungent aroma of incense. He couldn't believe it. He'd gone nearly twelve years without smelling that wrenching scent, and now he'd been subjected to it twice in a matter of days. He didn't like it. To him, it was a bad omen. He deliberated changing cabs, but they were already crossing the Potomac, and when the bridge merged with Highway One, it was only a few more miles to the airport. Aames sat silently in the back seat, trying to ignore the pulsing reggae beat of the radio. The heavy base line tormented him, mocking the mad thump of his heart. When the music gave way to the latest installment of the evening news, Aames was relieved, but only for a moment. The lead story concerned the recently discovered bodies of murder victims Andrew Hatch and Hunter Stead. The reporter eagerly described the sordid details of their death.

"Ooh, dat's pretty rude, mon," the cabbie opined as he weaved through the slowing traffic. "Sound like de voodoo mon done stick ees pins in dose boys, yes?"

When he overheard the reporter giving a description of the suspect in the murders, Aames raised his voice. "I don't know about that. Why would some witch doctor want to kill the President's son-in-law?"

"De voodoo mon, he got his reasons," the driver maintained. "And I don't fuck wid heem, mon."

The taxi had been swerving erratically since clearing the bridge, and Aames cringed when the beacons of a patrol car suddenly flashed on behind them. The cabbie mumbled incoherently as he pulled off to the side of the road and waited for the police officer to approach his vehicle. As discreetly as possible, Aames slipped his dart case from his coat and hid it under the back seat.

"Dem crazy baldheads," the cabbie groused as he rolled down his window. He grinned out at the man in blue hunched over the side of the car. "Good evening, sir. Rastafari."

The officer asked for the cabbie's license, then took a deep breath and peered into the car. "You tryin' to hide something with that stink, ace?"

"This is true, mon," the driver confessed as he pulled out his ID and handed it to the officer. "My supper is not being very kind, mon. I got de gas real bad."

"You also got de steering real bad, ace," the cop deadpanned. "I'm gonna have to cite you for that little exhibition of yours coming off that bridge."

"I got de immunity, mon," the driver boasted. "Dis guy I'm driving ees an ambassador. He told I to step on it, mon."

The officer looked back at Aames, who had turned pale in the back seat. "Is that true, sir?"

Aames shook his head. "No, I'm just a tourist."

"I thought as much." The cop turned back to the driver. "Stay put, rastaman. I'll be right back."

As the officer retreated to his patrol car to run a check on the license, the cabbie drummed his fingers on the dash and looked at Aames. "You're a real drag, mon."

"Come off it. You're the one who drove like a goddamn maniac. I don't have any diplomatic credentials!"

"Sheeeit!" The driver slumped in his seat. "Dat voodoo mon got it in for I, sure enough."

Aames ignored the black man's moaning and kept his eyes fixed on the rearview mirror. He was certain that at any second both officers in the patrol car were going to rush the taxi with guns drawn, having matched him up with the description of the man wanted in connection with the killings at the Diplomat. Inching closer to the door, he grasped its handle and prepared to make his break. He wasn't sure what kind of chance he would have fleeing on foot, but it had to be better than his odds if he stayed put and surrendered. To his surprise, however, only the driver of the squad car came back out of the car, and his gun was still in its holster as he returned to the taxi and presented the cabbie with his citation.

"Here you go, pal. I could have gotten you on five different violations, but I only put down one. Consider yourself lucky."

"Hah!" the cabbie snorted as he snatched the ticket and threw it down beside him. He rolled up his window and started the car, badmouthing the police force the rest of the way to the airport. Aames left his darts in the taxi. He felt fortunate to have escaped detection in the cab and wasn't about to push his luck further. As soon as he entered the terminal, he detoured quickly to the shop selling gifts and notions, where he purchased a baseball cap, tinted sunglasses and a travel-size bottle of No-Gray hair coloring. Retreating to the men's room, he wet his hair in the sink and applied enough of the coloring to tint the gray, then took a pair of scissors from his shaving kit and trimmed his hair a few inches. When someone came into the restroom, he loitered near the sink, fussing with his shortened hairstyle. Once he was alone again, he used the sheers to thin his beard, then lathered the remainder and shaved it off. The metamorphosis took more than half an hour, and when it was completed Aames felt changed enough to don the ball cap and brave the gauntlet of inspections that awaited him before he could board a plane back to Los Angeles.

Chapter Twenty

Tranquilizers dropped Jane into a sleep without dreams, but the dose wasn't strong enough to keep her from waking before dawn. Groggy from the drug, she also felt weakened and miserable with grief over Andrew's death. Lying still beneath the warmth of her down comforter, Jane stared up at the ceiling, trying to adjust to her waking state. At first she felt as if she were surrounded by absolute silence, but gradually she was able to pick out a whole spectrum of sounds, from the soft grinding of gears in the clock by her bed to the purr of intermittent traffic and the clattering of tree limbs in the outdoor breeze. Now and then the house itself creaked, and downstairs she could hear muffled coughs and the light buzz of conversation. Her parents had arrived within an hour of hearing about the murders, and she recognized her father's voice among the others. Closing her eyes, she recalled her childhood years at their house in Los Angeles, when she would fall asleep to the sound of that same voice downstairs, always just loud enough to assure her that he was close by.

Soon Jane was aware of another presence in the room. She craned her neck and opened her eyes again, spotting the silhouette of her sister sitting on the sill of the bay window, watching her.

"Regina?"

The younger woman stood up and drifted over to the edge of the bed. "Go back to sleep, Jane. It's still early."

"When did you get here?"

"A little while ago. Sis, I'm so sorry . . ." Regina sought out her sister's hand beneath the blanket and squeezed it tightly. "We're all here for you. You know that."

Jane smiled weakly. "Yes, I know. Thanks."

With her free hand, Regina stroked Jane's brow. "You really should try to go back to sleep."

"I don't think I can." Jane reached for the nightstand and flicked on a small reading lamp. She aimed its beam away from the bed as she sat up. "I can't believe this has happened."

"I can't either. Such a terrible thing."

"I'd really come to despise him, and yet —" Jane couldn't find the right words for her feelings. "I don't know, I almost feel responsible. I mean, if it weren't for my announcing the divorce, and —"

"Look, Jane, there's no way on earth you can be blamed for this, so stop talking like that!" Regina stared at her sister until she was sure she had her attention. "You've shouldered enough guilt these past few years, damn it. Don't do it to yourself again. Do you hear me?"

Over Regina's shoulder, Jane could see a grayness seeping into the night sky, washing out the stars and giving shape to thin, ragged clouds. "Regina, did you ever wonder how things would be different for you if Scott were to die?"

"No, of course not . . ."

"Come on, I mean it. Not even once?"

Seeing that her sister was shivering, Regina reached to the foot of the bed for a flannel robe and handed it to her.

"Well, okay, maybe a few times. Like after that time his plane made that emergency landing in Cleveland. I mean, the thought of losing him scared me half to death. He means so much to me."

Jane poked her arms through the robe and tightened the sash around her waist. "I thought about Andrew dying . . . a lot. Or what if he'd never existed? I always wondered if I'd be better off, and most of the time I was sure of it. Other times, though, I figured I was just playing games with myself, as usual. That if it wasn't Andrew, I would have hitched up with someone else just like him, because there's just something about me that draws me to the wrong kind of man. And now that he *is* dead and I've had my cry, I don't feel anything. I'm empty inside. There's nothing."

"That's only natural," Regina assured her. "You're in shock. After everything you've been through, your system just can't take any more stress."

"You're starting to sound like my analyst."

"I'm just stating the obvious. Look, Jane, I've talked things over with Scott, and we'd both like it if you could come out and spend some time with us in L.A. after the funeral. You know there's plenty of room at the house, and you're overdue for a visit anyway. It'd be a perfect chance for you to get away from here and put things into perspective."

Jane eased back on the bed, exhaling. Looking up at her sister, she said, "You've been talking to Jack Damascus, haven't you?"

"Jack Damascus?"

"Don't play dumb, Regina. He put you up to this, didn't he?"

"That's beside the point, Jane. It's a good idea. At least consider it, won't you?"

Jane threw off the covers and went to the window to watch the dawn. Out past the front yard, a handful of mobile television vans were parked along the curb, with crews setting up for shots. One cameraman was already panning the house, and when his camera swept up toward the second floor, Jane quickly pulled away from the window.

"Fucking vultures, can't even wait for the sun to rise."

Chapter Twenty-One

During the years before he had earned his reassignment to mobile patrol, Johnny White had worked at the observatory pit and enjoyed the experience. That had been before the new museum had gone up, with its fancy displays and documentary film clips. Back then, the crowds at the observatory had been constant and curious, eager for information about the phenomenon of the tar pits. He had given extensive talks near the railing at regular intervals, relating the history of the area and explaining in detail its more intriguing aspects. The job had appealed to the storyteller in him, and he'd always got a secret thrill from the wide-eyed wonder of children responding to his dramatic recreation of prehistoric La Brea, when the mammoths and dire wolves and saber-toothed cats had ruled this land. Now, after standing alone inside the old structure for more than an hour, Johnny White felt a sad nostalgia for those bygone days. His sadness, however, was gradually overshadowed by a profound boredom. No wonder Aames always seemed a step or two outside reality. A guy would have to be a little on the strange side to put up with this insufferable solitude for hours on end several days a week. White figured he'd be lucky to last the rest of the day without the claustrophobia driving him nuts.

A few minutes later, a young family wandered into the observatory with an older woman who appeared to be the grandmother of the two children, a boy and girl. The husband and wife, both in their late twenties, nodded a greeting at White as they escorted their children to the railing. The grandmother sniffed the air inside the enclosure and made a face.

"Whew! And I thought it smelled bad outside."

"Wow!" the younger child, the girl, gasped, pointing through the railing at the display of bones. "Check it out!"

"Oh, big deal," the girl's older brother yawned. "We saw a whole skeleton in the museum."

"So what?" the girl countered. "It's still cool."

"Kids, let's not fight, okay?" their mother pleaded.

The husband had a camera dangling from his neck and, while he changed lenses and fidgeted with his light meter, the grandmother joined the children at the railing. "I wonder how those buzzards got stuck in the tar? You see those bird bones in that cluster, children?"

Johnny White cleared his throat and stepped forward. "Well, there's an interesting story behind that," he said, trying to recall one of his old anecdotes. "You see, what would happen would be one of the animals — let's say a sloth — would accidentally wander too close to one of the pits while looking for water, and while it was struggling to get out of the tar, some wolves or maybe some sabertoothed cats would come up on it. Thinking they'd found themselves an easy dinner, the beasts of prey would lunge onto the back of the defenseless sloth, only —"

"Oh, mercy!" the grandmother interrupted.

"Shhhhh, quiet, Gram!" the girl hissed. "Then what happened?" she asked White.

"Well, after they'd killed the sloth and begun to eat, the wolves or tigers would realize they were stuck. They would try to jump back to land, and maybe one or two might make it, but the others would be trapped. That's when the vultures would swoop down, hoping to have a crack at what was left of the sloth. Before you know it, the birds were stuck, too, and —"

"Hey, we just saw a movie about all this at the museum!" the boy complained. "Gimme a break already."

"Tad, watch your tongue," the mother scolded.

"Okay, I'm ready," the father said, attaching a flash to his camera. "Let's all crowd in near the railing. You think you could take our picture?" he asked White.

"Yeah, sure," White drawled bitterly. "Why not?"

The father handed White the camera and showed him how to use it, then herded his family together. White peered through the viewfinder and took the picture on the father's signal. As the father was taking the camera back, his two children bounded down the spiral staircase to get closer to the pit.

"Be careful," their mother warned.

The grandmother saw a bench near the vending machine and sat down, placing her tote bag next to her. White went over to where he'd hung his overcoat on a nail by the main doors. In one of the pockets was a folded issue of the *Wall Street Journal*. He sighed and began browsing the front page. He was halfway through the lead article when, out of the corner of his eye, he saw two young men wander into the observatory. White's instincts alerted him to possible trouble, and he lowered the paper. As he did so, one of the youths veered sideways and grabbed for the grandmother's tote bag.

"Oh, no you don't!" The woman curled her fingers tightly around one of the bag's straps. She was jerked to her feet when the would-be thief tugged hard on the other strap. The woman refused to give up, and a tug-of-war ensued.

"Hey, damn it!" The husband lurched away from the railing, but before he could reach his mother, the other youth caught up with him and planted a fist in his stomach. The man doubled up in pain, and his attacker grabbed the camera from around his neck and headed for the exit, stiff-arming White, who was making a futile attempt to bar the man's escape. White reeled back against the wall and dropped to his knees, wheezing for air.

The grandmother held valiantly onto her tote bag until the strap broke in her attacker's hand. He staggered back, then quickly recovered and ran off as the grandmother fell to the floor. Her tote bag slipped from her grasp and skidded across the concrete, disappearing between the posts of the railing that overlooked the pit.

"That goddamn sonofabitch!" the older woman shouted as her son gave chase to the fleeing thieves.

"Grandma, please," the wife said, helping the older woman to her feet. "Get a grip on yourself!"

"Shit," Johnny White muttered as his breath came back to him. Constellations still obscured his vision slightly, and he stayed put until they went away. By then, the husband had returned to the observatory, empty-handed and furious.

"They got away." He glared at White. "Aren't you going to do something?"

White nodded miserably and reached for his walkie-talkie. As he was spreading word of the robbery, the girl at the bottom of the steps howled, "Gram! Gram! Your bag's sinking!"

"Oh, dear Lord . . ." The grandmother moved to the railing and stared with horror at her tote bag, which was quickly vanishing in the tar. "My purse is in there! And my traveler's checks!"

The younger woman turned to White. "You have to help us!"

"I'm trying!" White snapped back at her. He finished reporting the theft, then clipped his walkie-talkie back to his belt and grabbed a long pole with a double hook at one end that hung on the wall in readiness for emergencies like this. He trudged down the stairs and motioned for the children to move aside so he could lean over the lower railing and reach for the purse with the pole. The broken strap was exposed, and his repeated efforts to snare it just forced the bag further into the tar.

"Man, it's gonna be a goner!" the boy predicted.

"Listen here, sonny," White said as he jockeyed the end of the pole through the ooze. "I've seen my share of things dropped into this pit, and I haven't lost one of 'em yet." He probed deeper, trying to reach beneath the tote bag and catch the hook on the remaining good strap. Even when he felt he had the strap hooked, the resistance of the tar made it hard to pull the pole out, especially when White had to lean so far over the railing.

"Here, let me give you a hand," the husband said, coming down the steps and gripping White at the waist. "Okay, give it a good tug now."

White strained his arms and pulled hard on the pole. Slowly, a portion of the tote bag poked its way back up to the surface of the pit, snagged on one hook of the pole. But it wasn't the tar that had been causing the resistance. White's jaw dropped as he saw attached to the other hook of his pole the unmistakable form of a tar-covered hand.

Chapter Twenty-Two

In his haste to get out of Washington, J.T. Aames had taken a stand-by flight requiring a transfer in Kansas City to another aircraft bound for Los Angeles. Because of a heavy snowstorm in the Midwest, however, only two runways had been cleared in Kansas City, and in the resulting shuffle of schedules, Aames's westbound flight was postponed until morning. He spent the night at the nearby Hyatt, falling asleep to adult movies on his room TV after masturbating to ease the tension of his whirlwind mission at the nation's capital. After treating himself to a scalding bath and ordering up breakfast the following dawn, he felt considerably more refreshed and relaxed. His rescheduled flight left shortly before noon, and it was early in the afternoon when he arrived in Los Angeles. During the flight he read in detail about the murders at the Diplomat Hotel. Based on a description given to them by two children playing on the eleventh floor at the time of the killings, police had put together a composite sketch of the man they were seeking, and Aames was relieved to see that, even before he had so drastically altered his appearance, he bore less than a passing resemblance to the suspect.

Aames had spent nearly all of the money he'd brought for his trip. He took a series of buses from the airport to a bank, near the fossil pits, where he kept a savings account. There were no lines, and Aames deliberately went to one of the tellers he was least familiar with. As he was filling out a withdrawal slip, however, another of the employees, a young woman who wore her hair in cornrows, passed by and did a double take.

"My goodness, what a change," she said, looking Aames over. "I barely recognized you."

Aames completed filling in the slip and handed it to the other teller. "I spent a couple days camping out at Joshua Tree and got to thinking my looks were behind the times." He forced a smile. "So, what do you think of the new me?"

The woman smiled back. "I like. It makes you look at least ten years younger. Funny, though, I always thought men shaved for summer and grew their beards for winter."

"That's in places where the winters are a little colder than here, I think." Aames took his money from the other teller and wished both women a good day. Outside, he walked down to the bus stop. A scramble of activity across the street caught his attention and he looked behind the art museum, where a crowd was gathering around the observatory. Police were on hand trying to cordon off the area, and there was an ambulance parked at the nearest curb.

"Shit." Aames turned to face the building behind him, drawing in a deep breath as he observed his reflection. If the teller had recognized him, he would have to take extra precautions to disguise himself. Setting his suitcase on a planter that stretched the length of the storefront, Aames retrieved from it the sunglasses and ball cap he'd bought back in Washington. He donned them, inspected his reflection again, then raised the collar of his jacket and braved the crosswalk leading to Hancock Park. Wading into the throng at the observatory, Aames listened for clues to the reason for the commotion. He overheard that a body had been discovered in the pit just moments before a pair of ambulance attendants emerged from the rounded building guiding a wheeled stretcher between them. A contoured body bag glistened atop the stretcher, and the police officers flanking it waved their nightsticks to ward off press photographers and anyone else who strayed too close.

"I hear they found some Stone Age guy," someone ventured.

"Bullshit," another bystander scoffed. "If the body was that old, they would have found it a long time ago. My money says it's a suicide. Probably some babe jilted him."

"Him nothing. It was a woman!" a third party interjected. "I was one of the first people there, and I heard 'em call it in."

Aames watched the body being loaded into the ambulance, then looked over toward the observatory where Johnny White was locking the gates and putting up the "Closed" sign. He didn't wait for the older man to look his way. Police were shouting for the crowd to break up, and Aames followed part of the flock back to the intersection of Wilshire and Ogden, then crossed the street to wait for the bus.

All the way downtown he nervously mulled over the implications of the discovery. He didn't know how the body had been found, but he was sure that the coroner would soon discover that the woman had been murdered. They'd probably be able to determine when she had died, too, and accusing fingers would inevitably be pointed at him. Something had to be done.

He approached his building warily, circling around the block to see if any patrol cars were parked in the vicinity. He knew the make of undercover vehicles, too, and once he was sure the authorities weren't around, he went up to the loft and quickly checked his answer phone. There were two messages for him. The first was a call from a telephone solicitor wanting to know if Aames had considered subscribing to the *Times*. The second message was from Johnny White.

"Yeah, listen, J.T., you aren't gonna believe this, but we just found a stiff in the observatory pit. Man, it's fucking weird! Gimme a buzz at home when you get back. I think the cops are gonna want to ask you a few questions, too. Don't wig out, though, it's just routine. My number is —"

Aames shut off the machine and slumped back in his chair. What to do? What to do? His gaze fell on the wall before him, and he instantly sprang to his feet. After emptying his suitcase, he went around the room and refilled it with his dart board, his diary, all the paraphernalia dealing with Jane, and his darts. In addition to the ones he had left behind in Washington, Aames had two other sets of darts, which he kept in a kitchen drawer. He was barely able to fit everything into the suitcase. The dart board was too wide to lay flat, and he had to set it at an angle.

Aames snapped the suitcase shut and scanned the room one final time. He couldn't see anything else that might reveal his obsession with either darts or Jane Britland-Hatch, but he had the feeling he was overlooking something. On his way to the closet, his eyes fell on the heap of dirty laundry on the floor, and he dropped to his knees to sort through the shirts. In the pocket of one of them, he found Michael Gasner's business card and his scrawled room number at the Brea Hotel. As he was putting the card in his wallet, he was startled by a sharp rap on the door to his room.

Aames remembered he hadn't locked the door when he came in. He silently rose to his feet and padded across the bare floor, ignoring the second knock as well. He saw the doorknob slowly beginning to turn. Rushing forward, he quietly slipped the deadlock into place, then backed away from the door, snatching up the torso of the beheaded Venus de Milo that still lay on the floor.

"J.T.? Are you in there?"

It was Debra from next door. She repeated his name and fidgeted with the doorknob. Aames remained silent and backtracked to the suitcase, picking it up and taking it to the window. With patient care, he unlocked the window and pushed it open, then let himself out onto the fire escape before reaching back in to fetch his suitcase. Debra knocked a third time, but Aames was gone.

Chapter Twenty-Three

Jack Damascus and Seamus McTeague sat at the counter of Jack's favorite eatery, Hobbs Place, a diner within walking distance of the Metro line. Hobbs had first opened its doors when Warren Harding was in office. The walls were cluttered with faded photographs of Randolph Hobbs serving his famous Hobbsburger Supreme to senators, chief justices, Hollywood stars and even a couple of presidents, including George Britland. The jukebox selections hadn't been tampered with since V-J Day nearly forty years before, so the diner's nostalgic air was always enhanced by the scratchy tunes of big bands and croon soloists. "Moonlight Serenade" crackled in the men's ears as their waitress, a matronly woman in a stained white uniform, refilled their cups with fresh coffee. Jack mopped up stray egg whites with a wedge of cinnamon toast while Seamus stoked his pipe and stared thoughtfully at the cloud formations that rose from the gleaming bowl.

"Well, now, there's really no reason why we should suspect Jane might be a target, if you ask me, Jackie."

"And I think until we have more information, there should be more protection, not only for Jane but for the rest of the family." Jack downed the toast and stirred cream into his coffee.

"I'm sure it's already been taken care of."

Damascus wasn't sure what had his nerves more on edge, the lack of sleep or the coffee he'd been drinking all morning to counteract his fatigue. There was a third possibility, too, of course, and he continued to pursue it. "I think we can rule out robbery," he said. "I mean, nothing was taken from their wallets, and why the hell would a robber go to the trouble of stripping them both and stringing them up from the terrace? Damn it, Seamus, we're dealing with a nut case here, so who's to say where he'll strike next?"

Seamus's pipe was giving him problems, and he poked at the bowl with his tamper until he achieved a more even draw. Shaking out the match, he said, "You might have something with this psycho angle, but there're other possibilities, too."

"Such as?"

"Well, it's not a common M.O., but there's something about the hanging part that strikes me as an advertisement of sorts. You know, a warning."

"A warning from whom?"

Seamus shrugged. "I know we ran a check on Stead and he came up clean, but who's to say he didn't have something going on the side? The man was a lobbyist for one of the top five oil companies in the free world, for God's sake! That he should check out clean just doesn't ring true. Face it, there's too damn much wheeling and dealing that comes with his kind of territory. He had to have contact with some hardballers."

"And you think maybe Stead pushed his luck too far with them, is that it?"

"It would make sense. Somebody finds out he's double-dealing on them and decides to spread word that it won't be tolerated. What better way than to bump him off along with somebody who's sure to make the papers?"

Jack drained the last of his coffee and signaled the waitress for a final refill. He took the check along with it. "For what it's worth, I hope you're right," he told McTeague. "It'd make things a whole lot easier on our end."

Damascus finished his coffee, and they left their stools and headed for the door, nodding a greeting to several other regulars holding down places at the counter. There were stacks of newspapers near the cash register, and Jack paid for a copy of the *Post* along with the meal check. As they walked outside and started down Pennsylvania Avenue, Jack stared at the police sketch on the front page. It was an updated rendering from the earlier composite that had been sent out over the wires. Apparently the two young witnesses had given conflicting discriptions when first questioned by the police, and the new sketch reflected a more accurate consensus put together in a second interview. Damascus stopped walking to take a better look at the picture.

"Know him?" Seamus inquired.

"I'm not sure," Damascus said. "There's something familiar about him, but I'm not sure if it's just because of the earlier picture. I think it's his eyes."

"Well, I'll bet you dinner that when the guy turns up, he's going to be someone with mob ties to Stead or something of that order."

"What kind of dinner?" Jack said with a grin.

"Winner's choice. Ethnic."

"Okay, you're on."

They walked to the Metro link and took the escalator down to the pristine, futuristic-looking subway, with its curved, waffled concrete ceilings and unlittered rail beds. As they waited for the next train, Seamus said, "I suppose this isn't the timeliest question of the day, but is there something going on between you and Jane?"

"What?"

"Jackie, you and I have rubbed elbows for the better part of four years now. I know how to read you."

"That's debatable," Jack countered.

A flash of light announced the coming of their train, and the men let the topic pass for the time being. There was a large crowd waiting to board, and the agents waited until the others had entered the train before getting on. All the seats were taken, so they stood side by side, holding onto the uppermost railing as the train glided along to its next destination. After they'd been traveling for a couple of minutes, McTeague broke the silence between them.

"Take it slow, Jackie," he advised. "Especially now. She's a fragile one, you know."

Chapter Twenty-Four

... and there's not much I can do but follow through now. I can't say it isn't exciting, though. No more daydreams. Every moment is real. This is it!

J.T. Aames flipped back a few pages, then quickly read over what he'd just written. There were a few corrections to be made — in his haste he'd misspelled a couple of words and screwed up his punctuation — but on the whole he was pleased with it. More than pleased. Putting his thoughts on paper had helped to sort out the confusion, to impose some faint semblance of order on the chaos he'd made of his life. It gave him increased confidence, a firmer sense of purpose. He finished the last sentence of his entry and carefully underlined it.

This is it.

He was sitting on the toilet in a public restroom, closed off in a rank-smelling stall whose walls were scrawled with crudely drawn genitalia and scribbled bits of folk wisdom dealing with various things that could be done with said genitalia and certain complimentary orifices. As he waited for another man to finish at the sinks and leave the restroom, Aames doodled pubic hair around a penciled vagina awaiting the entry of a penis that looked something like a bloated toadstool. When he had the place to himself, Aames emerged from the cubicle and spent a few minutes before the mirror, parting his hair different ways. He decided he didn't like any of the variations and combed his hair straight back instead. He'd come to like his new look, thinking it projected a brasher, more confident image. He didn't have to hide behind a beard and long hair any more. It was just another example of the guiding hand the fates had given him during the course of this, his greatest adventure. And that's what it was. An adventure, a challenge that would reward him with those things he'd spent so many years only dreaming about. Yes, this was real.

"This is it," he told himself before leaving the restroom.

He was in Union Station. The cavernous main hall was loud with bells and the clop of feet on the tile floor. An emotionless voice droned over the loudspeakers, announcing the arrival and departure of buses and trains at the various gateways of the recently refurbished structure. Aames strolled casually amid the crowd, willing away his paranoia and defiantly meeting the gaze of anyone who cared to look his way. When he reached a long bank of storage lockers, he pulled out a key encased in bright plastic and fitted it into one of the locks. His suitcase was inside the locker, and he added the diary to its contents before shutting the door and feeding the lock mechanism another fifty cents to get the key back.

In a phone booth by the ticket counter, Aames dialed the number of the Brea Hotel that Michael Gasner had scrawled on the back of his business card. When he got an answer he asked for Gasner's room extension. The phone rang nine times before he slammed the receiver down and shoved his way out of the booth. He'd called three times in the past hour without getting through to the Rotarian. It was almost sundown now. Aames decided to catch a bus to the Brea and try again, but first there were a couple more things he needed.

Down the block from Union Station, Aames stopped in a camera store. A collegiate-looking young woman was stocking the shelves with a late-day shipment of fresh film. She greeted Aames with a smile and asked if she could help him.

"I hope so," he said politely. "I'm helping my brother edit a bunch of his old home movies, and I was wondering if there were some kind of special gloves we could wear so we don't get fingerprints all over the film."

"Oh, sure. You want some of these." She pointed out a stack of boxes containing cotton editing gloves. He bought one box, along with a roll of dated, discounted film. "That's a couple of months past expiration, so we can't guarantee it, you realize," the woman told him.

"I'll take my chances." Aames paid for the purchases with cash. Once outside, he tossed the roll of film into the nearest trash can. He pulled out one pair of the editing gloves, discarding the others, then proceeded down the block to a discount store. In the party section, he looked over an assortment of ice buckets with matching tongs and picks. He paid careful attention to the picks, judging the lengths and widths of the tips, trying to determine which one had the dimensions most similar to the darts he'd left in Washington. When he found the pick he was looking for, he purchased it along with the matching tongs and bucket. Leaving the store, he started for the corner to catch a westbound bus. Halfway there, he was accosted by a limping beggar seeking spare change. Aames gave him the ice bucket and tongs, keeping only the ice pick, which he slipped into his pocket next to the editing gloves. He reached the bus stop without further incident and stood waiting with a group of four other people. One of them was the old woman Aames had helped board the bus the night of Georgia's murder. He recognized her, but when she looked at him through squinting eyes, he was sure she couldn't place him. To be on the safe side, however, he let someone else help her onto the bus when it arrived. Taking a seat halfway back, he didn't even bother looking at the other riders. He already knew who his next victim would be.

Chapter Twenty-Five

After a simple, quiet supper with Regina and her parents, Jane excused herself and returned to her room, where she had spent most of the day. She tried to sleep, but her mind was too restless and she was wary of taking more tranquilizers. She went to the bay window and stared out at the night for a few minutes. A light rain was falling, and she idly watched a sparrow that had taken refuge on the window sill. The bird bounced back and forth on the ledge, chirping occasionally as its small head twitched about. Jane slowly moved her head closer to the window until she could see the bird's markings. When the sparrow flapped its wings, she noticed that one seemed to have less mobility than the other.

"Hey, little fellow," she whispered through the glass. "Are you hurt? You should be on your way south by now."

The bird continued to pace the ledge. Jane reached for the window latch and carefully unlocked it, but the moment she tried to open the window, the sparrow flew off, dipping awkwardly to one side as it favored its bad wing. There was a nest wedged in the uppermost branches of the old elm, and the sparrow took refuge in it. Home, Jane thought.

She left her room and walked slowly down the hallway, pausing to look at a framed photo collage on the wall next to the bathroom. There were a variety of shots showing her and Regina growing up back in Los Angeles. Jane crashing into her sister on the bumper-car ride at the Santa Monica Municipal Pier, with Dora standing in the foreground, feigning horror; a picnic out near the riding stables at their Malibu Lake home, with her parents arm-wrestling while she and Regina refereed; Jane's first picture after having her braces removed in tenth grade, grinning boldly for the first time in several years; Jane and Regina half-buried in a large mound of raked leaves, which they had just landed in after running jumps; Jane and Andrew the night they announced their engagement, sitting at their favorite Mexican restaurant while Jane flaunted the glittering diamond ring that had just been placed on her hand.

Jane tried to find comfort in the memories, but instead she was stung by what she found to be their bitter irony. To have grown up so happily, only to find herself now weighed down by a relentless melancholy left her feeling even more helpless and victimized. She finally tore her gaze from the photos and continued down the hall to the last bedroom on the right. When she and Andrew had purchased the house, this had been earmarked as the eventual bedroom for their first child, but during the interim it had become more of a family archive and glorified storage place. Unused wedding presents were stacked in boxes along one wall, precisely marked so they could be hauled out at a moment's notice and put on display should their givers be dropping by. An open closet was filled with old sporting gear, broken appliances and mothball-scented garments awaiting the day when they might come back into style. The heating duct for the room was closed, and Jane had to tighten her robe around her as she waded through the other stored goods and finally sat down in an old wicker chair with one missing leg replaced by a stack of old phone books and encyclopedias. She wept quietly, eyeing the memorabilia visible in the light through the open door. When she spotted the antique sewing machine that had been passed down to her by her grandmother, she blinked away her tears and rose from the chair. The old Singer hadn't been put to use in several decades, but the machine's ornate wooden stand had served a more recent purpose. Reaching underneath the main body of the stand, Jane ran her fingers along the inside cavity that held the sewing machine in its storage position. When she felt the cold smooth touch of rounded glass, she took hold and withdrew a miniature bottle of gin, the size sold on airplanes. She had hidden more than a dozen similar bottles throughout the house during the height of her drinking problem, and this was one she had forgotten about.

She blew dust off the bottle and stared at its clear liquid contents. Even without cracking the seal she could already imagine the juniper smell and the tart, biting taste.

Why not? she thought, fingering the cap. Surely she was entitled. After all she'd been through. Just this one, a little crutch to help her get by. To help her sleep, that's all. No one need know.

She backed away from the sewing machine and sat down in the chair again. Slowly she unscrewed the cap. Fresh tears crowded the corner of her eyes and trailed coldly down her cheeks.

"No," she said, suddenly casting the bottle aside. It thudded against the padded back of an upright vacuum cleaner and fell to the floor, spilling its contents across the old carpet. Sobbing uncontrollably, she drew her legs up and curled into a ball on the chair.

She was still crying when a shadow stretched through the doorway and drew her attention. Looking up, she saw

Jack Damascus standing in the hallway just outside the room.

"Jane?"

"Go away!"

Jack stepped into the room. "Christ, it's freezing in here!"

"Aren't you going to say something about how it smells, too?" Jane demanded angrily.

Jack ignored the taunt and held his hand out to Jane. "Come on."

"Leave me alone!"

Jack crouched until his eyes were level with Jane's. "Is that really what you want?"

Jane stared at Jack for a few seconds, then set her feet to the floor and shook her head. She and Jack stood up together and she walked into his arms.

"Oh, Jack, I feel so awful..."

As he continued to hold her, Damascus whispered in her ear, "It's not over yet, but you're going to make it, Jane. You're going to make it."

"Hold me tighter."

He obliged her, but also began walking her out of the room and down the hallway. She continued to weep, but by the time she was back in her bedroom, she'd managed to bring herself under control. Sniffing back the last of her tears, she said, "I must be making you feel like a baby sitter or something."

Jack shook his head. "I wouldn't put it that way. Not at all."

Chapter Twenty-Six

By now Aames knew Gasner's number by heart, and he dialed it again. Still no answer. He checked his watch. It was almost 1:00 A.M.

He'd been waiting nearly four hours now. He took his change from the phone and stepped out of the booth, which was located across the street from the Brea Hotel, a nondescript structure on an equally nondescript block of Wilshire. He'd already had supper at the adjacent coffee shop and had spent another hour lingering at the bar between phone calls to Gasner's room, and he was wary of going back inside and drawing attention to himself. Instead, he hiked a few blocks east to the restaurant where one of his would-be stalking victims waitressed. She was on duty, and he took a seat at a booth in her section.

"Hi, can I get you some coffee?" she asked as she came over to him.

"No, thanks." He grinned, looking her over. *I almost killed you the other night, sweetheart. What do you think* of that? I could kill you tonight if I felt like it, and you're standing there smiling at me like you want it.

"Well, what would you like?" she said, poising a Bic pen over her check pad.

"Pie," he replied, still showing his teeth. "I'd really like a thick slice of pie."

"We still have apple, cherry, and mincemeat."

"Meat."

She ignored his leer and scribbled the order. "I can heat that for you if you'd like."

"That'd be nice of you. Real nice."

"I'll be right back with it."

You're already here with it, his eyes told her. He said nothing, though. She walked off, stopping to refill another man's coffee cup. She wasn't what he'd expected when he'd watched her on the bus. He hated her voice, and close up her face didn't do anything for him, either. The thought of tracking her down no longer appealed to him.

"It's your lucky night, cunt," he murmured under his breath as he watched her carve a slice of pie and heat it in the microwave. He looked down at his watch. One-thirty. He went over to the wall phone between the restrooms and tried Gasner's number. Still no answer. The waitress had his pie ready when he came back.

"Here you are. Enjoy."

"Thanks, I will." As he ate, Aames looked over the other patrons. If he couldn't get to Gasner, he'd have to find another outlet for the anxiety building up inside him. Someone else might have to pay. He'd discounted the waitress, and the only other female that remotely interested him was the hostess, a middle-aged woman with curly blonde hair and a health-club physique. There was a problem with her, though. She kept talking with a man who'd come in a few minutes ago and hadn't left the cashier's counter. Aames figured she was probably going home with him. He briefly toyed with the idea of following them both when they left and killing the man before having his way with the blonde, but decided there were too many variables, too many chances for mistakes. The fates were warning him away from here. It was time to leave.

Aames finished his pie, paid his tab and strode back out into the night, scanning the street for prostitutes as he headed back toward the Brea. As Gasner had mentioned earlier, this section of Wilshire was a poor area for pickups. It wasn't until he had backtracked almost all the way to the phone booth across from the hotel that he encountered a tall brunette in a leather skirt and denim jacket, smoking a cigarette jammed into an onyx holder. She had a small star tattooed on her right cheek and faint traces of glitter clinging to her false eyelashes.

"I've seen you walking around here all night, handsome," she told him. "Found what you're looking for?"

"Not yet."

"What about me? I could show you a good time."

Aames looked her up and down. "Maybe. Maybe you could at that."

"What do you have in mind?"

"Would you do it with a wig?"

The woman frowned, staring at Aames's head. "Say what? You want me to hump your toupee? Now there's a new one on me."

Aames was in no mood for jokes. Unsmiling he said, "You know what I mean. I want it from a blonde. I know where I can get a wig."

The woman's cigarette had burned down to its filter. She snapped it off into the gutter. "Sounds like a big production. What's it worth to you?"

"I'll make it worth your while," Aames promised.

"How about being a little more specific."

Aames was reaching for his wallet when he saw a taxi cruise to a halt in front of the Brea. Michael Gasner got out of the cab and paid off the driver, then disappeared inside the hotel.

"Hey, friend, don't space out on me." The prostitute

snapped her fingers in front of Aames's face to draw his attention. "How much of a good time are you looking for? I don't have all night."

"I changed my mind."

As Aames started across the street, the woman followed, grabbing his arm. "Hey, we had a deal!"

"I told you I changed my mind!" Aames shook her hand away from him. "Look, I'm doing you a favor. I've got herpes, okay?"

"Herpes, my ass," the woman sneered. "Cold feet is more like it. Or cold dick. What's the matter, Casanova, can't you get it up?"

"I don't care what you think, bitch." Aames saw a police car heading their way and quickly ducked inside the hotel, ignoring the stream of epithets from the woman on the curb. He didn't look back until he had reached the second-story stairwell. Out by the curb, the officers got out of their patrol car to confront the prostitute, who harangued them in a voice loud enough for Aames to hear through the thick, tinted glass. After trading a few insults with the officers, the woman was ushered into the back of the cruiser and driven away. Aames waited until the car was out of sight before continuing up the steps to Gasner's floor. The Rotarian's room was halfway down the corridor. Aames knocked gently on the door twice and waited.

"Who's there?" came a muffled voice from the other side of the door.

"I'm the guy from the tar pits," Aames said. "You gave me your card, remember?"

"Step away from the peephole so I can get a look at you."

Aames stepped back, taking off his ball cap. "I had a beard and longer hair before," he explained. "Gray hair. You came in out of the rain on election night, and —"

"Okay, okay. What do you want?"

"I have a message from Georgia. She wants to meet with you again."

"Then why the hell isn't she here instead of you?"

"She gave me five bucks to come up and make sure you're on the level."

There was a pause, then Gasner unlocked the door and let Aames in. He had a gun in his hand. "Sorry, but I don't like to take chances, especially here in L.A. Lotta wackos running around, you know?"

Aames nodded as he stepped inside and closed the door behind him. "Georgia won't want to come up here if you're going to wave that thing around."

"Yeah, yeah." Gasner tossed the gun on his bed and walked over to the television, on top of which stood a bottle of Scotch and a bucket of ice. "How about a drink before you go get her?" he asked.

"Sounds good."

Gasner turned his back to Aames and started pouring Scotch into a glass with the hotel logo on it. "Well, I hope she's close by, 'cause I'm sure in the mood for a good lay. I just had one shit of a dinner date with a would-be business partner. Pissed me off so much I been out cruising for some piece that don't mind a little rough stuff. Georgia'll do the trick."

Aames quietly removed his hands from his pockets. He wore the cotton gloves and held the ice pick in his right hand. He strode forward, coming up on the other man from behind. As Gasner set down the bottle, Aames reached around him from both sides, pinning the Rotarian's arms and pressing the ice pick into his chest. Going through the motions of a Heimlich maneuver, Aames hugged the man tightly, forcing the tip of the ice pick deeper into Gasner's chest. The Rotarian struggled, but only for a few seconds, managing to kick the television stand and topple his drink. When Aames let go of him, Gasner pitched forward onto the carpet and stopped moving. Aames stepped away from the body, taking a plastic shower cap from the bathroom and wrapping the bloodied ice pick before putting it in his pocket. On his way out of the room he stopped by the bed and took Gasner's gun.

Chapter Twenty-Seven

In her dreams, Jane found happiness.
Jack Damascus was her husband now, and Andrew had been delegated to the Secret Service. The three of them were inside the Capitol Building, wandering from the Rotunda to Statuary Hall, where the chiseled likenesses of heroic figures from various of the nation's states stared down at them in stony, stoic grandeur. Another security officer came by with a message for Andrew, who apologized to Jane and Damascus before leaving them alone in the large chamber. Jack explained that this room's acoustics allowed sounds to carry with unusual clarity. To demonstrate, he took her to a given point on the checkered marbled floor and told her to stay there while he crossed the room to another point more than fifty yards away. With his back turned to her, Jack whispered that he loved Jane, heart and soul, and she heard the words as clearly as if he had been speaking them in her ear. She clapped with surprise and blew Jack a kiss, which he promptly ducked, calling

out that she'd have to catch him if she wanted to deliver such a romantic gesture. As she started across the room toward him, Jack darted behind the nearest group of statues and was quickly gone from sight. Calling his name, she continued the chase, which soon took them up into the maze of corridors that connected the House with the Senate and all the conference rooms and offices that lay between. Whenever she was ready to give up, Jack would appear just beyond reach, taunting her to keep on. She pursued him down one last hallway and outside, where, to her amazement, the entire area surrounding Capitol Hill was deserted. It was just her and Jack, free to frolic in the grounds. She found that she was now almost weightless, loping across the grass in fluid, effortless bounds. Jack was far ahead of her at first, rushing across First Street and rounding the Peace Monument, but she was catching up with him, and as he raced past the Capitol Reflecting Pool, which mirrored a view of the panoramic mall stretching out to the west, she laughingly grabbed the sleeve of his shirt and dragged him into the cool, inviting water. They grappled playfully, scaring off golden schools of koi fish, and came up laughing to the surface, joining in an embrace that stimulated her need for him. Climbing out of the pool, she suggested shedding their clothes and running naked until they were dried by the midday sun. Jack agreed and, by the peculiar magic of dreams, when he took off his shirt and pants they turned into brightly colored kites. Jane eagerly stripped as well and moved close to Jack, slyly suggesting that perhaps they should warm themselves before playing. But Jack shook his head and ran off with one of the kites, feeding out line as it rose higher and higher in the air. Jane followed with the other kite, racing alongside Jack down the center of the deserted mall. To their right loomed the National Gallery of Art and, on their left were the NASA museum and the distinctive castle that was the Smithsonian's trademark. In the distance, the Washington Monument stood tall and white. Halfway to that majestic spire, they stopped running and looked up to see their kites hovering high above them, swaying back and forth in the warm wind like scraps of color in an aerial mating dance. "Let them go free," Jane pleaded, and they released the strings, letting the kites drift further away, till they became mere specks in the deep blue sky. When there was nothing left to see, Jane and Jack turned back to one another and slowly drew together.

Jane trembled at the touch of Jack's body, the gentle pressure of his lips against her flesh. "I'm so happy," she told him, again and again, as he gently guided her to the luxuriant grass of the untrampled mall. His fingers trailed across the soft contours of her flesh, teasing her nipples to erectness before he took them in his mouth. Between her legs she became wet with expectation, and when he entered her, she reached around him, clasping his buttocks and pulling him further inside her as she closed her eyes and whispered his name. They stay fused for some time, with him rocking atop her in time to the swaying of her pelvis, gradually increasing their rhythm until he was pounding against the aroused bud of her clitoris so fiercely that she came several times in quick succession, whimpering with satisfaction as she felt his ejaculation bursting deep inside her. She had no idea how long it all had taken, but in its wake she felt a sated bliss, a state of sorrowless fulfillment that made her want to weep with joy. She wanted to lie there in the grass forever, with her eyes closed and Jack lying on top of her, matching her heartbeat with his own and running his fingers slowly through her hair. When she did open her eyes, there within the dream, she became instantly aware that something was wrong. A regiment of clouds had trooped above the mall, blocking out the sun, putting a chill into the breeze, leaving her suddenly cold. As Jack pulled away from her and she sat up, she heard sounds and looked to the side. Pouring along the mall toward them were dozens of Secret Service agents, clad in three-piece suits, their features obscured by dark-lensed glasses. All the rooftops of the buildings along the mall were crowded with agents, peering at her and Jack through binoculars. To the east, an unending stream of people surged out of a Metro entrance, as if the entire population of the city had been summoned to the mall to confront the two lovers on the grass. With no clothes to pull on, Jack and Jane were forced to cower close together as the mob circled around them and slowly edged forward. Some had cameras, and flash bulbs popped like small exploding suns, dazzling Jane's eyes until she could not longer see. She could only hear the murmur of the crowd growing louder every minute. Above all the others, she could hear Andrew's voice saying repeatedly what a scandalous thing she had just done. She called out for him to be quiet and for all the others to back away, to leave her and Jack alone, but her pleas were ignored. The mob closed in, their hands clutching and prodding at her naked flesh.

"Stop it!" she cried out, and woke up.

It took a few moments to shake the powerful hold of the dream from her mind. She was in her bed and, like the day before, it was not yet light. Closing her eyes, she tried to retreat back into the earlier part of her dream, the part that had brought her hands between her dampened thighs. But she was too wide-awake, and already the dream had begun to fade, leaving as its strongest impression only the last few moments, when things had begun to go wrong. Resigned, she pulled her hands free from the grip of her clasped legs and stirred. There was an unfamiliar rustling sound above the covers, and when she sat up, she saw wads of paper littering the bed.

Before she fell asleep, she had taken a legal pad from one of Andrew's drawers and attempted, for the first time in years, to commit her thoughts to paper. It was Jack's suggestion, and although she had resisted the advice at first, after he had left her she had spent close to an hour battling the plain lined pages with a ballpoint pen. She had slaved over an opening sentence numerous times, accounting for most of the crumpled pages before her, and once or twice she had finished the better part of a paragraph before being overwhelmed by the pretentiousness of her writing, the pathetic triteness of the thoughts she was trying to convey. Written down, her feelings struck her as the mournful whinings of an adolescent, embodying every weakness that Andrew had ever accused her of. She reached out and uncrinkled one of the pages, rereading the few sentences. If anything, they seemed even more insufferable than they had the night before, and she quickly compressed the paper back into a ball. Filled with anger, she swept all the wads off the bed, then gathered them into a heap before stuffing them into a wastebasket by the dresser.

The door to her room was partially ajar, and as she stood over the trash receptacle, an unmistakable aroma swept in from the hallway.

"My God," she murmured, plucking her bathrobe from the foot of the bed and putting it on as she left the room. The smell grew stronger as she padded down the steps and made her way to the kitchen, where she expected to find either her mother or Regina. Instead, she saw Jack Damascus standing before the range, a chef's apron around his waist and a spatula in his hand. On the counter next to him, a ceramic teapot rested on a wooden trivet, steam issuing from its spout.

"Sorry, I didn't mean to wake you."

"You didn't." Jane looked at the raisin bread in the skillet and sniffed the cinnamon tea, shaking her head with wonder. "I almost think I'm still dreaming. Jack, I haven't had this kind of breakfast since . . . I can't even remember when."

"You said it was your favorite breakfast in an interview once," Jack recalled. "This here's the trial run. I wanted to make sure they turned out all right."

"They're wonderful. But why? It's not even six in the

morning yet. Jack, you shouldn't have gone to all this trouble."

"I wanted to," he told her, flipping the toast. "You have one hell of a rough day ahead of you. You'll need all the help you can get. I wanted to do my part."

Jane put a hand on Jack's shoulder and waited for him to look at her. "Thank you. I . . . I don't know what else to say."

"As long as you're up, why don't you sit down and eat? Who knows, this might be the only batch that turns out."

Jane pulled up a chair and sat at the table, pouring herself a cup of the sweet-smelling tea. As she watched Jack finish the French toast, she said, "I never pictured you being the type to cook. As a matter of fact, I hate to admit this, but I've never been able to picture you doing anything but wearing suits and standing around being . . . watchful. I know that's a lousy thing to say, but —"

"That's because I'm good at my job," Jack cut in. "But there's more to me than that."

"Of course there is. I didn't mean to imply there wasn't."

"I know that, too. Here." He set before her a plate stacked high with slices of toast. After putting syrup next to her plate, he sat down across from her. "Look, I realize I'm stepping way out of line here, but I just want you to know that you can look on me as a friend as well as a bodyguard, okay? I care about you."

Jane didn't know what to say. She smiled and poured syrup over her toast. "Thank you," she finally managed to whisper, her voice cracking. "Again."

"I guess I'll make myself something, too." Jack got up and went back to the stove, dabbing butter into the skillet and watching it begin to melt. "We've made all the arrangements for you to fly out to L.A. with Scott and Regina," he told her, trying to sound more businesslike.

"You'll be heading out a couple of hours after the funeral. Unless you think that's too soon."

Jane shook her head. "No. No, not at all. I don't think it would be possible for me to leave Washington too soon. What about you? Are you . . . ?"

"Yeah, I'll be flying out, too. Along with Seamus and a few others."

Jane looked at Jack, recalling the better moments of her dream. "I'm glad," she said.

Chapter Twenty-Eight

It was a little past three in the morning when J.T. Aames climbed the stairs to his apartment. Debra's stereo blared, but her door was closed and there was no one in the hallway. Aames paused outside his door, waiting for his pulse to slow and giving himself time to think his plan through one final time. He'd had little else on his mind since he dropped off Gasner's revolver at the bus terminal, and each time he thought through the scenario, he considered every possible thing that could go wrong and plotted a way of dealing with it. No fuckups, he told himself. There was too much on the line.

Next door, he heard a brief lull of silence between songs, then the throbbing bass line resumed, punctuated by the staccato beat of drums. Aames withdrew his hands from his pockets and put on the editing gloves, then removed the reddened ice pick from the shower cap, which he tossed aside in a place where it was sure to be found. He braced himself before the doorway, then raised one leg and kicked it forward, putting all his weight behind the blow. His foot slammed hard into the door, wrenching the locks from their moorings. The door swung inward. Charging into his room, Aames rushed to the window facing the back alley and hurriedly opened it. Debra had heard the disruption and within seconds the rumbling of her stereo ceased.

"No!!!" Aames roared, kicking over the table closest to the window. As he continued to shout, he stabbed himself with the ice pick and his voice filled with pain. Blood began to spurt from wounds along his leg and torso, staining the floor as he pried off the cotton gloves and tossed them out of the window, along with the ice pick, which clattered on the iron grating of the fire escape.

Hearing Debra leave her apartment, Aames staggered from the window and reached for his phone. He was already feeling weak from his wounds, but he kept his eyes on the edge of the nightstand, gauging its distance from him. When Debra raced into his apartment and screamed his name, Aames tumbled forward, striking his head on the stand. By the time Debra reached his side, he was lying face down on the floor, his skull throbbing. He fought to remain conscious, wanting to be as alert as possible, so that he could monitor the events around him. He had to make sure everything went according to plan.

"J.T., J.T., are you all right?"

He didn't respond, and Debra's cold hands felt for his pulse as she kept repeating his name, asking him what had happened. She left him momentarily to go to the window, then knelt back beside him.

"You'll be all right, J.T. Just stay put." She picked up the phone and dialed the emergency operator. "I need an ambulance, quick! A man here's been stabbed, and he's bleeding real bad . . ."

The operator taking the call entreated Debra to calm down and give more specific information. Debra repeated that Aames had been attacked. It was the last thing he heard before he gave in to the blackness creeping over him, content that things were proceeding as planned.

"Hey, he's coming to."

Aames slowly opened his eyes. He was still on the floor, but he was now lying on his back, having been transferred to a stretcher. An oxygen mask covered his face. Leaning over him was a black man in a white uniform. Off to one side, another paramedic was wrapping Aames's arm with gauze.

Aames started to raise his head and open his mouth, but the black man eased him back onto the stretcher, saying, "You just take it easy, friend. You're in good hands. We're going to take you to the hospital."

When the other man had finished with the gauze, the paramedics lifted the stretcher and carried Aames out of the room. Debra walked out beside him, and in the background he could see two uniformed police officers and a plainclothes detective milling about in his room. The detective followed the paramedics out into the hallway.

"You're going to be okay, J.T.," Debra told him, stopping as they went past her room. She put a hand on his arm, adding, "Maybe I'll come visit you, okay?"

Aames nodded weakly.

There was a service elevator at the far end of the hallway, and the paramedics used it to bring Aames down to the ground floor. His breathing was easier now, and as he was being carried out to the waiting ambulance, the black man removed the oxygen mask. "If you start feeling dizzy or lightheaded, let me know right away."

"Yeah," Aames whispered. "I will."

Police and ambulance lights were flashing off the sides of the building, and several derelicts had been drawn to the scene, only to be warded off by the detective, a tired-faced late-fiftyish man with high cheekbones and disheveled tufts of fading brown hair framing his large ears. A thick mustache drooped well below the corners of his mouth stopping a fraction short of his double chin.

"Mind if I ride with him?" the detective asked the paramedics.

"Just don't wear him out with too many questions."

"Fair enough."

As the black man headed up into the driver's seat, his partner made sure Aames was stable in the back of the ambulance, then sat on a padded bench across from the stretcher. The detective sat next to him. They ambulance started up, and a siren announced its hasty roll down the street.

"How am I?" Aames wondered.

"You lost some blood and you have a slight concussion, I think. Let's hope that's the worst of it," the paramedic said. "We'll have a better idea once you've checked in at the hospital."

Aames turned to the detective. "Did you catch him?"

The detective shook his head. "We found his gloves and the ice pick, though. Did you get a good look at him?"

Aames shook his head. "Thin, short. Had a nylon stocking over his head. He might have been Mexican, but I couldn't be sure. He didn't say anything."

"We'll get more into that later," the detective said, raising his voice to be heard above the wail of the siren. "Do you remember anything out of the ordinary happening while you were on duty at the tar pits last Tuesday?"

Aames frowned, staring at the ceiling, wondering if he should pretend to black out. No, it would only draw more suspicion. He'd thought out an alibi already. He had to go through with it. "Tuesday," he moaned, then paused as if trying to place the date.

"Election night," the detective prompted.

Aames hesitated a moment longer. "No . . . well, wait a minute. I do remember something."

"What?"

"I was getting ready to close when some guy came into

the observatory. Said some kids were climbing over the fence at one of the outside tar pits. I went to check it out, but I didn't see anyone. When I got back, the observatory was locked from the inside. I used my keys to get back in, and the guy who sent me on the goose chase was there, trying to make off with one of the bigger bones. I told him to get out. He said something about it being part of his fraternity initiation."

"Did you report it?"

"No, I —" Aames closed his eyes and swallowed hard, making a wheezing sound as he struggled for breath.

"Okay, no more questions right now," the paramedic intervened, readying the oxygen mask for Aames. "You're going to have to wait until he's been admitted and taken care of.

The detective shrugged. "If that's the way it's gotta be." As the oxygen mask was placed back over Aames's face, the officer said, "I tell you something, though, Mr. Aames. You were duped into being part of more than some harmless frat prank. From the looks of it, while you were off on your wild-goose chase, this guy you're talking about dragged a whore into the observatory and dumped her in the tar pit there. We figure she'd been killed first, probably with an ice pick . . ."

Chapter Twenty-Nine

". . . and after his distinguished service in Vietnam, Andrew was honorably discharged and promptly turned his focus to the business world, where he pursued his entrepreneurial goals with the same vigor and zest that served him so well throughout his life."

The man at the lectern paused for breath, allowing his words to echo through the vast enclosure of the church, where more than a hundred people had gathered for Andrew Hatch's funeral service. Jane sat in the front pew. She was flanked by her parents and her sister, dressed in black and wearing tinted glasses to shield her eyes. The man eulogizing her husband was one of Andrew's uncles, a man Jane had met only a few times — and one whom Andrew had professed to despise. As Jane listened to the tones of his full, rich voice, tuning out the words, it almost seemed that she was hearing the recital of a lone horn player. The speaker was putting on a performance, she realized, flaunting his eloquence as he evoked an image of

Andrew Hatch that bore little resemblance to the man she had shared her life and bed with for the better part of seven years. Perhaps the uncle was only being kind. More likely he was deluded, conjuring up an image of his ideal of a favorite nephew. Jane looked away from him, casting her eyes down at the thin, pale hands folded in her lap. She hated her cynicism and the fact that she felt so little emotion for the man who lay in the coffin less than ten feet away from her.

From other pews, she heard muted sobs and the sniffing of mourners. One sorrowful outpouring sounded loudly above the others, and when Jane turned to trace its source, she saw the redheaded campaign worker she had watched with Andrew the night of her father's concession party. The woman was crouched slightly forward and leaning to one side so that her tears spilled on the shoulder of another woman who was trying to comfort her. Jane diverted her gaze once more, feeling a sudden flash of heat racing up her neck.

When the eulogy was over, the pallbearers helped guide the coffin out of the chapel and into the first of three black hearses parked by the front curb. Mourners slowly filed from the church. As Jane was following her family through the rear vestibule, she crossed paths with the redhead, who was dabbing at her bleared eyes with a dampened handkerchief.

"He was a wonderful man," she told Jane through her tears. "He had a right to happiness. If he had only listened to me —"

"Excuse me," Jane cut in harshly. "I don't care to listen to this." She whirled away from the woman and headed for the nearest exit. Regina hurried along beside her.

"Who was that, anyway?"

"Who do you think?" Jane snapped. "Damn her . . ."

Out on the front steps of the church, amid the mingling friends and relatives of Andrew Hatch, various members of the media went about their business as discreetly as possible. Ed Lobyia found his way to the First Family. "My condolences, Mrs. Hatch. I want you to know how absolutely terrible I feel about what's happened, especially after the things I wrote about your husband. I guess —"

"Spare me the theatrics, would you, Ed?" Jane said. "The only thing you're sorry about is that you won't be able to get as much copy out of my marriage problems as you had hoped for."

"Well, now, I know you're upset, Mrs. Hatch, but —"

"I think you'd better be moving along, sir," said Jack Damascus, appearing from out of the crowd.

Lobyia made a face and took a step back, letting the First Family walk past him. The President eyed the columnist. "You know, Ed, if you'd been around when they were drawing up the First Amendment, I think they might have been tempted to add some small print about protecting people against the likes of you."

"Oh, I don't know about that, Mr. President," Lobyia smiled. "You seem to forget that the people love their dirt and would never think of doing anything to deprive themselves of their right to read it. Just like you, I'm a loyal public servant, trying to do my job as best I can."

"If that's true, then I'm damn glad the people didn't vote me into another term."

At the bottom of the steps, Damascus held the hearse door open for Jane and Regina, then joined the sisters inside closing the door after him. As the long car followed the lead hearse away from the curb, Jane shook her head. "I feel like a time bomb with a short fuse."

Regina put her hand on top of Jane's. "The plane leaves in less than three hours."

"I just hope I can last that long." There was silence in the hearse for the next few blocks, then Jane added, "I feel like I'm on my way to bury a stranger."

Chapter Thirty

It was almost noon when the sedatives wore off and Aames found himself in the post-op recovery ward, sharing a room with two other patients. He felt dull pains in his chest and leg, but he wasn't sure if they were caused by his wounds or the tightness of the gauze covering them. A bottle of clear liquid hung upside down from a rack next to his bed, slowly dripping its contents through a plastic tube into his uninjured forearm. He vaguely recalled being wheeled into surgery the night before, but he had been put under anesthesia before he could get a clear idea of his condition. He knew only that this morning he felt well-rested if a little thick-headed from his medication.

Directly across from Aames, a heavily bandaged man snored lightly as his wife stood over him, pensive and worried. Her fingers worked at the beads of a rosary, and her lips moved in silent prayer. Above her head, a mounted television flashed the image of a somber-faced anchorman reporting the midday news. The volume on the set was barely loud enough for Aames to hear the man's voice, which was soon drowned out by the patient in the next bed.

"Morning," the frail, elderly man called out to him. He was propped up in bed, a lunch tray straddling his legs. His emaciated appearance was partially offset by a warm smile and a brightness in the eyes that stared out at Aames from behind wire-rimmed bifocals. "You have much better color today, I must say. That transfusion worked wonders."

"Thanks," Aames said. "I feel okay, all things considered."

"They told me what happened to you." The man clucked his tongue as he probed his Jello with a plastic spoon. "A shame that decent folk can't be safe in their own homes these days. A real shame."

"Yeah, isn't it, though . . ."

"Listen, the nurse was just by with lunch. If you're hungry, you might try buzzing her." The man pointed at his tray with his spoon. "For hospital food, it's not bad. At least you can recognize what you're eating."

Aames was aware of a nagging emptiness in his stomach, and he reached for the paging button. A jolt of pain shot along his side when he moved. As he waited for the nurse, he watched the television, which featured a brief segment on President Britland's recent budget battle with Congress. Aames wasn't interested and let his attention drift to the couple beneath the set. The woman with the rosary had stopped praying and was now gently rubbing her husband's arm. When the man opened his eyes, she leaned forward and gently kissed him on the forehead as they traded a few soft whispers.

The nurse entered the room on noiseless crepe soles, wearing a powder-blue jacket over her white uniform. She was young and petite, with dark hair pulled back in a ponytail. She smiled at Aames. "You look better this morning, Mr. Aames."

"So I've been told," Aames replied. "How am I doing?"

"Quite well for someone who's been through what you have," the nurse told him. "If you like, I can tell the doctor you're up so he can come by and give you more details."

"I'd like that. Also, if there's an extra tray of food around, I'm starved."

"Sure thing." The nurse paused long enough to adjust the flow from the bottle feeding Aames's forearm, then left the room. Aames was adjusting his bed so that he could sit up when he heard Jane's name mentioned on the television. He glanced up and saw a mini-cam picture of the cemetery where Andrew Hatch had been buried. Leaning forward, he ignored the pain in his side as he tried to pick Jane out in the crowd of mourners. Before he was able to find her, the channel suddenly changed to a football game.

"Hey!" Aames turned to the man in the next bed, who was holding the remote control. "Turn it back, damn it!"

The man was shocked by Aames's outburst, and the couple on the other side of the room also looked his way. Without waiting for the man to respond, Aames grabbed his own remote unit and changed the channel back to the news. The funeral scene had been replaced by a head-and-shoulders shot of the anchorman, who was saying, ". . . a gathering of several hundred. There has still been no arrest made in connection with the murders of Hatch and oil lobbyist Hunter Stead. Following funeral services for Hatch, the President's elder daughter announced plans to take a brief vacation from Washington. Although no specific details were given, informed sources report that Mrs. Britland-Hatch will be traveling to Los Angeles to spend some time with her younger sister, Regina, who lives with her husband and son at the Britland ranch near Malibu Lake . . ."

As Aames turned down the volume on the set and let the news soak in, the man beside him, said, "I'm very sorry. I just thought it might be upsetting for you to hear about that poor man. I mean, he was attacked just like you, and, well, I thought you —"

"That's okay," Aames said. "And I'm the one who owes you an apology. I guess my nerves are still a little on edge."

"Who can blame you?" the man responded. "I'd be a nervous wreck, I'm telling you."

The nurse returned, carrying a tray, which she set across Aames's lap. Behind her, a middle-aged woman in a white outfit entered the room, carrying a clipboard. She came over to Aames and said, "I'm Dr. Corwin. I have to say you look much better than when we last met."

"Hi," Aames said. "I guess I don't remember . . ."

"You were already unconscious. I was part of the team that helped sew you back up. You were very lucky. You had a lot of wounds and a lot of bleeding, but no major organs were punctured. You needed two units of blood and a few dozen stitches."

"I feel a jabbing sort of pain when I move from side to side," Aames said.

The doctor nodded. "You'll have to put up with that for some time, but it's nothing serious. If you can avoid infection or breaking the stitches, you should heal just fine."

"That's a relief," Aames said. "How long do I have to stay in here?"

The doctor set down her clipboard and checked Aames's pulse. "Well, normally, we'd keep you an extra day as a precaution, but we're pressed for beds. I can release you this afternoon, but you'd be wise to restrict your activities for the next few days. Definitely no running or lifting. Nothing strenuous."

Aames smiled. "I don't feel much like trying out for the Olympics anyway."

"Good." The doctor made a notation on her clipboard. "Well, I have to complete my rounds. I'm sorry about what's happened to you, but if it's any consolation, you came out of it in better shape than a lot of victims we deal with."

"I can imagine."

Once the doctor had left, Aames raised the lid from his plate and his nostrils were greeted by the bland fumes of cooked veal and steamed vegetables. As he was getting ready to cut into the meat, the nurse stopped by and set a business card on the tray, saying, "I almost forgot. Detective Traburn would like to speak to you as soon as you feel up to it. He has a few questions about what happened last night."

Chapter Thirty-One

Jane waved out the window to her parents, who stood on the tarmac next to their limousine, staring up at the private jet that was about to fly their daughters to Los Angeles. Her wave was returned by both the President and Dora as the jet's engines revved to a high whine, ready to drag the plane out onto the runway for takeoff. A wind was blowing across the airfield, and Dora had to hold down her dress as she followed her husband past their Secret Service escort and back into the limo. Jane secured her seat belt as the jet began to roll. Regina was sitting next to her; Scott and Darren were one aisle over. Jack Damascus, Seamus McTeague and three other agents sat in back.

"California, here we come," Regina announced.

Jane remembered the song and whispered the next line, "Right back where we started from . . ."

The engines thundered even louder, and the jet began its race down the runway. Jane closed her eyes and gripped the armrests tightly. She had never cared for flying, and there was always that telltale moment as the plane lost contact with the ground and she felt her stomach drop when an overwhelming sense of despair would come over her. As always, it was only a fleeting torment, and when the jet managed to remain aloft and gain altitude, the panic left her, replaced by the dull ache in her ears from the change in cabin pressure. By force of habit, she opened a pack of gum and folded a piece into her mouth, confident that within a few minutes the steady chewing would force her ears to pop.

As the jet banked to one side, making a wide arc that would put it on its westward course, Regina looked past Jane and pointed out the window. "My God, isn't it just beautiful?"

Jane looked and saw the Capitol Building and the long stretch of grassy mall extending beyond it. With the sunset in the background, it was truly a breathtaking sight. She could see small roving dots of tourists and, off near the Washington Monument, a softball game in progress. Rush-hour traffic trickled around the periphery of the mall. The view triggered something inside her, and the more she thought, the more she began to recall fragments from her dream of the night before. She remembered emerging from the reflecting pool with Jack, their embrace as they shed their clothes, and the transformation of those clothes into kites that had flown as high as the jet she was on now. She smiled at the memory, dwelling on details that had eluded her all day.

"What're you thinking about, Jane?"

She looked at her sister. "Nothing much. Just enjoying the view. You're right, it is beautiful."

"Looks a lot better from here than when you're down there in the thick of it."

"I can't argue with that."

A light flashed overhead, telling the women they could undo their seatbelts. "I'll be right back." Regina left her seat and headed to the restroom. Jane got up and stretched in the aisle. In the back of the jet, Seamus was starting up a chess game with another of the agents while Damascus looked on. He noticed that Jane was alone and came over to her.

"There's an extra chess set in back," he said. "Care to play?"

Jane shook her head. "I'm a bad enough player when I can concentrate. I don't think I'd be much competition."

"So who's competing? It's just to kill time. We're going to be up here quite a while, you know."

"That's true, but still, I don't think so. Thanks for the offer, though." Jane yawned. "Maybe I'll sleep all the way there."

"Okay, but if you need anything . . ."

As Jack headed back to his seat, Regina emerged from the restroom and motioned to Jane that she was going to sit with her husband and son. Left alone, Jane sighed and adjusted her seat so she could lean back slightly. She had packed a few books with the idea she might be able to lose herself between their covers, but after thumbing through a few pages of her first two choices, she realized she still had too many things on her mind. Setting the books aside, she stared vacantly out over the wing of the jet. The sunset lingered above the horizon for well over half an hour because of their westward flight pattern. As her mind wandered, she found herself mulling over the passages she had written the previous night before falling asleep. In retrospect, she was able to see the flaws and, to her surprise, she began to edit the isolated sentences in her mind, scrutinizing them with a writer's eye. It was something she hadn't felt like doing in years, and she let the impulse carry her, sorting through her purse for a scrap of paper and beginning to write out her revised thoughts.

"That's it," she murmured as she reread the first sentence, marveling at its new power and clarity. She moved on, tapping the voice that was now putting her thoughts into words. It was an old, familiar voice, one she had lost touch with in recent years. It was a voice that spoke with conviction, with courage. A voice that dared to speak with hope.

Chapter Thirty-Two

J.T. Aames walked with a slight limp. Entering the police station, he presented Detective Traburn's business card to a desk sergeant and waited calmly while the officer made a quick call to Traburn's office. After considerable deliberation, Aames had decided his best move would be to come here directly and fearlessly, in a spirit of cooperation with the authorities. He reasoned that if he were under suspicion, more of an effort would have been made to keep an eye on him.

"Okay, he'll see you." The desk sergeant gave the card back to Aames and gestured down the hallway. "He's halfway down, right side. Name's on the door."

When he entered Traburn's office, Aames recognized the man who had ridden with him in the ambulance the night before. The detective was on the phone, and he motioned for Aames to have a seat across from his cluttered desk. It was a small office, with corkboard walls holding up mug shots, news clippings and various notes and reports waiting to be filed in the row of battered metal cabinets behind the desk. The room had an air of comfortable anarchy, and Traburn exuded the confidence of someone in command of the mess surrounding him.

"Good to see you up and about," Traburn said as he hung up the phone and reached across his desk for a handshake. "Quite frankly, I didn't expect to see you so soon."

"I don't like hospitals," Aames said.

"Like 'em or not, if we hadn't gotten you to one when we did, you might not be around."

"True."

"You were one stuck pig, let me tell you."

"I still feel like a pincushion," Aames responded, then added, "What did you want to see me about, detective?"

Traburn rummaged around on his desk, finally unearthing a Manila envelope. As he put on a pair of reading glasses, he said to Aames, "Backing up to a couple of hours before you were attacked, could you tell me how you spent last night?"

"Let's see . . . I'd spent a couple of days camping out at Joshua Tree National Monument, and I got back into town a little after sundown. I stopped off at my place to shower. I'd decided to get a haircut and have my beard shaved off, and I had all this loose hair inside my shirt, itching me like crazy. After I cleaned up, I went back out . . . no, wait. Before that, I checked my answer phone and there was a message from Johnny White. He works at Hancock Park with me, and he said I should call him right away about something that happened at the fossil pits while I was gone. I tried calling, but he wasn't in, so I went out for supper and then stopped off at a couple of bars on the way back. It was a little after two when I returned. The girl next door to me must have been having a party or something — the stereo was playing real loud. I didn't mind, because I wasn't that tired. I started reading, I'm not sure for how long, but I was just nodding off when the door burst open and this guy came after me with the pick. Like I said before, he was kinda short, on the thin side, but he had a stocking over his head so I couldn't get a good look at him."

Traburn had been jotting notes all along. When Aames stopped talking, the detective asked, "Do you think there's a chance it might have been the same guy who pulled the prank on you at the fossil pits?"

Aames stalled, pretending to think it over. "It might have been," he decided finally. "I mean, as near as I remember, they had similar builds. But I couldn't swear to it."

"Do you remember the face of the guy from the observatory enough to help us come up with a composite?"

"I can try."

Traburn excused himself for a moment and used the phone, asking a police artist to come to the office. While they waited, Traburn said, "I just have a few other questions, if you don't mind."

"Anything to help."

"Why did you shave your beard and cut your hair short?"

Aames raised a quizzical eyebrow. "Beg pardon? What does that have to do with anything?"

"At the moment, not much," Traburn admitted. "But I'm trying to fit things together, and when the pieces don't quite take shape, I need to know why. Now, then . . . ?"

Aames sighed. "Why the haircut and shave? I guess it had something to do with a party the girl next door had a couple of nights ago. It was a sixties party, and everybody was supposed to come in costume. A lot of the guys there were wearing wigs and fake beards because they'd outgrown that hippie look years ago. It sort of opened my eyes, and I got to thinking about it while I was camping. I finally decided the first thing I wanted to do when I got back was to clean up my act a little. I also bought some color rinse to do something about the gray hairs I'd been growing lately."

Traburn scribbled a few more notes, then took a long look at Aames. "And you think you look a lot different now?"

"Well, yeah. Nobody's going to mistake me for Mel Gibson, but I think it was a change for the better."

"Okay." Traburn leaned back in his chair and crossed his legs. "For the sake of theory, let's say the guy who attacked you is the same guy who got you to leave the observatory. He's a stranger, probably didn't get a much better look at you than you did at him. When he bursts into your apartment and finds a guy who looks completely different from the guy he was looking for, why does he still try to kill you?"

"Maybe because I jumped out of bed and tried to be a hero by going after him?" Aames speculated. "If I hadn't been half asleep, I might have thought better of it. I might have had a better chance of defending myself, too."

"Perhaps." Traburn pulled a photograph from one of his files and passed it to Aames. "You ever seen this man before?"

Aames looked at the photo. It was a morgue shot of Michael Gasner, looking very dead. "Yeah, I was talking with him at the observatory when the other guy came by with that story about the kids climbing fences at one of the other pits. Who is he?"

"His name's Michael Gasner," Traburn said. "He was killed at the Brea Hotel about an hour before you were attacked. Ice pick to the heart."

"Jesus..."

"You see, Mr. Aames, the way I figure it is this: Our mystery man gets you and Gasner out of the observatory so he can dump the body of this whore he's just ice-picked in the head. He figures the body will sink and he'll be off scot-free because who's gonna miss a whore besides her pimp, right? Only problem is, we get a fluke and the body gets found by your cohort, Johnny White. The murderer finds out about it in the papers and figures either you or

Gasner will be able to finger him, so he decides that as long as he's got one killing to worry about, what's a couple more if it'll give him a shot at getting off the hook."

Aames took a few seconds, supposedly to let the theory take hold in his mind. "That seems to make sense," he conceded. "But how did he know where I lived? And this other guy — what's his name again?"

"Gasner," Traburn repeated. "As to how he knew where you lived, well, that's something we're going to have to figure out. Nasty thing about murder cases, they don't always come to us in tidy little packages."

Another officer came in with a sophisticated identification kit that used a variety of facial traits printed on clear plastic so they could be superimposed on one another to create any number of combinations that would help in drawing up a composite sketch. As Aames helped the officer assemble an arbitrary likeness of a scar-faced Latino in his early twenties, Traburn said, "Since he botched his first attempt on you, it's not unlikely that he'll come after you again. We can provide you with some additional security if you'd like. Surveillance, things like that."

Aames considered the offer, but only briefly. "Thanks, but I don't think I want to let this thing run my life, if you know what I mean. I have an uncle who had his pocket picked three years ago and still hasn't gotten over it. He's practically a basket case now. I don't want that kind of trip."

"There's worse alternatives," Traburn reminded Aames. "This guy's on the loose and he's playing for keeps, you realize."

Aames nodded. "All the same, I'll take my chances. If I come across anything suspicious, I'll get in touch with you, okay?"

"Well, of course, it's your decision, Mr. Aames." Traburn checked his watch, then rose from his chair. "I don't have any more questions for you right now, and I have some other business to attend to. You can leave after we've got a good make on our man."

Aames nodded. "Thanks for all your help."

"It's a little early for that," Traburn said as he took his leave. "If we come up with anything on our end, we might be calling you to come in again, all right?"

"Sure, fine."

It took a few minutes to finish putting together the composite. After leaving the station, Aames took a wandering route through the heart of the downtown area, ducking periodically into stores and office buildings and looking out to see if he was being followed. He wasn't ready to believe that Traburn hadn't gone ahead and placed him under surveillance. The interview had seemed to go well enough, but in retrospect Aames did wonder whether the detective was just playing along with him, trying to trip him up. Not till he'd zig-zagged about the city for close to an hour did he finally feel confident enough to venture to Union Station, where he picked up his suitcase and the gun he'd stolen from Michael Gasner.

Chapter Thirty-Three

Malibu Lake was a manmade body of water nestled in the Santa Monica Mountains nearly forty miles northwest of downtown Los Angeles. Created in part as a resort area in the twenties, the resort club quickly drew attention to the area's potential as a getaway spot, and the lake was now surrounded by homes clinging to the rolling hillsides. Although development had been slow over the past fifty years, newer, more lavish estates were now springing up along the winding roads that led to the cloistered community. There were rumors that the modest peak of Sugarloaf Mountain, which overlooked the lake, had been the inspiration for Paramount Studios' longstanding logo — rumors fueled by the fact that a neighboring expanse of land had, years before, seen wide use as a location for westerns and other cinematic extravaganzas requiring an outdoor setting that boasted lush meadows and stunning slopes of chaparral and manzanita. More than a few movie people had bought property in the area for a mere pittance during the thirties and forties, including cowboy star Rusty Kramer, who had built a five-bedroom, two-story ranch house and riding stable for his family and housed a collection of thoroughbred race horses on a twenty-acre lot during the height of his screen popularity. Fame had been fickle for Kramer, however, and when his star declined, he packed up his family and horses and moved to Montana. He had sold his Malibu Lake property to George Britland, who, at the time, was an up-and-coming real estate agent with only a vague notion of running for political office. George and Dora raised their two daughters on the ranch over the next twenty-three years and, when George joined the cabinet of then-president Luther Dawkins and established a Washington, D.C., residence, he turned over the deed to Scott and Regina, who had lived on the property ever since.

A sandstone gateway marked the entrance to the ranch. As Scott drove the family wagon past the Secret Service agents already on duty near the gate and headed up the twisting asphalt drive, Jane rolled down her window and took a deep breath of the midday air. She already felt less tense than she had in Washington, and her mood was nostalgic as she took in the subtle landscaping that blended with the natural growth on the property. It was a clear day, and towering oaks filtered the harsh rays of the sun that hovered above the canyons.

"It's as beautiful as ever," Jane said. "The air's still fresh, too."

"We get maybe a handful of smoggy days a year now," Regina said, "but that's usually during midsummer. We won't have anything to worry about on that count while you're out here."

A fern-clotted knoll blocked their view of the house until the station wagon had negotiated the sharpest turn in the driveway, and then the two-story structure seemed to leap into view, looking paradoxically both cosy and sprawling. It was built near the base of the highest mountain on the property and shaded by a stand of eucalyptus trees that had vaulted to twice their height and width since Jane had last seen them.

"It's been too long," she remarked thoughtfully.

The driveway forked, and Scott veered to the left, parking in front of a smaller guest cottage situated fifty yards away from the main house. "Welcome back, sis," Regina said. The sisters were sitting next to one another, and they shared a momentary embrace. Jane began to weep, softly at first, then with exorcising abandon. As they remained in the car, Scott and Darren got out and waited for the arrival of the four-door sedan carrying secret service agents Jack Damascus, Seamus McTeague and Phil Brockwell. The other car was only a few seconds behind the wagon, and when the agents piled out, Scott pointed to the guest house. "There's your base of operations," he explained, mostly for Damascus and Brockwell's benefit. McTeague was already familiar with the layout from previous visits. "A couple of your men are already settled in there, but there's still plenty of room, plus we have an extra guest room in the basement of the main house if you guys want to fight over it."

"We just might do that, Scott," Seamus grinned as he filled his hands with luggage and started for the cottage. As Damascus was loading up with his things, he noticed Jane and Regina getting out of the station wagon and walking slowly toward the house.

"Is she okay?" he asked Scott.

"Yeah, she'll be all right. I think it's all just catching up with her. Regina will keep a good eye on her, I'm sure."

While Scott got back into the station wagon and drove up to the main house, Darren ran through the lush grass as fast as his short legs could carry him, calling out to get his mother's attention. "Lookatmeeeeee!!"

Regina turned and, seeing her son, squatted to wait for him. "Here he comes, my son the track star!"

"That's a big boy!" Jane cheered along, putting aside her deeper emotions for the time being. Darren ran into his mother's waiting embrace and Regina carried him the rest of the way to the house, where Scott was just pulling into the garage.

"I gotta pee!" Darren told the world.

"Then we'd better get you to the bathroom," Regina said, climbing the front steps. She called over her shoulder to Jane, "I know it's been a while, but I'm sure you can find your way around."

Jane nodded, slowly coming up onto the porch, then turning around to survey the rambling front yard. An old croquet set from her childhood was still in place with rusty hoops and wooden balls poking up through the grass. A thick rope hung from a lower branch of the only oak in the yard, its end tied around an old tire that swung in the breeze, waiting for its next rider. There had been times when she had spun the tire around and around in place until the rope was about to double up from the tension, then raised her feet to spin effortlessly the other way, leaning back and watching the world race by her, upside down.

Scott and Regina had redecorated much of the interior of the house, but there were still enough reminders to sustain Jane's feeling of *déjà vu* as she wandered from room to room, pausing to pick up an item here or stare out a window there. She was upstairs when Scott and Regina caught up with her, carrying her luggage.

"We've been using your room for guests," Regina told her sister, "so why don't you go ahead and take it while you're here?"

"That'd be great. Thanks."

One of the things Jane had always loved about the room was its southern exposure, which allowed the sun to brighten things for the better part of the day. As Scott set her larger suitcase on the neatly made bed, Jane walked to the far window and pulled aside the drapes, looking out at the back of the property, where a few horses, corraled near the old stables, stood in a clearing just past the eucalyptus trees.

"I can unpack later," she said. "Right now I'd like to take a walk around the property. You guys want to come with me?"

"Sure, we'd love it."

"Why don't you girls go ahead," Scott suggested. "I promised Darren I'd help him put together that train set Gram and Gramps bought him."

"I think I'll just change my clothes first," Jane decided.

"Sure thing," said Regina. "I'll meet you downstairs when you're ready."

Left alone in the room, Jane shoved aside the suitcases and sat on the edge of the bed.

"Home," she whispered.

Chapter Thirty-Four

Although it was the newest addition to the Britland property, the guest cottage was still more than thirty years old. Its walls of knotty pine and the antique rugs on the oak floor gave it a rustic air. A black Franklin stove stood off in one corner, with kindling and small sticks of firewood visible inside its opening like twisted teeth. A topographical map of the property was tacked to the wall next to the stove, with different colored pins indicating potential problem areas and spots where agents could be posted for the most advantageous perspective of the grounds. Seamus McTeague knew the map well and pointed out certain areas as he spoke with Damascus.

"There's a sudden dip into a creek bed over here, and we've had a few cases of people wandering onto the property. Usually they're just day hikers who picked up the stream where it feeds into Malibu Lake, but once we ran into a real nutcase who had this idea that if he traced the creek to its source he'd find the old Vasquez treasure."

"I seem to remember that," Jack said. "Isn't he the one who was dressed in buckskins and packing an old Winchester?"

"Yeah, that's the one. I think he wound up in a padded cell in Camarillo."

"Anybody ever see if he was right about the treasure?"

McTeague pointed to a spot a few inches off the map. "The creek starts up here, a couple hundred yards from the property. It's a big drinking hangout. Only treasure you'll find there is if you're into recycling empty beer cans."

Phil Brockwell came in from the porch, loosening his tie. "The ladies are off on a hike around the grounds. You want me to cover 'em for you?"

"Nah," Jack said. "Remember, Seamus and I are off all day tomorrow. We'll go. I want to get a better feel for the place, anyway."

When Jack and Seamus went outside, they found Regina and Jane each holding a small picnic basket.

"Let us carry those," Damascus offered.

"That's all right, we can manage," Regina said, starting off down a dirt path that led to the stables. Jane walked beside her, and the two men brought up the rear. The recent rains had left the surrounding hills greener than they would normally have been at this time of year, and the hearty grass sprouted high on either side of the trail. As the two women looked around them, admiring the beauty of the surroundings and trading memories of times spent playing there, Jack and Seamus viewed the terrain with a more professional eye. The joined trunks of two thick eucalyptus trees might have been the starting point for many a childhood game of hide-and-seek, but to the agents they represented only an ideal sniper outpost. The winding stream bed, with its waist-high reeds and high-pitched banks, interested them not because Jane and Regina had captured their first tadpoles and held their first secretive discussions about the mysteries of the opposite sex there, but because it could afford intruders easy access to the house.

When they reached the corral, Jane climbed the first rung of the fence and Regina called out to the two horses loitering near the water trough. The animals responded to their names and slowly clopped over to the fence. Regina reached into her picnic basket, pulling out two carrots. She handed one to Jane, who fed it to the older of the horses as she stroked its massive head.

"It's been a long time, Bandit. I missed you."

The horse snorted through its nostrils and nuzzled closer to the fence, allowing Jane to reach behind its ears.

"We'll go riding in a couple of days, okay?" Regina suggested. "The trails are still a little muddy right now."

"I'd love to." As Bandit backed away, Jane climbed down from the fence and retrieved the other picnic basket. "Listen, I'm absolutely starved. How about if we eat here?"

There was a hand-hewn picnic table near a raised fire pit a dozen yards away and, after draping a checkered cloth over the tabletop, the foursome sat down and Regina began taking out provisions for lunch. She had packed tins of oysters and sardines, a small box of crackers, fruit, and an assortment of jellies, cheeses, and condiments. In Jane's basket were bottles of wine and sparkling cider, along with plastic cups.

"Before we dig in," Regina said, "I've got a present for you, Jane."

"What? Out here?" Jane was confused. "But you didn't even know I was coming."

"Never mind that." Regina circled around the table and shifted her sister so that her back was turned to the stables. "You just stay put right there. Seamus, I'm going to need your help."

McTeague got up and followed Regina to the stables, leaving Jane alone with Damascus.

"Are you in on this, Jack?"

He shook his head and opened the bottles. As he started filling glasses, he looked out at the property. "This sure is a nice place. You must have had some great times growing up here."

"I certainly did. Of course, until I was in my teens, I assumed everyone lived like this, so I didn't really appreciate how fortunate I was. What about you? Where did you grow up?"

"Downtown Chicago," he told her. "City boy, born and raised. Had a set of grandparents who lived on a farm, though, and we drove our folks crazy asking them when we were going to go visiting again."

"So you're from a big family?"

"Not really. I have an older brother and a younger sister. They both still live in Illinois."

Jane looked at Jack. "I swear, we've been around each other for nearly two months, and I hardly know anything about you. It's terrible."

Jack shrugged. "We've been through this before. It's my job to hang out in the background, you know. The strong silent type."

"Doesn't it ever bother you, though? It's not like you're a robot, for crying out loud."

"I know that." Jack shifted in his seat. He was relieved when he saw Regina and Seamus coming up from behind.

"Okay, Jane," Regina called out. "I want you to close your eyes and count to five, then turn around and look."

"What is this?"

"Just do it," her sister told her.

"All right." Jane followed the instructions, battling her curiosity as she went through the countdown and swiveled around. When she opened her eyes and saw what Regina and Seamus had brought out from the stables, she gasped, "My God, it can't be!"

Resting on the ground in front of her was an old, partially charred footlocker, covered with dust and ash. The last time she had seen it was in the fire pit next to the picnic table, where she had set it afire and then walked away from it. That had been years ago.

"Dad and I sneaked back here and rescued it the night you tried to burn it," Regina explained. "We put it in the stables for safekeeping, figuring that at some point you might want to give it another try. When I saw you writing on the plane, I figured this would be as good a time as any..."

"This is incredible," Jane whispered, leaning forward and carefully unsnapping the latches. She took a deep breath, then raised the lid. Inside the locker, unravaged by the flames that had licked at the exterior, was her old portable typewriter and a thick, bound stack of papers comprising the bulk of Jane's literary output up to the day she had decided to quit. Tears came to her eyes as she reached in and touched the typewriter's keys, then ran her fingers across the bound edges of the old manuscripts.

"I hope you're not mad at us for saving it," Regina said.

"No," Jane said softly. "No, not at all. Oh, Regina, how can I ever thank you?"

Her sister smiled. "Put it to good use, and I'll consider myself more than thanked."

Jane was still stunned. Taking the stack of papers from the footlocker, she flipped through the top few pages. "My God, it's like a reincarnation..."

Chapter Thirty-Five

The first thing Aames noticed when he reached his apartment was that the door had been repaired. There was a note taped to it.

J.T. —
 I busted the landlord's chops and got him to fix things so your place could be locked up while you were gone. I came by the hospital this afternoon, but they said you checked out already. Hope you're okay. Let's talk when you get back.
Debra

Aames could see light crawling out from beneath Debra's door, and her stereo was playing, though not as loudly as usual. Leaving the note posted on his door, he quietly let himself into his room. Without turning on any of the lights, he moved slowly to the side window and peered out through a slit in the curtains. It was dark outside, and in the blackened alley Aames thought he detected the glow of a cigarette across from the fire escape. He drew the curtains tight, then crossed to the kitchen area, where he flicked on a light and raided the mini-cooler for a supper of chilled beans and beer. He had a cigarette for dessert and carefully opened his suitcase on the kitchen counter. There were two old yearbooks packed in with the wigs and dart paraphernalia. Aames took out the more recent of them, the one from his senior year. Turning to the back of the book, he located Jane's graduation picture. So lovely. As he stared at her beaming countenance, Aames sorted through the wigs in the suitcase until he found the one that most closely approximated Jane's hairstyle in the picture. Idly fingering the wig's curls, Aames read over the cryptic handwritten message beneath Jane's picture. It read: "James, we couldn't get much higher . . ."

The line was from a song by the Doors and had prompted Aames to write under his picture in Jane's yearbook "Come on, baby, light my fire . . ." The endearments had been exchanged shortly before their falling out, but Aames was seldom able to hear any music by the Doors without remembering those few shared moments of intensity that had been the highlight of their short-lived romance.

Turning the page, Aames stared at his own senior picture. Was that really him? It seemed inconceivable that he could have changed so much, that so much time had passed since he'd sat for that picture. There was a sense of excitement and expectation in those photographed eyes, and Aames remembered that the picture had been taken the day before his first date with Jane. They had planned to spend an entire Saturday with friends, putting the final touches on a homecoming float before going to Santa Monica Pier and then on up the coast for a clambake at the old stone lighthouse on Stony Point. He'd masturbated twice before showering for the date on the advice of a friend who had told him it would help him keep it up longer if he had a chance to score with Jane. As it had turned out, they had only ended up necking on that first date, but enough of a spark had been ignited for him to accept her initial reluctance to go all the way. There had been more dates in the ensuing months, interspersed with long, passionate phone calls and secret correspondence. They had carried out a romance inspired by characters of D.H. Lawrence, their favorite author. Eventually they had made love, triggering a three-week outburst of sexual exploration that had abruptly ended when Jane had stood him up for a scheduled rendezvous and then sent him a letter calling their relationship off. He had refused to believe she could have lost her feelings for him so suddenly, and he still looked upon their parting as a temporary phenomenon decreed by the fates for reasons he could neither understand or accept. He knew that it was their ultimate destiny to be reunited, and at long last he felt sure that the moment he had waited for all these years was close at hand.

Taking the yearbook into the bathroom, Aames propped it up over the sink so that he could refer to his picture as he filled the basin with hot water and then lathered his face. He shaved off what was left of his mustache, then took scissors to his hair, making the necessary snips to alter his part and bangs into a style that matched the one he'd worn throughout high school. The activity caused some of his stab wounds to throb burningly, but he steeled himself against the pain. As he was washing loose hairs down the drain, Aames heard a knock at the door.

"J.T., I know you're in there!" It was Debra again. "Come on, let me in! Don't make me have to break down this door just after it's been fixed!"

Aames strode to the kitchen counter, stuffing the yearbook and wig into his suitcase, then closing the lid. "Just a second."

After sliding the suitcase under his bed, Aames went and opened the door. Debra was wearing a bathrobe and not much else. Aames could tell at once that she was either stoned or drunk. Before he could respond, she stepped past him into the apartment and looked him over.

"J.T., you look great! I don't believe it, after all you went through. I expected you to be in a wheelchair. Or worse."

"I'm still a little sore." Anticipating her curiosity about his new look, he quickly repeated the story he'd told Detective Traburn at the police station.

"Well, I like it," she flirted. "It makes you look sexy."

Aames blushed. "What was it you wanted?"

"I just thought you might want some company that's all," Debra said, deliberately moving so that Aames could see she was nude beneath the robe. "I have a nice Chablis over at my place. Maybe you'd like to come over?"

"I don't know, Debra. It's been a rough day for me."

"All the more reason to just kick back and take it easy, right?" Debra laid a hand on Aames's shoulder, and he could smell both wine and marijuana on her breath. "Come on, I'll make sure you stay nice and comfortable. Okay?"

Glancing over Debra's shoulder, Aames eyed his suitcase, still visible beneath his bed. A few strands from one of the wigs dangled out, tempting as blonde snakes in Eden. Debra didn't look anything like Jane, and they were built completely differently, but Aames thought Debra might be willing to don the wig and do things his way. The more he thought about it, the surer he became, and the prospect aroused him.

"Well?" she purred. "What do you say? We can have a drink, then maybe you can tell me about that fantasy you were having the other night when you were in the raft, hmmmmm?"

Aames backed away from the woman, trying to think things through. Something bothered him about the arrangement, but he wasn't able to pinpoint it until he reached for his cigarettes and remembered the glimmer in the back alley. What if it was one of Traburn's men? He couldn't take any chances of getting carried away by a diversion, especially tonight. Too much was at stake. He forced himself to smile at Debra. "Any other time, that'd be an offer I couldn't refuse," he said. "But I'm still on medication, and my stitches are giving me problems if I move around too much. Look, how about a raincheck?"

"Oh, J.T...."

"Tomorrow night? I should be in a little better shape by then." Aames matched Debra's sly wink. "I think we'd have a better time when I can move around a little, don't you?"

Debra walked over to him and stood on tiptoe to kiss him. "Well, if I don't have a choice, that will have to do, won't it?" Her hand wandered down his midsection and lingered on the bulge between his legs. "Save something for me."

She broke away from him and flitted to the door, her robe billowing loosely around her. She turned and blew him another kiss, then left the room. Aames ached to have her. If he could only do it without arousing suspicion. Without the wig. No deviations. There were plenty of ways she could please him. He opened his mouth to call her back, but stopped himself as he heard her close the door to her apartment. He dropped his hand to his waist and began unfastening the belt buckle. He would have to content himself with his own embrace and his mind's-eye visions of his truly beloved.

"Jane..."

Chapter Thirty-Six

A fire roared in the hearth of the main house, beating back the November chill. Jane had pulled an old rocker close to the flames, and now sat sifting through the trove of papers in her charred footlocker. She'd been at it for several hours, caught up in the material. It took her back to what seemed another lifetime. There were naive compositions written for fifth- and sixth-grade English classes; loftier collegiate term papers dripping with academic pretension; a few fragmented journals filled with tedium and containing the ripped edges of pages that had been censored in moments of anger or embarrassment; and numerous fictional endeavors ranging from hastily scrawled scenarios to short stories and scraps of would-be novels awaiting some unifying inspiration. She'd given all of these a cursory once-over, then settled in to look over folders filled with her attempts at journalistic writing. She found the process disturbing, primarily because she could only vaguely recall the sense of conviction and self-assurance that had allowed her to write so forcefully. Granted, some of the strength had been an illusion fostered by youthful vanity and self-righteousness. But beyond that, there was also a genuine, well-founded confidence that seemed foreign to her now. How could she have lost so much of that confidence in just a few years? Cynicism? Bitterness and self-pity? An overwhelming helplessness?

Lost in thought, Jane gazed into the shifting play of flames in the fireplace. Minutes passed as she changed her focus from the past to the uncertain future. She was at a point in her life where change was inevitable. With Andrew dead and buried, things would have to be different now. To what extent could she control the course of her life? In reading through her old writings, she found herself longing to regain the parts of her personality that had fallen by the wayside. How wonderful to recapture that joyous spontaneity, to have faith in other people, even to indulge in moments of charmed innocence . . .

"Jane?"

She turned and saw Jack Damascus standing in the doorway at the top of the basement stairs. He was out of his customary suit and dressed in a flannel shirt and jeans.

"Looks like you caught me daydreaming again," Jane apologized. "How long have you been there?"

"Not long. I was just setting up my things down in the basement and thought I'd come up for some coffee."

"I have a pot over here." Jane pointed to the metal pot resting on the hearth. "There's plenty. Help yourself."

Jack disappeared into the kitchen to find a cup, then returned to the main room and poured himself some of the coffee. "So how's memory lane?" he asked Jane.

"Quite an experience," Jane confessed. "I keep expecting to hear the theme from 'The Twilight Zone.' "

"Read me something, " Jack said, crouching near the rocker, his back to the fire. "That is, if you don't mind."

Jane glanced at the literary archives. "Most of what's here would probably be boring to you."

"Try me."

Jane smiled. "Okay, you asked for it. I'll grab something at random, and we'll play 'This Is Your Life.' "

"Better yet, let me pick," Jack suggested. "It'd be more random that way."

"All right. I can live dangerously."

Jack burrowed his hand down into the midst of the collected papers and came up with what looked like a short story. "Here you are."

Jane looked at the selection and let out a short laugh. "My God. Now, this one goes back a *long* way. Tenth-grade English. We were supposed to retell 'Goldilocks and the Three Bears' in the style of our favorite author. I was crazy about Emily Bronte back then, so this will probably be written in very purple prose."

"I can take it." Jack sipped his coffee and watched as Jane began to read.

" '. . . and it was to the lush, exquisite manor that the fair Goldilocks wandered, her mind alive with the fervent thoughts of some fair prince or valiant nobleman that she might have the good fortune to chance upon, a man of rugged virility and yet possessed of a gentility of the soul that would allow him to see that she was a woman requiring a delicate touch.' " Jane laughed again and looked up from the paper, shaking her head. "This is awful! Let me read something else. Anything, please!"

"No way. A deal's a deal. Besides, I don't think it's that bad."

"Flatterer," Jane accused before turning her gaze back to the paper and venturing on. " 'No one greeted the waifish child as she approached the imposing door, and a tremble of fear shook her daintiest of hearts as she dared to knock upon it. Weary from her journeying, Goldilocks was also aware of a growing hunger, and when the distinctive odor of a well-cooked porridge wafted forth from somewhere within the seemingly deserted mansion, she turned the doorknob and, finding it was not locked, walked inside . . .' "

Jane's voice trailed off when her peripheral vision

caught Jack's movement toward her. As she raised her head, he was there beside her. Their lips drew together. She lowered the paper and let it drop to the floor, then put her arms around Jack, pulling him into her embrace. He held her tightly as well, guiding her down from the chair and onto the thick rug before the fireplace. The kiss lasted for some time. At length, as their lips parted and they broke their embrace, they gazed at each other, mutually startled by their actions.

"I don't know what brought that on," Jack said.

"I liked it," Jane told him. "I hope you don't plan to apologize."

"No, it's just that . . . I don't know. The timing doesn't seem right."

"You mean because of Andrew?"

"Partly." Jack sat up. "But there's more to it than that."

"Maybe you're right," Jane sighed. "But I still want to thank you. You're a good person, Jack. I know it wasn't out of pity."

"That was the last thing on my mind." They looked at one another silently. A few feet away, the fire crackled in the hearth, blazing openly in ironic comment as both strove to suppress the passion between them. Finally, Jack stood and grabbed his coffee. "I think I should be going."

"Okay."

Jane stayed near the fireplace and watched him walk out the door. Her fingers strayed absently to her lips, as if to hold his kiss in place.

Chapter Thirty-Seven

After lying in his darkened room for more than an hour, Aames was no closer to sleep than when he put the lights out. His mind seethed with a plan that had taken root while looking through his old yearbook. The bold simplicity of the plan taunted him. It seemed the surest way for him to be reunited with Jane, and yet there was a chance it might prevent him from ever getting close to her again. The choice was too difficult for him to make without consulting with his connections amongst the fates.

Over the years, Aames had employed various means of decision making that had their roots in either superstition or games of chance. During childhood there had been the Ouija board and an oversized, store-bought eight ball that flashed snippets of advice on its underside when he turned it over. When these oracles proved cumbersome, he had flings with astrological forecasts printed in newspapers, but finally rejected them because they tended to be too vague in dealing with his specific concerns. Now, of course, his primary reliance was on signs and omens gleaned from his environment, which he felt had a more direct bearing on his particular fate. And, too, there was the dart board, his current Ouija. He could ask the board questions and have the various target areas act as his advisors, accepting his throws in a way that would give him a firm, irrevocable course of action.

Aames pulled on his jeans and stole to the window. He peered through the curtains until he was sure he was no longer under surveillance, then took his dart board from the suitcase and mounted it on the wall. He decided he would play to choose among three possible options. He selected three sets of darts, assigning one potential choice to each set. For the next twenty minutes, the only sounds in the room were those of darts ramming into the pressed corkboard or occasionally bounding off target wires to the floor. As always, the rhythm of play helped calm Aames, assuring him that the fates were indeed at hand to guide his aim and make certain his decision would be the right one.

One of his options was to wait, on the theory that it was too soon after Hatch's funeral for him to make his move, as well as too soon after his own self-inflicted injuries for him to undertake any extensive activity. He was already enduring twinges of pain every time he threw. His second set of darts were also flung in favor of delaying any move toward Jane, but were those darts to prove victorious, he would go next door, where he heard Debra still moving about her apartment. He would have his way with her, and if it became necessary to kill her afterward, he would think of a way to do it without casting suspicion on himself. Most likely he would invite her over to his room, where she could be passed off as another victim of the mystery assassin who had supposedly tried to kill him the night before.

In the end, a pair of deftly tossed bullseyes decreed that Aames would pursue his third option. He was pleased, because his own personal inclination had already been to proceed with this, his latest master plan. With the move now sanctioned by fate, he went confidently to the phone and dialed for an operator servicing the Malibu Lake area.

"Yes, I'd like the number of Britland Ranch," he requested. "It might be listed under either Scott or Regina Kendall."

There was a pause on the other line, then: "I'm sorry, sir, but I have no listing under either name."

"But I know they're still living there."

"Would this be *the* Britland Ranch? The one owned by the President?"

"Yes! That's the one."

"Well, sir, naturally that's an unlisted number."

"But I'm a close friend of the family," Aames pleaded. "It's imperative that I get in touch with them."

"I'm sorry, sir, but I can't give you the number. You have to understand that I —"

Aames slammed down the receiver and paced a quick circle in the center of his room, beating a fist against his opened palm. This wasn't right. He had to make his move now, tonight. He had to make contact, set the plan in motion. If he couldn't reach her by phone, then perhaps a letter . . . no, that wouldn't do. What if she left for Washington before it got to her? Besides, he didn't have the mailing address of Britland Ranch . . . or did he?

A wave of hope carried him back to his suitcase, where he snatched up his old yearbooks and thumbed wildly through the pages until he found what he was looking for in the book from his junior year. In the section of blank pages set aside for autographs, Aames had stapled a list of the names and addresses of everyone in his class. He'd stolen the list from the principal's secretary one day when he'd been sent to the office, because a friend had once told him that it was possible to earn money by providing names to an outfit that in turn passed the information along to junk mailers. He'd never found out who to send the list to, however, and it had remained in his yearbook. Fate's helping hand again.

Aames found not only Jane's old address, but her phone number as well. It seemed unlikely that the same number would still be in service, particularly now that the Britland phone was unlisted, but Aames knew that the path of destiny was often paved with improbability. He went back to his phone, yearbook in hand, and smoked a quick cigarette as he collected his thoughts. After crushing out the butt, he held his hands out and waited for them to stop shaking. It was important for him to be calm, in control.

It was not quite ten-thirty when he dialed the number. There was an answer on the third ring.

"Hello?"

"Uh, yes, is this Jane?"

"Who's calling, please?"

There was a distinct difference between the sisters' voices, and Aames was able to guess whom he was speaking to. "Regina, this is J.T. Aames," he told her politely. "I'm not sure if you remember me, but I went to high school with your sister, and —"

"Yes, of course I remember you." The cheerfulness in her voice took Aames by surprise. "This is really strange that you should be calling tonight of all nights."

"I know it's late. Maybe this isn't a good time."

"No, no, I didn't mean it that way. It's just that Jane's been going through a lot of her old things today and reminiscing about 'the good old days,' if you know what I mean."

"That *is* strange," Aames told her. "How is she doing? I was calling to give my condolences about her husband, but maybe you can tell me whether I should wait to talk with her, or — ?"

"Tell you what, if you want to hold, I'll go check on her downstairs. Are you calling long distance?"

"No, I'm here in town,"

"Okay, just hang on."

"Thanks."

As he waited, the receiver to his ear, Aames gloated at his good fortune. He opened his senior yearbook to the page with Jane's picture and was unbuttoning his jeans when he heard her voice.

"Hello, James?"

"Hi, Jane. Yeah, it's me."

"Amazing! Did Regina tell you I was knee deep in nostalgia when you called?"

"That must have been why my ears were burning, huh?" He was going out of his way to sound warm, friendly. His fingers idly fondled his flesh as he spoke. "I saw the news that you might be coming to town, and I just wanted to call. Jane, I'm really sorry about all that's happened to you."

"Thank you, James."

Aames shivered and grabbed himself tightly. James again. God, did it feel good to hear her call him James. The years fell away, taking him back to high school and that one stretch of passion when life fell into place for him. He felt a tightness in his throat, and his jaw was quaking so hard he couldn't speak.

"James? Are you still there?"

Snap out of it, Aames, he chided himself, forcing a deep breath down his throat. Take control. He let the breath back out. "Sorry, I just dropped something," he said, his calm returning. "How are you holding up?"

"As well as can be expected . . . maybe even a little better. What about you? Are you still working at that dude ranch? Where was it, in Nevada?"

"Yes, it was in Nevada, but no, I'm not working there any more. I'm back here in town. I've got a nice loft apartment downtown, and I'm doing odds and ends to make ends meet. Still haven't figured out what I really want to do with my life."

"You and me both, James. I suppose you know how

much of a wringer I've been through lately. I got your letters, but I . . . well, I just couldn't bring myself to write back. I'm sorry."

"Don't be ridiculous." Aames was close to ejaculation, but his voice held steady. He let go of himself. "I was way out of line on some of that stuff I sent you. Truth is, I can't even remember most of it."

"Oh . . . ?"

"You see, Jane, I was having a few drinking problems of my own, and I always made the mistake of writing you when I was, well, not in a right frame of mind. But I've sworn off it. The booze and all the other stuff I was taking."

"That's wonderful, James."

"It's been four rough weeks, but I think I'm going to make it."

"Congratulations, and I wish you luck. I know what kind of hell it can be."

Aames leaned over and picked up the blonde wig from his suitcase. He dangled it above his groin until the hairs teased him back to erection. "I was wondering if you might want to get together some time while you're out here, Jane. It's been a long time."

"Well . . ."

"If you don't want to, I understand. No hard feelings."

"That's not it, James. I was just realizing how few plans I have. Sure, I'd like to get together. As a matter of fact, how does tomorrow sound for you?"

"That'd be great. How about if we meet for lunch somewhere?" Aames waited a few beats, then added, "Or, even better, if you've got some time and want to keep being nostalgic, we could check out some of the old high-school hangouts. You know, the pier, the beach . . . maybe Stony Point."

"I'd love to," Jane told him. "The only thing is, I'm not too crazy about attracting a lot of attention. One reason I'm out here is to shake the limelight."

"I remember reading about that." Aames wrapped the wig around his erection and used it to stroke himself. He let a little of the excitement creep into his voice. "Listen, I have an idea. It's a little off the wall, but . . . why don't you disguise yourself? We can go around incognito."

Jane laughed in his ear. "I see you haven't changed completely."

"Maybe so. What do you think?"

"I don't know . . ."

"Come on," Aames badgered good-naturedly. "I'll make all the arrangements. It'll be like 'Mission: Impossible.' You'll fool everybody."

There was another pause on the line, then: "Okay, you have a deal."

"Great! How about if I drop by the ranch some time around noon?"

"That would be fine. This could be exciting!"

"I'll try not to let you down."

"Okay, then. I'll see you tomorrow."

"Right, Jane. I'm looking forward to it."

" 'Bye, James."

" 'Bye."

Aames slowly placed the receiver down on the cradle, then closed his eyes and brought himself to ejaculation. A smile crossed his lips as he cast the wig aside and lay back on his bed.

"Tomorrow," he whispered.

Chapter Thirty-Eight

The sun was well into its eastward trek past her bedroom windows when Jane awoke for the fourth time in the past hour. The comfort of the bed was lulling, and its warmth was welcome against the chill that lay waiting outside the covers. But it was after nine, and she didn't feel she could put off getting up any longer. Enduring the room's temperature, she hurried to the refuge of a warm shower. The hot spray helped wash away much of the jet lag that sleep had failed to overcome, and by the time she had toweled off and slipped into some casual clothes, she felt ready to face the day.

The house seemed strangely quiet as she walked down the stairs. When she called out to see if anyone else was home, there was no break in the silence. Through the kitchen window, she saw Regina helping her young son into the station wagon. Scott was already behind the wheel, starting the engine.

"Oh, hi, Jane!" Regina called out when her sister emerged from the house. "We didn't wake you, did we?"

"No, not at all." Jane waved to Scott and Darren. "Where are you guys going?"

"Over to visit with Scott's folks in Thousand Oaks. You want to come with us?"

"Thanks, but I'm meeting James at noon."

"Oh, that's right. Should be interesting, hmmmm?"

"Definitely."

"Well, with your trusty Secret Service chaperones, you won't have to worry that he'll get fresh," Regina chuckled.

"Very funny." Jane noticed two unfamiliar agents waiting in the sedan that was going to follow the station wagon. "Hey, where's Seamus?"

Regina got into the wagon and rolled down the window. "He and Jack had the day off, remember? They left a couple of hours ago to go golfing. The L.A. office sent out some men to take their places for the day."

Jane traded a few parting words with Scott and Darren, then stepped away as the station wagon backed out into the driveway. The sedan followed close behind. Another unmarked coupe was parked near the cottage. Agent Brockwell stood near it, walkie-talkie in hand. He waved to Jane. "I just got a call that some news station's got a chopper heading this way. We're heading it off, but you might want to go inside just to be safe. Don't want to risk them finding out you're here."

"I'll say. Thanks."

Brockwell got back on the walkie-talkie as Jane headed up the front steps of the main house. Even as she was letting herself in, she heard the faint din of a helicopter headed their way. The sound grew louder, and from the kitchen window she saw the chopper swing past the property, with a cameraman poking a zoom lens out the side.

"They never give up, do they?" she muttered to herself as she went to the refrigerator and took out some eggs and milk for French toast. Making breakfast, she was reminded of Jack Damascus, and she smiled at the memory of their brief moment of intimacy the night before. He was such an enigma to her. In a way, the one-sidedness of their relationship was disturbing. He knew so much about her. He had witnessed her at her best and at her worst. And yet, until last night, she hadn't had more than brief glimpses of the man behind the three-piece suit.

As she began musing about their possible compatibility, Jane also began to think about her upcoming meeting with J.T. Aames. She smiled at the thought that she could be having contact with two such radically different personalities in the space of less than twenty-four hours. As even-tempered and disciplined as Jack was, to the same degree J.T. was mercurial and unpredictable — traits that had initially appealed to her own rebellious spirit in high school. From the letters he had written to her after their breakup, she assumed that Aames had followed his reckless, foolhardy impulses to their logical, perhaps dire, conclusions. Was his decision to swear off booze and "illegal substances" the result of some desperate need for rehabilitation? She had to admit that on the phone Aames had seemed surprisingly subdued. Perhaps his wildness arose entirely from his use of drugs and alcohol? Maybe, maybe not. Of course, she knew that her own personality had undergone changes every bit as pronounced because of her drinking.

It was well after ten when she finished breakfast. Leaving the kitchen, she returned to her footlocker and decided to spend the next hour browsing through more of her old writing. She needed the time to lounge around to help her feel at home. She wanted to explore a growing feeling that this was where she belonged. She picked up a couple of stories and moved to a chair near the window, stopping to look at a pair of bronze booties resting on the television set. Darren's name was on the stand that held them, and Jane remembered picking the memento up for Regina and Scott. She'd become especially close to her sister during the pregnancy, and seeing the changes Regina went through as she prepared for motherhood, Jane's own yearning to start a family had increased. It seemed like the ideal course for her life to take. To become pregnant would have forced her to focus her thoughts and efforts on wholesome living, on becoming a less selfish person. She'd thought it would bring her and Andrew closer together, too. But, however much they tried, Jane did not get pregnant. She visited specialists to see if there was anything wrong with her, and Andrew assured her he had done the same. It wasn't until the evening of that idyllic day they'd spent working in the garden that the truth came out; Andrew told her that, a few months before, pretending to be on a weekend fishing trip with friends, he had actually checked into an out-of-state hospital for a vasectomy. He tried to gloss over the operation as a medical necessity, pointing to a history of family problems with certain ailments, but she'd seen through his feeble excuses. It was his way of making sure that he wouldn't get other women pregnant when he was sleeping around. He denied the accusation, but Jane knew when he was lying. His betrayal had triggered her drinking problems again, and had destroyed what little love remained between them.

Jane had been troubled for days about her failure to embrace the role of the grieving, mournful widow, but as she ran a finger across the bronze booties, any guilt over her would-be lack of sensitivity was crowded out by more powerful emotions. What had the woman at the funeral said? Something about having tried to convince Andrew to follow her advice. To do what? Divorce Jane and move in with her? It didn't matter. Andrew was dead. Jane was alive, with her own life to lead. There was no valid reason to let him torment her from the grave. What had happened to him was terrible, but she was better off without him. Cling to that thought, Jane, she told herself as she settled into the chair.

Life is for the living . . .

Chapter Thirty-Nine

J.T. Aames awoke with his diary in his lap. He'd fallen asleep, while writing, not more than a few hours ago. He sat up in bed, massaging away a stiffness in his neck, and flipped back through the pages. He'd filled both sides of six pages with his most recent entry. He whispered the opening passage aloud.

" 'There's much I have to say so that people will understand and properly appreciate why I've done the things I've done and am about to do . . .' " He set the diary aside and lay back for a moment, closing his eyes. His body was sore from his wounds, and lack of sleep held him in a tense fatigue. Getting up, he took some of the painkillers that had been prescribed for him at the hospital and, while he waited for his morning coffee to percolate, went back to his journal, making a few minor corrections to what he considered to be a masterpiece of persuasion. Anyone reading this would have to understand and even admire the forcefulness of his vision.

The pills were starting to take effect by the time he finished the coffee, and although he couldn't shower because of the wrappings around his wounds, a sponge bath with near-scalding water helped revive him even further. He hummed an old Doors song as he filled a canvas tote bag with items he would be needing in the course of the day. When he was ready to go, he carefully set out the diary on his nightstand, propping the book open to the start of the last entry.

Debra was home next door, and she answered at Aames's second knock. She looked tired and hungover, but managed a weak smile. "Morning, starshine," she said. "You're early."

"I know, but I have some errands to run," he told her. "I was just wondering if I could borrow some of your old tapes from the party. You know, the sixties stuff."

Debra yawned and opened the door all the way. "Sure, come in, help yourself."

Aames went to her stereo and sorted through the tapes, picking out the ones he wanted.

"J.T., do you mind if I ask why?"

Slipping the cassettes into his tote bag, Aames offered Debra a wicked smile. On his way to the door, he told her, "Who knows, maybe I'm checking out new sound tracks for another initiation ceremony, hmmmm?"

"Oh, really?" Debra perked up slightly. "In that case, I can hardly wait until tonight."

"It will be special," Aames promised.

"I'm sure it will."

Bounding down the steps, Aames slapped the hidden cassettes. So far, so good. Love those willing fates. He stepped out into the harsh light of morning and paused in front of the building to light a cigarette. He casually glanced up and down the street to see if he was being watched. The block seemed deserted, so he took long strides to the nearest corner and boarded a westbound bus, which took him to a rental agency on Beverly Boulevard that specialized in custom cars. He searched the lot until he found a 1966 Mustang convertible in near-mint condition. It was a different shade of red from the one he'd owned during high school, but it was close enough. He filled out the necessary forms, this time using his own identification. Leaving the lot, he drove the Mustang down Highland to Melrose, marveling at the familiar feel of the vehicle, even after all these years.

As he was parking in front of a second-hand clothing store, the first in a formation of ominous clouds heading inland from the coast blotted out the sun. He put the roof up on the Mustang, then entered the clothing store carrying his high school yearbook. Showing a few select photographs to the salesgirl, Aames was able to purchase an outfit similar to the one he'd worn to his senior prom.

"I can't match the girl's dress, though," the clerk confessed between smacks of bubblegum. "You might try the shop down the street. They handle that kind of swanky stuff."

Aames bought the used clothes and changed into them before leaving the store. The sun was fighting its way through the clouds. In an appliance store halfway down the block Aames purchased a portable tape player for Debra's cassettes, then ventured into the clothing store next door. He showed the prom picture in his yearbook to a matronly woman with horn-rimmed glasses and asked if she could match the dress Jane was wearing.

"My, now, isn't that President Britland's daughter?" the woman asked.

"Yes, ma'am," Aames conceded nonchalantly, although he was instantly on his guard.

"And this young man looks like you, am I right?"

"Yeah, we're old friends," Aames said. "I want to do something to help cheer her up, if that's possible. I figured I'd try to track down a special dress for her to wear to our high-school reunion next year. 'Those Were the Days' is the theme, and we're supposed to come looking as much like we did then as possible."

"What a charming idea. And I can see you're already well on the way to getting your look down pat." The woman took a second look at the dress in the yearbook, then beamed at Aames. "You're in luck, because I have a couple of dresses very similar to that style. Not the same color, but you can't have everything, you know."

"Yes, ma'am, I know."

"They're in back. Just wait here and I'll get them for you to look at."

"Thanks." As he waited at the counter, Aames looked over a display of old perfume bottles. He tried to recall the scent Jane had always worn, but its brand name escaped him. Going from bottle to bottle, he unscrewed caps and smelled each fragrance. Most of them were repulsive to him, floral and overpowering. On the bottom row of shelves, though, he recognized a bottle uniquely shaped in the form of a praying insect. "Mantis," he whispered with affirmation as he sampled the perfume, which was light and subtle, smelling more like ripened fruit than flowers. It brought back memories of his face against Jane's flesh, the scent arousing him.

"Here we are." The woman came back with a dress held aloft in either hand. "This one's closer to the right color, but the size is way off, I'm afraid. Of course, we could have it altered . . ."

"No, that's okay," Aames said. "I'll take the other one, along with this perfume."

"Very well." The woman started writing up the sale. "It's certainly a shame what's happened to that poor girl these past few years. I hope this will perk her spirits up a little."

Aames said, "So do I."

Chapter Forty

Jane was sitting on the front porch when the clouds came. She'd been enjoying the sun, and the sudden dip in temperature caused her to shiver. Her sweater was draped over the back of her chair, and she put it on before turning back to her typewriter, which rested on a small table in front of her. She'd dusted and oiled the machine, finding to her pleasure that this small bit of maintenance was sufficient to return it to working order. A blank sheet of paper rested in the carriage. All that remained was for her to put her fingers to work. The sound of the keys striking the paper at first seemed loud and obtrusive, and she quickly pulled her hands away, glancing up to apologize to the agent, Phil Brockwell, for the noise. He was standing at the far edge of the porch, gazing contemplatively out at the sprawling yard. He didn't appear to be disturbed by the typing. Jane decided her apprehension made the machine sound louder than it actually was. No excuses, she told herself. You won't get off that easy. When she summoned the nerve to proceed, it was with caution. At first she typed her name, then the date, then a sentence she remembered from typing class that incorporated all the letters of the alphabet. "The quick red fox jumped over the lazy brown dog." She typed it eleven times before it appeared without error on the page.

"So far, so good."

She had one of her old short stories with her, figuring she'd retype it and perhaps make a few minor changes, as an exercise to get her back into the rhythm of typing. Then, when she had shaken off the wariness, she would branch out and begin putting new thoughts onto the page. A step at a time.

As she was starting on the second page, Brockwell responded to a call on his walkie-talkie, then relayed a message to Jane. "J.T. Aames. That the name of the guy you're waiting to see?"

"Yes, that's him."

"He's at the gate."

"Well, let him drive in, please."

As Brockwell brought the transmitter back to his mouth, Jane rose from her chair and walked down the steps. The sun was now lost behind the clouds, and the breeze blew through her loose-knit sweater. She crossed her arms in front of her for warmth. At the sight of the Mustang, Jane smiled and an involuntary gasp spilled from her lips. She took a few steps forward when Aames pulled to a stop next to her. As he got out of the car, she exclaimed, "This is too much! James, you've been hiding in a time warp all these years! My God, you've hardly changed!"

Aames grinned shyly, patting the canvas roof of the convertible. "It's a beaut, isn't it?"

"Yes, but you aren't going to tell me it's the same one you had in high school."

"Oh, no, this is a different one. All part of Operation: Disguise."

When their eyes met, they shared a lapse of silence.

Aames longed to move forward and embrace Jane, but he knew better than to push things at too fast a pace. He kept his distance, waiting for her to make the next move.

"It's good to see you, James," she said. "I didn't mean you to go to so much trouble on my account."

"Who said it was trouble? And you haven't seen half of it yet, Jane." Aames leaned inside the Mustang to retrieve a shopping bag, which he held out to Jane. "Here's your cover. I hope it all fits."

Jane peered inside the bag and laughed as she withdrew the wig and held it out to look at. "Oh, this is great!"

"Not that you don't look wonderful the way you are now," Aames said. "But you'll be harder to recognize this way."

"And the dress . . . James, I don't believe it!" Jane was genuinely elated. Clutching the bag, she bounded up the steps. "Look, you just make yourself at home. I'll change into this and be right back."

"Take your time."

Joining Brockwell on the porch, Aames introduced himself and shook the agent's hand, making a mental note of the bulge where Brockwell wore his gun in a shoulder holster. As they waited for Jane, Aames stared out at the graying sky above the mountains. "Looks like we might be in for some rain."

"That's what the forecast calls for," Brockwell said. "Couple inches, maybe some thunder."

"Good thing I made sure the roof works on the Mustang."

Brockwell nodded and watched Aames light a cigarette. "What's your profession?" he asked casually.

"Odd jobs right now," Aames said. "I spent a few years knocking around Nevada as a cook, but I don't see any real future in it. I figure I'm due for a career change. Something in computers, maybe."

"Can't go wrong there if you've got the aptitude for it,"

Brockwell said. His walkie-talkie buzzed and he picked it up. "Excuse me," he said.

Aames blew smoke and ambled over to Jane's typewriter. He picked up the papers next to the machine and skimmed through them, smiling at their familiarity.

"Well, how do I look?"

Aames spun around and saw Jane standing before him on the porch. She was a few pounds heavier than in high school, and the wig didn't match her old hairstyle as much as he had thought, but her similarity to the yearbook photos was none the less haunting. She'd draped her shawl over her shoulders against the cold.

"Perfect," Aames said, beaming his admiration.

"Nobody's going to recognize me unless we run into some alumni," Jane said. "You're remarkable, James. You even remembered my perfume."

"Memory's my strong suit," Aames said, crushing out his cigarette and pointing his finger at the papers next to Jane's typewriter. "For instance, isn't this short story the one you wrote for Severenson's class during Easter break our senior year?"

"Now *that's* spooky," Jane said. "How on earth did you remember that?"

"You took me out to Stony Point one night and read it to me by flashlight," Aames reminded her. "For effect, I think you said."

"That's right!" She'd forgotten until he mentioned it, and then the memory came back to her vividly. It was their second date, and she wanted to test his literary sensibilities, since at the time it was a crucial criterion for deciding if she wanted to become involved with someone. The short story was a period piece, heavy on melodrama and filled with metaphors about the open sea. Aames had listened patiently as she had read the story to the backdrop of waves crashing off the point, and then calmly critiqued the material, pointing out its overall heavy-handedness. She had defended herself with a self-righteous fury that brought the date to an early end, but a few days later she had reread the story and seen the merit in Aames's criticism. When her rewrite of the story earned her an A in the class, she had called Aames to apologize and ask him out, marking the true beginning of their short-lived romance.

"I was thinking we might drive out to Stony Point later on, provided the weather holds up," Aames said. "Why don't you bring it along and see how it stands the test of time?"

"Hey, I like that idea," Jane said. "We've got stuff here we can pack for a picnic supper."

"Sounds great." Aames followed Jane inside the house, where she took him to the kitchen pantry and brought out a picnic basket.

"Look in here. You can tell my sister was a Girl Scout. Always prepared." Jane pulled up the lid of the basket, revealing that it was already stocked with nonperishables. "All we have to do is buy some cheese and something to drink and we'll be set. What do you say we head out?"

"Fine with me." Aames took the basket as they went back onto the porch.

"We're taking off," she told Brockwell.

"Okay, just let me get another one of the guys to come along with me."

Aames frowned. "That disguise isn't going to fool anyone if you've got a Secret Service escort on your heels, Jane."

Jane smiled, undeterred. "Oh, I'm sure they'll be discreet. Right?"

Brockwell nodded. "We'll follow in the other car and try to keep our distance. Where are you headed first?"

"I think we'll hit the pier," Aames said. "Or what's left of it." Aames put the basket in the trunk of the Mustang. As he walked past Jane to open the door for her, he smelled her perfume in the breeze and felt his flesh raise with goosebumps. So close. He had only to reach out to touch her, to run his fingers along the smooth white flesh of her arms. But he held back and merely opened the door.

"Thank you, kind sir," Jane said as she slipped into the front seat.

"My pleasure," Aames assured her. As he closed the door, he glanced across the roof of the Mustang at the sedan by the guest cottage, where Brockwell and another man were getting ready to pull out. Just a minor snag, Aames thought. He was ready for it. He'd get around them, one way or another.

Chapter Forty-One

Jack Damascus crouched on the green, gauging the slope of the cropped grass before leaning over his ball. Like a human pendulum, he waved his putter back and forth ten times, then deftly poked his Titlest across its trademark. The ball made a slight whirring sound as it rolled across the green, following the contour to the right before slipping gracefully into the hole. Seamus was close by, holding the flag, and he shook his head sadly as he retrieved the ball and passed it back to Jack.

"Nice shot, Jackie. When did you take up prayer?"

"Prayer, nothing," Jack scoffed. "Don't you know talent when you see it?"

Seamus added up their scores, but they already knew the outcome. "One lousy stroke."

"That's all it takes, right?" They left the green and carried their clubs toward a large, shrub-surrounded building with golf carts parked along its side. The Rancho Park Golf Course was located across the street from the 20th

Century Fox Studios on Pico Boulevard. The upright edifices of the office buildings lining the main thoroughfare stood high in the background, dull against the bleak sky. "My guess is it won't rain for a couple more hours, Seamus. You up for the back nine?"

"No, thanks. You beat me fair and square." As they entered the clubhouse to return their equipment, McTeague added, "Besides, I still want to drop by the station to check on the guys."

"The guys" were downtown Los Angeles police officers Seamus had worked with for five years before opting for the Secret Service. He hadn't seen most of them since leaving L.A. eight years ago, and paying a visit was one of his top priorities while he was in town. Leaving the course, the men drove down Motor to the Santa Monica Freeway and headed east toward the downtown cluster of skyscrapers rising from a thin, dirty-looking bank of smog. Jack was silent, tapping one finger softly on the steering wheel as he drove.

"You have that lovesick look, Jackie."

"Bull. Would you get off that kick, Seamus?"

McTeague dipped his pipe into a tobacco pouch and packed the mixture tightly inside the bowl as he decided whether to pursue the subject further. He chose pursuit. "I don't want you to get the idea I'm a voyeur, but I was on the guest cottage porch last night. I saw you with Jane over in the main house. I might be wrong, but she seemed conscious when you tried mouth-to-mouth on her."

Damascus flicked his turn signal and changed lanes. "All right, so we're on friendly terms. Nothing in the manual says you can't be."

"I'm on friendly terms with Regina," Seamus countered, "but I know where to draw the line."

"Look, Seamus, you've made your point, more times than I can count. Spare me the 'Dear Abby' routine."

Seamus waved a match above his pipe, producing smoke. "Whatever you say, Jackie."

They turned to small talk the rest of the way to the station. There was parking space in the visitor's lot. Damascus had no other plans, so he followed Seamus inside. Most of McTeague's acquaintances worked Robbery-Homicide, and one of the agents' first stops was the office of Detective Traburn. He and McTeague bear-hugged one another and traded the obligatory good-natured insults, then Seamus introduced the older man to Jack, adding, "Traburn broke me in when I was a green recruit."

"I'm not sure if I wanna take credit for that," Traburn said with a smirk.

As McTeague and Traburn caught up on old times, Jack lingered in the background, gazing at the memoranda covering Traburn's wall. One particular item caught his attention, and he examined it closely. When McTeague and Traburn reached a lull in their reminiscing, Jack interjected, "This string of ice-pick attacks sounds damn familiar to what we had in Washington, you know?"

"It's crossed our mind," Traburn confessed. "The M.O.'s close, but we have a lot of logistical problems. There'd have to be a strong link to put both cases together, what with the time and distance factors."

McTeague skimmed over the report Jack had been looking at. "Copycat, maybe?"

"We don't think so. The lady was done in and dumped in the pits a couple of days *before* the Washington thing, though it didn't come out until afterward."

"What kind of leads do you have?" Jack asked.

"Not much," Traburn said. "We have the weapon, but no prints. No clear-cut motive, but we're leaning toward the theory that only the whore was supposed to die. When the body turned up, we figure the killer went after witnesses. Got one of 'em, nearly another."

Damascus glanced back over the report. "James Theodore Aames . . . Now why does that name sound familiar?"

"There was a Willie Aames in that movie we ended up watching on the flight over," McTeague said.

"Yeah, but I don't think that's it."

Traburn gave a brief rundown of what he knew about Aames, but none of it registered with Damascus. McTeague and Traburn wrapped up their reunion, and the two agents headed down the hall for their next stop. Damascus mulled over Aames's name a while longer, then let it pass.

Chapter Forty-Two

A series of devastating storms had ravaged the Santa Monica Pier in recent years, whipping up frenzied waves that had undermined pilings and dragged down large sections of the boardwalk. The water in the bay was rough now, too, and row after row of foaming whitecaps drove toward shore, filling the air above the pier with a misty spray that smelled of brine. The long stretch of beach running away from the pier was almost deserted. A lone jogger plodded determinedly through the sand, leaning to one side to compensate for the wind. His dog barked after the sandpipers that skittered across the tide line.

"That guy sure is disciplined," Aames said, as they watched the jogger from the pier. Jane stood beside him, holding the collar of her sweater up tight around her neck.

"Crazy is more like it," she said. "It feels like we're in for a hurricane."

They were at the end of the pier, near a barricade blocking off the area where construction was underway to replace the portions of the boardwalk that had been claimed by the sea. True to their promise, the two agents were standing off to one side, trying to look inconspicuous in front of a souvenir shop whose specialty was knick-knacks made out of seashells.

As they started back, Aames said, "How do you feel about your husband's death?" Seeing Jane flinch, he added quickly, "You don't have to say if you don't want to. I didn't mean to pry."

"No, that's all right," she answered. "I don't know. I guess I mostly feel numb. I didn't love him any more, but still, to have had such a horrible thing happen to him..."

Aames longed to tell her Hatch had gotten what he deserved. Instead, he said, "I think I know that feeling. I always hated my parents, but when they died in that plane crash when we were freshmen it still tore me up. I remember even feeling a little guilty."

"Yes, that's it exactly. I guess it can't be helped, under the circumstances. I'm trying my best just not to dwell on it." It sounded as if she were talking to herself as much as to Aames. "I have to look to the future, not the past."

Aames broke out laughing. Jane asked him what was so funny. "Sorry, but I couldn't help it. I mean, just take a look at you. If you don't look like something out of the past..."

Jane paused to regard her reflection in the window of a shopfront, and she had to smile at the sight of herself in the wig and old dress. She changed the subject. "I remember when we took our staff pictures for the yearbook out here. There was a fortune teller in this shop back then."

"Yeah, I remember that, too," Aames said. "She told me the key to my success was that I had to know what I wanted and then work for it. Hell, she sounded just like the school guidance counselor."

"Back then you wanted to be a photographer," Jane recalled as they headed past the idle bumper cars. "What became of that?"

"Lost interest. I spent too much time screwing around to really stick with it." Aames checked his own reflection and patted a few stray hairs back into place. "Now that I've cleaned up my act, though, I might just get back into it."

Although their clothes were from another decade, Aames and Jane easily blended in with the diverse mix of humanity on the pier, which ranged from bag ladies and transients to punk rockers and Madonna lookalikes. Adjacent to the main arcade, which buzzed with the electronic bleeps of video games and the shouts of boisterous teenagers, was a row of small booths that featured various games of chance. Hawkers manned the booths, touting their wares. A gray-bearded man standing between pyramids of plastic milk bottles caught Aames's eye and howled, "Three tosses for four bits. Win a nice prize for the lady, pal."

"What kind of prize?"

"Anything on the shelf if you get 'em all down with one toss," the barker said, tossing a ball up and down in his hand. "Even if it takes all three, you still win something."

"You're on."

"James, really!" Jane veered over to the booth with him. "How hokey can we get?"

Aames gestured to the stuffed animals. "Which one do you want?"

"How about the big frog?"

"You got it." Aames paid the man and took three balls.

"Here's where you want to aim," the hawker told him, pointing at the stacked bottles.

"That's what you say." Aames aimed at a different spot, took his dart-throwing stance and concentrated on the targets before letting loose with the first ball. It hit the bottles squarely, toppling them all from the stand.

"You did it!" Jane gasped.

"It gets hokier all the time, eh?" Aames grinned as he waited for the barker to hand him the frog.

"You maybe wanna try double or nothing?"

"Sorry." Aames took the frog and handed it to Jane. "Kermit, meet Jane. Jane, Kermit."

Jane laughed as she hugged the stuffed amphibian and walked with Aames down to the vintage carousel housed in a brightly painted building close to the mainland. The sound of calliope music reached their ears, and through the open doorway they could see the merry-go-round slowly rotating, with children and young lovers riding its polished horses. "Let's go in here," Jane suggested. "I hear it's been totally refurbished."

Aames balked, glancing over his shoulder at the bay. "Maybe we ought to be getting to Stony Point before the storm breaks."

"Come on, just one ride," Jane said. "Kermit insists."

"Okay, fair enough," Aames conceded. "Anything for Kermit."

They entered the building and joined the line for tickets. As they waited, Jane squeezed the frog and smiled at Aames. "Thanks again for suggesting this, James. It's just what I needed."

Aames smiled back at her. "I'm glad."

Chapter Forty-Three

Having lost at golf, it was up to Seamus McTeague to treat Jack Damascus to supper. He chose a posh Moroccan restaurant on Sunset Boulevard, with North African decor and a central open-roofed courtyard and landscaped reflecting pool. Sitting on thickly padded cushions, the men enjoyed a prolonged seven-course meal, featuring a variety of spiced vegetables, quail stuffed with wild rice, baby back ribs in a special African sauce, and a cornucopia of fresh fruit. They shared a bottle of crisp Chardonnay with the meal, and the time went by with pleasant ease. Jack watched the daylight slowly fade from the courtyard, to be replaced by colored beams illuminating the gentle spray of water shooting up from the center of the pool.

"One more bite and it's gluttony," Seamus declared as he peeled a fig and helped himself to its sweet, sticky meat. "I feel like I've been plumped for slaughter. I'm going to end up roasted on someone's Thanksgiving table, I'm sure of it."

"They sure don't skimp on their portions," Jack agreed, divvying up the last of the wine. He leaned back against the cushioned wall and took in the other diners. Some were dressed in harmony with the restaurant's African background, but far more prominent was evening dress ranging from casual to Yuppie, and the snatches of conversation Jack was able to pick up were primarily in English. When he looked back at Seamus, he felt obliged to make a confession. "You're right, you know."

"How's that?"

"About Jane," Jack said. "I . . . there's a definite spark there. No use denying it."

Seamus chuckled and sipped his wine. "Spark? Is that what you call it? For my money, it's more in the order of spontaneous combustion."

"I don't know what to do about it."

"You already have my advice, Jackie. Go ye slowly. She's taken a hell of a beating, that girl. She needs time to recuperate."

Damascus watched the Chardonnay roll back and forth in his glass like an unruly sea. "You're probably right."

"Of course I'm right." Staring across the room, Seamus chortled sardonically. "In the meantime, what you need is some diversion."

Taking a five-dollar bill from his pocket, Seamus waved the money in the air and, moments later, a voluptuous dark-haired dancer was undulating before their table, whipping gossamer veils about herself and accompanying the music with the chiming of small cymbals tied to her snapping fingers. She smiled flirtatiously at both men as she demonstrated her forte, rocking to and fro so that her stomach rolled from side to side with frenetic abandon, threatening to dislodge the gleaming gem in her navel. Jack blushed as the woman draped one of her veils around his head and slowly pulled it away, leaving the lingering scent of some exotic perfume. As the music increased in tempo, the other diners clapped their encouragement, and the woman gyrated with increased speed, creating a mesmerizing din with her cymbals. Then, when the music abruptly stopped, the woman sank gracefully to the floor in front of the two men. As the room filled with cheers, she slowly rose and acknowledged the ovation, thanking Seamus as she took her tip and glided quietly out of the main room.

"My, my, my," Seamus said. "Now there's a woman that sets *my* heart to thumping!"

The waiter appeared with the bill and hot, moist towels for the men to clean their hands with. As Seamus looked over the tally, Jack heard a faint rumbling above the collective banter in the dining room. "Sounds like the storm's on its way," he told his associate. "Maybe we should be heading back to the ranch. I hear the mountain roads can get pretty slick once it starts to rain."

"Afraid so," Seamus sighed. "What a shame. I was hoping we could sample a little night life as long as we were so close to the Strip."

"I don't think it's our type of crowd, anyway, Seamus."

"Speak for yourself."

Outside, the thunder was louder, but it still sounded far off. It was dark now, and no trace of the sky was visible behind the cloud cover. On the way back to Malibu Lake, the men were able to tune in to a radio broadcast of the Lakers, who were now playing the Washington Bullets at the Forum. The reception weakened as they approached the coast, and by the time the ocean came into view, they were getting nothing but static. Seamus shut off the radio.

"Jackie, I hope you didn't get the impression I don't think you and Jane could hit it off well, under the right circumstances."

"I know that."

"Good." Seamus got out his pipe and began his routine of filling it. "This isn't without precedent, you know. There was that Ford gal a few years back. She ended up marrying the guy, for crying out loud."

"I know that, too," Jack said evenly, keeping up with

the flow of northbound traffic on Pacific Coast Highway. Near Pepperdine University, a scenic school situated on a bluff overlooking the ocean, he turned onto Malibu Canyon Road, which cut through the mountains, eventually linking up with Mulholland Drive. A stiff wind was blowing through the canyons, and Jack slowed down as he took the endless series of tight turns leading to Malibu Lake. As they approached the gate to Britland Ranch, an uprooted tumbleweed bounded eerily out into the road like a portly ghost, almost forcing the car into a ravine as Jack swerved to avoid it.

"It's heading for the ranch," Seamus managed to joke. "Do you think we should pull it over and ask for some ID?"

"I'm sure Brockwell will intercept it if it tries to get on the property."

The other sedan was gone from the driveway when Jack pulled up to the cottage. Scott's station wagon was parked near the main house, and the agents walked over, finding another agent on guard instead of Brockwell. He showed Jack and Seamus into the family room, where Scott and Regina were playing Scrabble before a roaring fire while young Darren busied himself with his collection of toy trucks.

"We were wondering if you guys would beat the storm back," Regina said. "Has it started yet?"

Jack shook his head. "Any minute, though. Say, where's Jane?"

"She's out with an old friend from high school." Regina pondered her game tiles and made a move on the board. "I was expecting them back by now, too, but they probably got bogged down on memory lane somewhere."

Scott got up to tend the fire. "It's a wonder to me that she even went out with the guy. From everything I've heard, I would have thought they were oil and water."

"Wait a second!" Something in Jack's memory clicked into place. "What's the guy's name? Isn't it Aames?"

"That's right," Regina confirmed. "James Aames. Or J.T., as the rest of us called him."

"Holy shit..."

"Jackie," Seamus scolded. "There's children here."

"Regina," Jack said, ignoring McTeague. "Do you have any of your old yearbooks here?"

Regina pointed to a bookcase next to the fireplace. "Top row, over on the left. Why?"

As Jack went to the bookcase, he said to Seamus, "Go grab a strip of plastic wrap, would you?"

Seamus glanced at the married couple and shrugged his shoulders. "Don't ask me," he told them. "It must have been something he ate." He disappeared into the kitchen to track down a roll of clear wrap. When he brought it back out into the family room, Jack had found the yearbook and was looking for a specific page. Taking a strip of the thin plastic from Seamus, Jack stretched it tautly over the senior picture of J.T. Aames, then took a felt-tip pen from his pocket and began lengthening Aames's hair and filling out his lower face with a beard and mustache.

"Does he look familiar to you, Seamus?"

McTeague scratched his chin as he observed Jack's handiwork. "Not particularly."

"Think back to Washington. The suspect in the Hatch-Stead murders."

Thus prompted, Seamus was quick to see the resemblance. "Good Lord, I don't like this. Not one bit."

"What?" Regina inquired nervously, sensing the man's sudden concern. "What's wrong?"

"If we're mistaken, nothing," Seamus replied gravely. "If not..."

Chapter Forty-Four

Stony Point was a desolate spit of land thrusting out into the Pacific with the same tenacity as the Santa Monica Pier. Unlike the pier, however, Stony Point was a natural formation, braced by a perimeter of jagged rocks that had claimed more than its share of errant boats over the years. Because the peninsula acted as a breakwater for nearby Chumash Cove, home to many a well-heeled entertainment figure with a penchant for sailing, there had been an attempt in the late forties to erect a functioning lighthouse at its far end. The elements had had other ideas, however, and while Stony Point itself was sturdy enough to endure seasonal storms, the lighthouse wasn't. Just five months after its construction, it was irreparably damaged by wind and the tidal fury of that winter's first bout of bad weather. The hired keeper, a retired seaman and part-time character actor, had been washed off the point while trying to flee from the lighthouse, and had never been seen again. What was left of the structure's stone shell remained as a grim monument to the old sailor. A fence had been put up to keep the curious away, but Stony Point had become, over the years, a hangout of lengendary proportions for thrill-seeking teenagers. Inevitably there were rumors about the sailor's ghost haunting the ruins; and occasionally, resourceful bands of youths would start bonfires in the lighthouse tower and fill the night with mournful wailings in hopes of giving the rich folks of the cove a good fright.

Agents Brockwell and Nye were adamantly opposed to Jane and Aames's desire to explore Stony Point with the night's storm so imminent. Waves were already pelting the reefs so hard that their spray covered the thin strip of flatland leading from the coast to the old lighthouse. Far out to sea, jagged shafts of lightning touched down like spindly legs carrying black clouds to shore. The young couple persisted, however, and the foursome cleared the short fence, then made their way along the pathway. They had agreed to retreat with the first fall of rain, which Brockwell felt was only minutes away.

Enough of the lighthouse's walls remained standing to block the cold wind, and Jane led Aames to a back corner of the structure where it was possible for them to coax a standing fire from a small can of Sterno they had picked up at a store on the way, along with the potato salad and deli sandwiches that were passed around for dinner. Brockwell and Nye took their share to an adjacent room, which was littered with evidence of the party rituals that had taken place on more accomodating nights. Little remained from the days of the sailor, and in the darkness that lay beyond the flame's reach, the cold stone enclosure felt as if it might have been centuries old. That had been the primary theme of Jane's short story, which dealt with the widow of a sea merchant slain by pirates, a woman who lived out her days in the isolation of a bleak house overlooking the bay where she'd last seen her husband alive. A believer in reincarnation, the widow had made a habit of standing out on the terrace whenever a ship came in, hoping that one day she would see a young man who embodied the spirit of her long-lost soulmate. At the story's end, she was on her deathbed when a magnificent pelican mysteriously flew into her room. Bound around its webbed foot was a ring that the woman had instantly recognized as her husband's wedding band.

"One thing I always wondered about but never asked you," Aames said to Jane between bites of his sandwich. "Why a pelican in the story?"

"I don't know; it just seemed right. I wasn't about to make it an albatross, and maybe I had a premonition that somebody else would come along and corner the literary market on seagulls."

They both laughed, and Aames said, "Good thing you didn't call the story 'Jonathan Livingston Pelican.'"

"Har har." Jane looked at the manuscript lying in the bottom of the picnic basket. "You know, I really don't feel like reading it right now. Just look out that window, would you? God, what a lovely looking storm!"

The shaft-spitting clouds were closer, blowing fiercer winds before them. Brockwell and Nye emerged from the other room, turning up the collars of their coats. A clap of thunder rolled noisily past the lighthouse, and in its wake Brockwell announced, "I think it's time we moved on."

"In a minute," Jane said, reaching inside the picnic basket for her camera. "I want to take a few pictures."

"Well, I can't insist, but I still think —"

Another blast of thunder drowned out the rest of Brockwell's advice.

"You go ahead," Jane said as she went to the glassless window and peered out through her viewfinder. "I'll be there in a flash. Promise."

Brockwell shrugged. Nye was the first one out of the lighthouse, and the other agent followed, while Aames blew out the Sterno's bluish flame and put the unfinished food back in the basket. "I'll go put this stuff away and start up the car," he said. "Do you think that film's slow enough to catch anything?"

"Positive." Jane clicked the shutter release. "Aw, damn, just missed that one!"

"Don't rush yourself," Aames suggested. "Try to time how long it takes between hearing thunder and seeing the next batch of lightning, then try shooting a half-second or so faster."

"Will do."

"I'll be in the car when you're finished."

The sky erupted again as Aames left the lighthouse. The first drops of the storm chilled his skin. In the brief glow of lightning, he saw that Brockwell and Nye were already inside their sedan, with the engine running. He climbed the fence, opened the trunk of the Mustang and put away the picnic basket. Glancing over his shoulder, he had a clear view of the point and saw no trace of Jane in the next flash of lightning. He counted off the seconds before there was more thunder, then grabbed something from behind the wheel well of the trunk before slamming down the lid. The rain was coming down harder now, stinging him as he walked to the other car and gestured for Nye to roll down his window.

"We're going to take the Pacific Coast Highway back into town," Aames began to explain. When lightning brightened the sky, he pulled out the gun he'd stolen from Michael Gasner, and when the next roll of thunder pounded the night air, he fired two shots in quick succession, striking Nye point-blank in the face and hitting Brockwell in the chest as he reached for his own revolver. Both men slumped lifelessly forward, and Nye's shoulder struck and sounded the car's horn. Aames reached in, pulled Nye back to an upright position, opened the door long enough to roll up the window, then slipped Brockwell's revolver inside his jacket and hurried back to the Mustang.

Jane rejoined Aames a few minutes later, her hair dripping with rain and a smile on her face. "I got a couple of great shots!" she announced excitedly as she climbed into the car. "Where to now?"

"That's a surprise."

As Aames backed up and pulled out onto the dirt road leading from Stony Point, Jane looked back and said, "Why aren't they following us?"

"I asked them to stay back a ways so I wouldn't have their headlights flashing in the rearview mirror when we're taking curves."

"Smart thinking, James."

"Thanks," he replied. "I like to stay on top of things."

Chapter Forty-Five

"God damn it, why don't they answer?"

Jack and Seamus were at the guest cottage, trying to raise Nye and Brockwell on the radio. A third agent, seated before the radio console, worked a few more switches in an attempt to improve both their transmission and reception, but the small speakers mounted to the radio continued to emit nothing but a wavering flow of static.

"Let's hope it's just the weather screwing things up," Seamus said.

"Don't count on it." Damascus turned to the other man. "Where did they say they were headed when you were in touch with them last?"

"They called from Santa Monica Pier and said they were headed to Stony Point."

"Where's that?"

"Five, six miles from here, on the coast. Near Chumash Cove."

"How long ago did they call from the pier?"

The radio operator checked his log. "Little over an hour ago. Just after dusk."

"Let's go!" Jack bolted to the door just as Regina rushed into the cottage.

"What's going on?" she demanded. "Is my sister all right?"

"That's what we aim to find out," Jack said. "Do you know the quickest way to Stony Point?"

"Yes, but . . . why?"

"Then come with us."

"I'll drive," McTeague volunteered as the three of them headed out into the rain and piled into the sedan.

Sixties music filled the Mustang as Aames negotiated the winding road leading away from Stony Point. The rain streaked down in torrents, blurring the windshield between swipes of the wipers. He leaned forward in his seat, trying to see beyond the range of the car's headlights.

"It's really coming down," Jane remarked, raising her voice to be heard above the storm and the music. "Maybe we should just head back to the ranch and wait until it blows over."

"We'll be okay once we reach the highway," Aames assured her. "We can just take our time heading back into town. The concert doesn't start for another hour or so."

"Concert?" Jane looked at Aames. "What concert?"

Aames grinned. "That's the *coup de grâce*. There's a big reunion of old sixties groups at the Amphitheater tonight. The Turtles, the Association, Jay and the Americans you name it, they'll be there."

"You're kidding!"

Aames shook his head. "Nope. Actually, that's what gave me the idea for this nostalgia trip. I bought tickets this morning."

Jane laughed. "You're something else, James. I have to hand it to you."

Aames was about to say something when he saw the

glimmer of other headlights a few bends ahead of them, coming their way. He reached over and turned down the volume on the radio, then steered the Mustang off the road, pulling between rows of shrubs that hid the car from view of anyone who might drive by.

"What's the matter?" Jane asked as Aames shut off the motor and killed the headlights. Although the storm was no longer directly overhead, the sound of thunder still reverberated loudly enough to be heard above the pelting of raindrops on the car's roof.

"Alternator's acting up," he said. "I tinkered with it before I picked you up, but I can hear it's on the fritz again." He opened his door. "It'll only take a second to fix it. I'll be right back."

"Don't you need a flashlight or something?"

Aames shook his head. "Remember, I had one of these babies for seven years. I could work on 'em blindfolded if I had to."

"Well, be careful."

"I will."

Outside the Mustang, Aames squinted his eyes against the fall of rain and quickly raised the car's hood so Jane couldn't see him. He took out the revolver and turned to face the road. Moments later, the headlights of the other car came back into view, visible through the shrubs. As the vehicle slowly drove by, Aames tensed, ready to start firing if his suspicions were confirmed. No one in the other car had seen the Mustang, however, and the sedan continued down the road toward Stony Point. Aames waited until the taillights were no longer visible, then put the gun away and lowered the hood. Returning to the driver's seat, he shook the rain from his hair and started the engine.

"Good as new," he boasted, shifting into reverse and backing up to the road, waiting until the last minute before putting on his lights.

Jane smiled with relief. Although James had been on his best behavior the entire day, when he had pulled off onto the side of the road, she had felt wary. But her unease was clearly without foundation. She turned up the music, determined not to indulge her suspicions further. As she hummed along with the music, she forgot that agents Brockwell and Nye should be bringing up the rear. All she knew was that she was enjoying herself, and she owed it to herself not to spoil the mood.

Chapter Forty-Six

The storm's center had moved inland, leaving only a thin drizzle to fall on Stony Point. Two vehicles were parked near the sedan where agents Brockwell and Nye had been gunned down. One was an ambulance, which a pair of attendants were loading with the dead men's shrouded bodies. Their job on the scene completed, the paramedics climbed into the ambulance and drove away, turning off their rooftop flashers. They were in no hurry.

Seamus, Jack and Regina were in the other car, trying not to let the implications of what they'd found at the point throw them into a collective panic. Beneath the thin veneer of calm, however, there were tell-tale signs of truer emotions. McTeague fretted with his pipe, doing everything but light it. In the back seat, Regina's eyes were as wide as her lips were tight. She stared silently at the radio beneath the dashboard, rallying her dim hopes that it would soon crackle to life with good news about her sister.

When a transmission did come through, Damascus was the first to grab the microphone.

"Yes?" he barked anxiously.

The news was neither good nor bad. Several minutes before, there had been a report of a Mustang convertible parked just off Pacific Coast Highway near Will Rogers Beach, halfway between Malibu and Santa Monica. A check on the vehicle's plates had revealed the owner to be an antique dealer whose wife confirmed that he routinely parked the Mustang in the area. He had clients in the luxury homes nearby and was, at that moment, having dinner with a set designer who wished to use some of his antique cars in a film. No, the car hadn't been stolen earlier that day, and no, neither the wife nor the owner of the car knew James Theodore Aames.

"Damn it to hell!" Damascus slammed down the microphone, then quickly picked it back up and summoned the dispatcher, asking if there was any news from the people staking out Aames's apartment building.

"Negative."

Jack put the microphone back more gently this time, then stared bleakly out through the windshield. The wipers swept back and forth in a mesmerizing rhythm. "They could be anywhere," he whispered helplessly. "Anywhere."

"You have to quit sounding like it's your fault," Seamus told him. "It won't help matters."

Jack wasn't convinced. "Damn it, if we'd been at the ranch when he showed up, I would have been tipped off."

"But we weren't."

Tears began to fill Regina's eyes. "If anyone's to blame, it's me. I took his call last night. Knowing him, I should have been on my guard right away. I should have told him Jane wasn't home. But he sounded so different." She laughed bitterly. "I thought he was sincere, concerned. And all the time he was scheming, planning some . . ."

McTeague cut in. "None of this is getting us anywhere."

When a tow truck slowly drove into view, he said, "Let's finish up here and head back to the ranch."

As McTeague got out to arrange for the other sedan to be towed to the Malibu sheriff's impound yard, Jack and Regina sat quietly. Damascus was trying to recall everything in the one conversation he'd had with Jane about Aames that day back in Washington when Hatch had moved out. It seemed impossible that less than a week had passed since then. So much had happened.

"Jane told me that she and Aames had a pretty abrupt falling out, but she didn't go into specifics," he told Regina. "Do you know what it was all about?"

"Of course I do!" Regina snapped. "I was her sister. She told me everything."

"I didn't mean to offend you, Regina. I'm just trying to get a handle on it all. Any information you can give us would help." Damascus paused, wondering if he should say more. He decided it was necessary. "You know, I . . . your sister and I, that is . . . we were starting to get close."

"*Were?*" Regina was livid. "She's still alive! She has to be!"

"Yes, yes, of course. I . . . I'm sorry. Everything's just coming out wrong. But you have to know I care about her. I need to know anything that might help us figure out where Aames might have taken her."

Regina grew calmer. "I know you two are close," she sighed. "We talked about it a little last night, as a matter of fact. She was shocked at first when you kissed her, but I think she'd been hoping something like that might happen. For a long time."

"I'm glad, but that's not important right now," Jack said. "What about her and Aames? Their falling out?"

Regina took a tissue from her purse and dabbed at her eyes. "It was after they'd been going together for a few months. They fancied themselves as wild and passionate lovers; like characters in a D.H. Lawrence novel. Only

Jane began to realize he was more interested in the sexual part of their relationship than the romance.

"One night, when they'd both had a little too much to drink at a party down in Beverly Hills, J.T. drove her over to the La Brea Fossil Pits in Hancock Park. I don't remember all the details, but somehow or other he talked her into helping him break into the old observatory. He had this kinky idea that they should try making it while leaning out over the pit. Jane was afraid, but she was drunk and she went along with it. They almost fell in, and that was when Jane realized that —"

"Shit!" Jack interrupted. "Of course! Why the hell didn't I think of it before?" He started up the car and honked the horn, waving for McTeague to rejoin them. Grabbing the microphone below the dash, he put in a quick call. "Look, I think we know where they've gone . . ."

Chapter Forty-Seven

They'd sung their way through the rain and were now heading east on Wilshire Boulevard. The storm, which had followed them in from the coast, was just beginning to sweep across the city. The Turtles were on the tape player singing "Happy Together" with considerably more harmony than the duet of J.T. Aames and Jane Britland-Hatch. Aames was tone deaf, although what he lacked in tunefulness he made up in enthusiasm. When he flubbed a line of the song, he laughed, and Jane sang on, shaking her head gaily from side to side. Aames looked over at her. She was still wearing the wig, caught up in the moment he'd laboured so painfully to bring about. Perhaps the rest might not be as difficult as he'd feared. Perhaps she'd go along with him willingly . . .

They passed the Wilshire-San Vincente intersection, leaving Beverly Hills. The song ended, and Jane caught her breath, gasping, "That was a good one!"

Aames reached beside him and turned off the tape

player. "I remember us dancing to that at the prom," he said. "It was the first song after the court dance. I told you they could crown whoever they wanted to, but you were my queen."

Jane smiled, remembering. "You were a real Romeo when it came to smooth talking, James." She leaned back in her seat and sighed. "Oh, we were so naive back then, weren't we? Young and foolish, heads in the clouds..."

"I don't think we were so naive," Aames countered. "Or foolish, either. And I meant all those things I used to say to you."

His sudden seriousness caught her off guard, and the smile left her face. A faint feeling of uneasiness began to creep over her. "James," she said. "Let's not spoil things, okay?"

Aames shrugged, cursing himself inwardly for discarding caution. "You're right," he apologized. "Sorry."

"I just don't think we should drag up certain things, that's all."

"I understand."

The light changed, and Aames drove on, passing the old May Company and approaching Hancock Park. Aames's ironic grin, caught Jane's attention.

"What's so funny?"

"Your timing," Aames said.

"What do you mean?"

"I mean it's ironic you should say something about not bringing up touchy subjects right now." He widened his smile, trying to project as much good-nature as he could muster. There could be no more delays, and he had to proceed as expertly as possible. This was it. "You won't believe this, Jane, but we have to stop by the fossil pits to pick up the concert tickets."

"What?"

"Afraid so. I had a friend who works here buy 'em for me. I was too busy tracking down the Mustang and our outfits to get to Ticketron."

"You can't be serious," Jane said. "This is a joke, right?"

Aames turned off Wilshire onto Ogden, which ran past the art museum and the observatory pit. There were several parking places along the curb, and Aames guided the Mustang into one of them. When he turned off the engine, the sound of rain grew louder. "Come on," he said, opening his door. "It'll only take a minute."

"I'll wait for you here." Jane looked out at the park grounds. "Besides, it seems to me everything's already closed up. Where are you supposed to get the tickets?"

"At the observatory," Aames told her, producing his keys. "Ready for another kicker? I work there."

"I don't believe you."

"I'll show you." Aames was standing outside the car now, letting the rain fall on him. "Hurry up before I catch pneumonia. I promise you, no funny business. Scout's honor."

"All right, all right." Jane got out on the other side and walked beside Aames down the path to the observatory, ducking raindrops. "You're as diabolical as ever, James."

There was a playfulness to the accusation. Aames was relieved. "Oh, you're just saying that," he said lightly. Reaching the entrance, he fitted a key into the lock and turned the latch. They were sheltered from the rain now, and he pointed up to a newer section of the observatory's roof. "They fixed the air duct we sneaked in through, see?"

Jane looked up and nodded, but said nothing. Aames opened the door for her and she warily stepped inside, feeling uncomfortable with the rush of memories the pit set loose in her mind. "It hasn't changed much," she managed to say after Aames had turned on the lights.

"That's the best part about it," Aames told her. His mood shifted as he pulled the door closed behind him. While Jane looked around, her back turned to him, Aames quickly locked the door from the inside.

"Why did you do that?" Jane said.

Aames smiled at her. "You know, Jane, I've never had it better than that night we were here. You feel the same way, don't you? Deep down?"

At the look in Aames's eyes, Jane was momentarily startled into silence. She stepped away from him. When she found her voice, it was strained, hoarse. She had to clear her throat to let a note of annoyance hide her sudden anxiety. "There aren't any tickets here, are there?"

"That's right," Aames admitted. "A small white lie, I'm afraid. Look, I'm sorry for all the deception, but I had to get you here one way or another without tipping you off. You know, the element of surprise. Now just let me explain . . ."

Jane looked in the direction of the locked door. "Don't you think you should open that, so our chaperones can get in when they show up? Or didn't you bother to mention this little side trip to them?"

"I told them to go ahead to the theater to make sure they could get in without tickets."

Jane tried to fight off a growing panic. "That wasn't them following us here, was it? It was just some other car, maybe a few different ones, right? You really sent them off on the wrong track and made sure you lost them in traffic, didn't you?"

"It's not important, Jane. We're here, alone. That's what counts."

"Well, you'll excuse me if I'm not all that thrilled about it." Jane yanked off her wig and threw it on the floor. "Damn it, James, we could have had a good time — we *were* having a good time, and then you had to go and pull a stunt like this. A stupid, juvenile prank."

"Put the wig back on, Jane." Aames was calm, but his voice was firm, demanding.

"Forget it!" Jane was equally insistent. "This has gone too far, James."

"I said put the wig on!"

"And if I don't?" Jane shot back, circling behind the donation box. "Look, James, let's quit with the games and call it a night, okay?"

"This is no game." Aames shook his head, leisurely strolling after Jane as he looked around him. "You have no idea how much time I've spent in here, mulling over that one night. This place is like . . . it's like a shrine. I'm the lone worshipper, always in here paying tribute to —"

"That's enough! It's more than enough!" Jane backtracked to the door, confirming that it was locked. "Let me out of here, this instant!" she demanded, turning back to Aames.

He sighed and lit a cigarette. "I hoped that once I got you here I'd be able to make you understand." He blew smoke and stared at Jane through the cloud. "Think hard. Have you ever been happier, more carefree, more *alive* than when we were together?"

"James . . ."

"No, of course you haven't. And do you want to know why? I'll tell you. It's because ever since we've been apart, you've been selling yourself out. Always doing what other people made you think you ought to do. Always sucking up to that herd instinct, then wondering why you never seemed to fit in with everyone else, why you always felt different, no matter how hard you tried not to be."

"You're talking about yourself, maybe, but not me." Jane willed herself not to show her fear, although she could now sense that Aames had trapped her here with far more serious intentions than she had at first imagined. "I've had my problems, but it's not because of anything to do with us."

"You're wrong, Jane." Aames took another step toward her. "If you had stayed with me, you wouldn't have ended up with that scum you called a husband. He didn't know your needs like I do. He treated you like shit, like a rug he could wipe his feet on when they got dirty. He got what he deserved. You have no idea how good it felt to put him out of his misery."

Jane felt a sick rush low in her stomach. Her knees felt ready to give out on her. "You . . . ?"

"I would have done it sooner, but I didn't have the nerve," Aames said. "I was like you. I couldn't face up to what needed doing. But once I decided there was no other way, everything started falling into place. I had a purpose, a destiny. Can't you see that, Jane? We were meant to be together."

The storm raged outside the walls, and Jane let out a cry of terror when a drop of water dripped from the ceiling and landed on her arm like the cold touch of someone tapping her from behind. Whirling around, she ran across the concrete floor to the emergency exit, but it was also locked. She pounded on the door, competing with the thunder as she cried out for help.

"There's no one out there, Jane. Save your breath." Aames crushed out his cigarette, and his footsteps echoed off the rounded walls as he approached her. "You don't have to worry, I won't harm you. At least, I don't want to."

"Damn you!" Jane saw the hose mounted on the wall next to her and grabbed a few yards of the loose end, waving it like a whip in front of her. "Get away from me and open the door! Now!"

"Are you threatening me, Jane?" Aames seemed amused.

"Take another step near me and find out!"

Aames laughed lightly, reaching into his coat. "Remember on the pier when I won the frog for you? Did you notice how good my aim was?" He removed his dart case and calmly started to assemble the projectiles. "Your husband and the other guy weren't killed by an ice pick, Jane."

"You wouldn't hurt me, James. You know that."

"That's what I just finished telling you a few seconds

ago. I don't want to have to do anything like that. I love you, Jane. I just want what's right. For both of us."

Reaching behind her, Jane turned on the faucet, but no water came out. "What's right is for you to let me go, James," she bartered, softening her tone.

"I can't do that, Jane. Not now. You know that."

"I need to think about what you've said. Don't you realize that? I mean, you've been figuring it out all these years, but to me it's like a bolt out of the blue. I need time."

Aames attached the flights to his dart shafts, taking his time. "It's not that difficult to understand, Jane. I've already explained it to you. You'll never be happy until you own up to who you are, what you are. You have to be true to your passions, and to hell with the rest of the world. It's the only way."

He fell silent. The storm was passing overhead. Then Jane slowly put the hose back on the wall and took a tentative step toward Aames. "Would you be willing to help me?" she asked. "I mean, to be patient with me? I know what you're saying, and I want to believe it, but I've been through so much these past years . . . I'm confused. This is all happening so fast."

Aames regarded Jane suspiciously. "You're lying," he decided. "Just trying to fast-talk your way out of trouble."

"No, that's not it!" Jane's face tightened from the conflict inside her. Two tears slid down her cheeks as she stared at Aames. "Please, James. Try to put yourself in my shoes. Please."

Aames rolled one of the darts between his fingers, twirling its flights. "You mean it?" he asked. "About wanting my help?"

"Yes!" Jane said. "What you've said is true. I *have* been afraid to be myself. I mean, last night, when I was reading through all my early writings, I was jealous at how self-confident I'd been back then. And you're right about us, too. I was never happier than when we were first going out. I let myself get scared off, just like tonight. Look at what a good time we were were having before I put a damper on things. James, I'm sorry."

"I still don't know if I can believe you," Aames told her, shifting his hold on the darts to warn Jane that his guard was up.

"What do I have to do to prove it?" Jane pleaded. "I already told you I was sorry."

"You know what you have to do," Aames said.

Jane stared at Aames, then let a smile slowly bloom across her face. It was a knowing smile, vixenish and playful, a smile she hadn't worn in years. "All right, Mr. Aames. I'll prove it to you."

She was only a few yards away from the upper rim overlooking the pit. She went to the railing and took off her coat. Like a model flaunting the latest fashion, she turned from side to side, bending slightly to accentuate her figure beneath the old-fashioned dress. Winking at Aames, she pursed her lips, teasing Aames with a distant kiss.

"James, we couldn't get much higher," she whispered before turning to climb the railing.

"Yesssss," Aames murmured as he watched her assume the same position he had taken when he had propositioned Georgia a week before. She leaned backwards so that the black pool was directly below her.

"Come and get me, James," Jane taunted. "It's your turn to do it to me."

Aames slowly approached the railing, thanking the thunder and the fates for having brought this long-sought moment into being. Keeping his darts in his right hand, he reached out with his left and gently stroked Jane's cheek. She turned her head and kissed the back of his hand, then licked one of his fingers before taking it all the way inside her mouth.

"Nice," Aames whispered, slowly drawing the finger from her mouth and running it through her hair. "You're going to have to let your hair grow out to the way it was."

"Of course," Jane told him. She was beginning to shake from the strain of supporting herself. "Now, hurry while I still have some strength. I can't wait to feel you inside me."

Aames stroked her other cheek, then let his free hand fall to her shoulder. He slowly fingered the strap holding her dress up and pulled it off to one side, then repeated the motion with the other strap.

"Reach around and unzip me, James," she encouraged.

Aames leaned over the railing, bringing his face close to the scented material of Jane's dress. He groped behind her, seeking out the zipper.

Jane kissed the top of Aames's head, then looked over his shoulder, judging the angle at which he was leaning across the railing. As she felt his fingers close around the zipper and begin to pull it down, Jane abruptly released her grip on the rail and grabbed at Aames's coat as she began to fall. Aames tried to catch himself, but Jane's weight pulled him over the railing, and together they plummeted down toward the pit, bounding once off the concrete walls before landing in the tar.

Stunned by the fall, it took Jane a few seconds to regain consciousness. She found herself mired near the edge of the pit, lying in the tar at a half-prone angle so that only one leg and half her torso were caught in the cold grip. Aames was behind her. He had landed feet first, burying both legs, and the tar was already as high as his waist.

"You bitch!" he raged, clawing at her.

"Leave me alone!" Jane screamed back, swatting at his hands. He leaned away from her and grabbed her leg, trying to pull her toward him. Jane spotted one of the darts lying on the cement near the pool's edge. Acting on instinct, she grabbed it and turned to her attacker. Before he could draw back, she rammed the pointed tip into the back of his hand. He roared with pain, pulling his hand away.

The fossil display was also within Jane's reach. By securing a firm hold on one of the larger bones, she was able to drag herself away from Aames and, with extreme effort, out of the pit. Aames's howling gave way to an anguished string of curses. Jane ignored them, gasping to regain her breath. Her right leg felt as though she'd broken it, and her left arm was bleeding from where she'd scraped it along the rough walls when she fell.

Aames dipped one hand into the tar, trying to get at the gun inside his submerged coat, but he only lost the use of the arm, which he was unable to pull free. "Help me, Jane," he called out from the middle of the pit, holding his free, bleeding hand out to her. "You have to help me." The anger and power was gone from his voice, replaced by a piteous whimper. "Please..."

Jane stared coldly at Aames as she watched him slip further into the tar. Up at ground level, someone was pounding on the doors of the observatory. Aames raised his voice, calling for help.

"They probably can't hear you over the storm. Remember?" Jane told him calmly. Rising to her feet, she limped over to where the blonde wig had fallen. She picked it up and tossed it at Aames, just missing him.

Aames had sunk as far as his chest. Realizing he sank faster when he struggled, he forced himself to remain still. "You can't let me die," he told Jane. When she refused to answer him, he said, "I'll haunt you forever, you bitch. Just watch."

Jane said nothing.

Outside the observatory, two police officers waited impatiently for Johnny White to fit the right key into the lock of the main door. One of them finally took out his revolver and pushed White aside. "We don't have time for that, pal." He leveled his gun at the lock and fired three times.

Out near the curb, Seamus pulled to a stop, and Jack Damascus bounded out of the sedan, rushing across the rain-drenched grounds to join the officers as they charged inside the observatory, guns drawn. At first they saw nothing out of the ordinary, but the sound of muffled weeping drew them to the railing. They advanced cautiously and stared down at the pit. Jane was sitting near the edge of the pool, her legs bent so that she could weep into the crossed arms resting on her knees. Out in the middle of the pit, a single hand protruded from the surface, clutching a tar-stained wig. As everyone in the observatory watched, the hand and wig slowly slipped the rest of the way into blackness. A lone ebony bubble appeared for a moment, then popped, leaving the pit's surface smooth as glass.

Epilogue

Some of Jane's things hadn't even been taken out of her suitcase yet, so it didn't take her long to pack. Scott had brought up her old footlocker, and she sat on the edge of the bed, staring at its time-worn contents. Regina quietly entered the bedroom, but it was several seconds before Jane saw her and broke from the near trance she had slipped into.

"I'm so sorry, sis," Regina said, coming up next to Jane. "Are you really sure you want to leave so soon, though? You're welcome to stay longer. The rest might be a good thing..."

"Thanks, Regina, but I have to go." Jane bent over, taking the typewriter from the footlocker and closing the lid. "I think I'd like to take this along, but if you could store the rest for me, I'd appreciate it. I've had my share of the past for now."

"I understand." Regina squeezed her sister's hand.

"Can you at least tell me a little more about this place you're going to?"

"I don't know that much about it, really," Jane confessed. "Jack just said it's his brother's summer cottage on some lake outside of Chicago. There's hardly anyone out there at this time of year. Just a few hunters. I didn't have to hear any more."

"Well, I hope you'll have nothing but peace and quiet."

"And time to think," Jane said. "There's a lot of decisions I want to make, a lot of changes in the way I do things."

"It'll work out. I'm sure of it."

From elsewhere in the house, the plaintive whine of young Darren sounded like the yelp of a coyote. "Mom Mahhhhhhhhhhhhhhhhhmmmmmmeeeee!!!"

"He's certainly in good voice today," Regina groaned. "I think I'd better check him out. I'll get Scott to help take some of your stuff down to the car."

When she was alone, Jane found room in her luggage for the portable typewriter, then carefully secured all the latches. Just as she finished, Jack Damascus, not Scott, appeared.

"How are you holding up?" he asked.

"Fine, thanks."

"I talked with my brother, and everything's all set. He doesn't have anything planned at the cottage for another six weeks, and he says you're welcome to put up there the whole time if you want. I have his word that he won't mention you're out there. No media this time, let's hope."

"Amen."

As Jack grabbed the two largest suitcases, he said, "I also made arrangements for someone else to be covering you while you're there."

Jane put a hand on Jack's shoulder and looked him in the eyes. "Last night you said you understood my reasons for not wanting you around. Did you really mean that?"

"Of course," Damascus said, though he sounded less than convinced.

"Jack, I feel strongly about you, but there are so many other emotions tearing at me, I can't trust my feelings at this point. If I can sort things out as objectively as possible, then maybe I'll be able to make some right decisions for a change."

"I can wait," he assured her. "And I *do* understand. Okay?"

"Okay."

Jane kissed him lightly, then picked up her carry-on bag and started for the door. Jack followed and they proceeded downstairs. Outside, Scott and Regina were appeasing their son with a game of croquet on the drenched lawn. There were mud puddles on the driveway, but little threat of more rain in the white patchwork of clouds overhead. The sun beat down warmly as Jack loaded the luggage in the trunk of the sedan.

Jane went over to exchange farewells with her family. Two new agents had arrived earlier that morning and would be taking her to the airport.

"Good luck to you," Jack said before Jane got into the car. "I'll send you a postcard, if you won't think I'm lobbying."

Jane smiled. "I'd like that. You take care of yourself, too."

The two new agents looked like twins off the Secret Service assembly line. Pressed suits and sunglasses, faces that could be lost in a crowd. They both sat in the front seat as Jane took the back. As the car started down the driveway, Seamus came out of the guest cottage and waved. Jane waved back, then tensed as she looked ahead and saw the clot of media people gathered just beyond the gateway to the ranch. Flashbulbs were already beginning to pop, and several reporters broke from the ranks, ignoring orders from other Secret Service agents to stay away from the departing vehicle.

Averting her gaze, Jane picked up a copy of that morning's *Times* from the seat next to her. The front-page headline caught her attention, as did photos of her and

J.T. Aames, separately and together. Much was being made of their former relationship, and the discovery of Aames's diary promised a wealth of lurid details about the romance and the murders of Andrew Hatch, Hunter Stead, Michael Gasner and the prostitute who had been found in the fossil pit where, ironically, he too had met his final fate.

Jane cast the paper away from her and bit her lower lip. Aames had been right after all. He would haunt her forever. The sedan drove on, leaving the media behind.

Innocent People Caught In The Grip Of TERROR!

These thrilling novels—where deranged minds create sinister schemes, placing victims in mortal danger and striking horror in their hearts—will keep you in white-knuckled suspense!

_____ **DEATH OF A PROM QUEEN,**
Marie Oliver 7701-03308/$3.95
As the class reunion drew near, only one person still cared who had been "in" and who had been "out"... and the time for revenge was now!

_____ **WIREMAN,**
Billie Sue Mosiman 7701-03030/$3.95
He's out there tonight. A dark and deadly presence, he has struck before. And with each new killing he becomes less human

_____ **BABY KILLER,**
Joy Carroll 7701-02964/$3.95
A series of mysterious baby deaths at Bonsante Hospital triggers off an investigation and hopefully a conviction... before it's too late!

_____ **A LILY FOR LILA,**
Robert Weverka 7701-03294/$3.50
The hottest love goddess since Monroe, she was hooked on sex, religion... and trouble!

BOOKS BY MAIL
320 Steelcase Rd. E.,
Markham, Ontario L3R 2M1

*In the U.S. - 210 5th Ave., 7th Floor
New York, N.Y., 10010*

Please send me the books I have checked above. I am enclosing a total of $_____ (Please add 75 cents for postage & handling.) My cheque or money order is enclosed. (No cash or C.O.D.'s please.)

Name_____
Address_____Apt._____
City_____
Prov._____Postal Code_____
Prices subject to change without notice. (CP102)

Have You Missed These Great Horror Bestsellers
by J. ROBERT JANES?

____ **THE TOY SHOP (7701-0191-7) / $2.95**
"A stunning blend of terror, sex and innocence."

____ **THE WATCHER (7701-0223-9) / $3.95**
"An hypnotic tale with the awful terror of *Psycho* and the intimate secrets of *Peyton Place.*"

____ **THE THIRD STORY (7701-0226-3) / $3.95**
"A chilling tale of danger uncovered."

____ **THE HIDING PLACE (7701-0291-3) / $3.95**
"Behind the pretty face was a terrified victim desperate for somewhere to hide!"

Prices subject to change without notice.

BOOKS BY MAIL
320 Steelcase Rd. E.
Markham, Ont., L3R 2M1

In the U.S. -
210 5th Ave., 7th Floor
New York, N.Y., 10010

Please send me the books I have checked above. I am enclosing a total of $_____. (Please add 75 cents for postage and handling.) My cheque or money order is enclosed. (No cash or C.O.D.'s please.)

Name_____
Address_____ Apt._____
City_____
Province_____ Postal Code_____

(CP16)

WHITEWATER POLICE

JOHN BALL
AUTHOR OF **IN THE HEAT OF THE NIGHT** INTRODUCING, **POLICE CHIEF JACK TALLON** IN THESE EXCITING, FAST-PACED MYSTERIES.

WHEN RAPE IS THE CRIME, EVERY MAN IS A SUSPECT. EVEN THE NEW...
___ **POLICE CHIEF**   7701-03561/$2.95

A MIDNIGHT RENDEZVOUS BECOMES A DATE WITH DEATH.
___ **TROUBLE FOR TALLON**
                 7701-0357X/$2.95

A DOUBLE DOSE OF SEX AND MURDER SPELLS DOUBLE TROUBLE FOR...
___ **CHIEF TALLON AND THE S.O.R.**
                 7701-03588/$2.95

BOOKS BY MAIL
320 Steelcase Rd. E.,
Markham, Ontario L3R 2M1

In The U.S. —
210 5th Ave 7th Floor
New York N.Y. 10010

Please send me the books I have checked above. I am enclosing a total of $_____ (Please add 75 cents for postage & handling.) My cheque or money order is enclosed. (No cash or C.O.D.'s please.)

Name _____
Address _____ Apt. _____
City _____
Prov. _____ Postal Code _____
Prices subject to change without notice.   (LTM8)

FREE!!
BOOKS BY MAIL
CATALOGUE

BOOKS BY MAIL will share with you our current bestselling books as well as hard to find specialty titles in areas that will match your interests. You will be updated on what's new in books at no cost to you. Just fill in the coupon below and discover the convenience of having books delivered to your home.

PLEASE ADD $1.00 TO COVER THE COST OF POSTAGE & HANDLING.

BOOKS BY MAIL

320 Steelcase Road E.,
Markham, Ontario L3R 2M1

In the U.S. -
210 5th Ave., 7th Floor
New York, N.Y., 10010

Please send Books By Mail catalogue to:

Name_____
(please print)

Address_____

City_____

Prov._____ Postal Code _____

(BBM1)